RUM OWD BOYS

I.S.B.N. 0 900227 16 8
Printed and published in England by
East Anglian Magazine Ltd
6 Great Colman Street
Ipswich, Suffolk.

Drawings by Peter Kemplay
Dust jacket design by Lynn Sheridan

Rum Owd Boys

– on Poachers, Wildfowlers, Longshore Pirates, Cut-throat Islanders, Smugglers & 'Fen-tigers'

BY

JAMES WENTWORTH DAY

EAST ANGLIAN MAGAZINE LIMITED IPSWICH SUFFOLK

CONTENTS

INTRODUCTION

HERE IS a book about those most English of all Englishmen - that unique breed which flourishes in the Fens, on the seaward farms and marshes and in the fishing villages of East Anglia.

Unquenchable, invincible, fiercely independent, cunning as foxes, wise as owls, sharp as a wagon-load of weasels, hardened by the hazards of the sea. A race apart, sweetened by rare humour.

The Vikings left their blood-marks in the breed. Napoleon feared their forbears. Nelson loved them. Winston Churchill praised them in more recent wars.

I have lived my life with them, know them, love them. In this book one tries to give sharp, endearing pictures of this utterly English breed. It is a book of laughter. All the characters are drawn from life. None are larger than life.

None are rich. None are poor. All have the springs of happiness. They have mastered the art of living, tapped the secret fount of laughter and found the wells of quiet content.

The gull's way is their way - the way of the sea-wind and the magic of new dawns. For they are of the English, utterly English.

Their's is a life lived in the half-land, between the settled order of upland farms and villages and the constant hazards of Fen floods or the deadly tricks of tide and tempest in the opal land of sea-lavender and shining creeks.

'The Admiral', 'in his nineties', until a year or so ago, jetted his white torpedo beard, snapped his hawk-eyes and danced a hornpipe.

Half the yachtsmen of England knew him as Bill Wyatt, of Mersea Island, boat-builder, shipwright, wild-fowler and the proud descendant of a race which had been building boats since the reign of Elizabeth I when they were turning out men-o'-war to fight the Armada from Bucklers Hard on the Beaulieu River in Hampshire. They came to Essex two centuries ago and have been men of salt-water note ever since.

As for the Councillor, he also departed this life not long ago. Shortly before he was 'called aloft' he fixed me with those beady, cocksparrow eyes and said: 'Yew've bin a-writin bits in the paper about me, hevn't you, marster?'

'Not by your name,' I replied.

'No, Councillor Art Bugg, ain't it? I know what that stand for - Artful Bugger! I allus was one. I allus will be.'

Until a year or so ago he still travelled the marsh-land roads in his rattle-trap car or, on economic occasions, 'put the old hoss in the shafts' and trotted off in his high-wheeled trap to buy and sell anything from hens or donkeys to ships' anchors.

The gulls still mew and swoop above the masts of anchored smacks off the foreshore of that noble inn *The Nelson's Eye* where iniquity is brewed.

Others of the old crew have up-anchored and gone aloft. Old Zebedee Milgate lies with his Breton forbears beneath the green turf of the churchyard. But there are still Roman bricks in the church tower and 'pinched gin' for those with tongues to sample it and mouths to shut.

Ephraim still livens this life with guile. His deeds are legend. His cunning remains a model for younger men to emulate.

Charlie sails the seaways and swatchways of that treacherous coast from Harty Ferry in the cattle marshes of the Isle of Sheppey to the seal-dotted sandbanks of the Wash. He is known in Amsterdam, feared in certain bistros in Calais, loved in Bruges and Walcheren, Texel and the Scheldt.

'The boy', Lennox Leavett, now past 50, is still a boy. He has a chestful of war medals and earned Winston Churchill's personal commendation during the last conflict. He remains the poacher in excelsis, the wildfowler without peer, the scourge of gamekeepers.

His father, Will Leavett, descendant, as he proudly boasted, of smugglers and pirates, died a year or so ago well in his 80's. Now here is a strange tale. On that night of stars, when I did not know that death was near to him, I dreamed that he was calling me. I woke certain of the fact. Promptly I cancelled all other matters and motored instantly the 30 miles to his house on the edge of the saltings. His wife met me at the door. She was in tears.

'He's dying - but he's just said "I know Mr. Day'll come". And you have.' Twenty minutes later the old seaman-wildfowler, my devoted friend for 40 years, was dead. That call in the night was a cry from the heart.

Others flourish like oaks. William, that shrewd cattle-dealer and yeoman farmer drops in for tea on Friday after market. He still hunts the fox, shoots with the Squire, judges at horse shows, rides like a centaur, tames bulls which terrify me and takes half a a day of tortuous verbiage to seal a tortuous deal.

Jim Rodd, the hunting groom, half-fox, half-man, remains immortal. He and I set out to ride 1000 miles on horse-back through the broad, bright fields of East Anglia when I was recovering from a tiff with the enemy in the last World War. We ended by riding more than 1200 miles, which, I believe, is an English record. Record or no it remains a memory imperishable, set down in a book called *Farming Adventure.*

Bert Bailey, boyhood hero of Wicken Fen, is still 'fit and fierce as a fleet o' lions', at well past 80.

As for the islands of the Essex coast, the long, luminous marshes, the saltings purple with sealavender, these, the lonely places of sea-mystery, are at the mercy of the Maplin menace. The scheme seems scotched for the moment but, if Maplin does come, beauty will be slain. Thus, England the mother of humble heroes, destroys their birthright.

JAMES WENTWORTH DAY,
INGATESTONE, ESSEX.1974

DEAD MEN'S BONES

CHARLIE, small, wizened, crafty as they come, his face graven by salt spray and sea winds, crooked a knee against the tiller as the fishing smack drew out of Thames-mouth and squared away northwards. Ahead, the Main sea glittered in stippled silver. On the port side lay the low, flat horizon of Foulness Island. A dragline reared its skeleton arm against the sky. Two mighty tractors chugged laboriously across a flat marsh.

Today, Foulness, which the Romans christened 'the Isle of Birds' is a secret place, guarded by sentries, visited only by passport. It has always been a place of secrets. The smugglers knew it. When the Crimean War was fought thousands of Russian prisoners were herded in its bleak solitude. They died of ague by the score. They buried them in a long-forgotten mass cemetery. Charlie drew back the curtain on the dead.

Peering at the clanking tractors he spat into the wake of the ship, and said suddenly:

'Scientific farmin'! They're at it agin. Same as they did in me granddad's day.

'All long words, fancy names and white-collared chaps givin' orders instead o' workin' - an' they don't grow no better crops in the end.

'Bone-meal was all the go in granddad's day. They was all a-hollerin' out for it. Payin' fancy prices too. Any owd bones 'ud do.

'Well, granddad knowed where them owd Russians laid. Other people had forgot about 'em. Granddad never did howd with hard work. So he reckoned them owd Russians could keep him in beer, and help the farmin' job as well.

'They'd died like flies. Couldn't stand the island weather. Got the ague or summat. They buried a rare parcel on 'em in a gret owd cemetery on the island. Me granddad knowed where they laid.

'Well, that might hev been about the late 80's when

they was all a-goin' in for this here high-falutin' farmin'.

'Well, me owd granddad never did hold wi' hard work if he could git round it. He'd bin on the island a time or two with some o' his rum owd mates on other business. You understand? Night work! Work what had plenty o' spirit in it! Well, me owd granddad reckoned that if they could run cargoes on to the island he might just as well run a cargo or two off it.

'So he started a-diggin' up these here owd Russians - cartloads on 'em. Sweated his owd guts out at it, night arter night. He barged 'em away up the creek, leg-bones, ribs, skulls, kneecaps, backbones - everything he could lay hold on, 'ceptin' their medals.

'He done pretty well at that game for a week or two. Got a tidy bit o' brass out on it. Set me owd grandma up in a new silk shawl and bonnet, forever o' whalebone corsets, got hisself a new double-breasted pilot jacket for Sunday worship, put half a quid in the plate jest to please the parson and stifle his own conscience - and then what do you think happened?'

'He tripped up on a skeleton and broke his neck,' says I.

'Not him! Not that artful owd davvle. He was as double-cunnin' as a wagon-load o' weasels! He could outthink a fox! No, that was his owd mates, the smugglin' chaps, what done him. They was all ready set to run another cargo on to the island when they go wind o' this here grave-diggin' job' of me granddad's - bone-meal merchant he called himself. 'That looked too much like competition. 'sides, all this here grave diggin' might draw attention to them, not that chaps on Foulness in them days cared two damns what went on arter dark. Still, they reckoned they'd better shut down me owd granddad's bone-meal business.

'So three on 'em got in the graves he dug one moonlight night, with long, white nightshirts on 'em, white nightcaps on their hids and rubbed their owd phizzogs with phosphorus so as they glouted like a lot o' damn tomcats on the walk.

'Across the marsh from his boat comes me owd granddad, whistlin' to hisself, thinkin' o' nothing but bonemeal an' brass, hops over the fence into the graveyard, draws his owd shovel out of a bush and marches over to a grave, spittin' on his hands.

'All o' a sudden three gashly white ghosts rose up out o' the earth, their faces all blazin' with fire, waves their owd arms an' shruk out like owd owls.

'Lor! Me owd granddad hulls down his shovel, crosses that owd graveyard in two bounds like a Jack-on-spring, clears the fence like a hoss and goes roarin' across the marsh to his owd boat like a long dog.

'He'd have won any race they hev at Newmarket or anywhere else. They warn't a hoss in the parish could ha' ketched him that night.

'He get to the saltings, springs off like a hare in a gret lep for his boat, ketched his foot on the gunnel, come down like a sack o' wheat in the boat, split his owd skull open on the thwart, busted his snout on a oar, picks hisself up, gets out the oars, rows off like one o'clock, all blood and sweat - Ha! He bled like a hog on a pig-killing day - and then . . . backside-over-snout he goes in the boat.

''Cos why? He'd forgot to pull up the anchor. He ketched a crab all right - more like a lobster.

'He gets home all o' a muck-sweat, chatterin' like a monkey, white as a sheet, took the pledge and never went nigh of Foulness agin.

'That done him o' scientific farmin'.'

Foulness, as Charlie says, is a rum old place - the Ultima Thule of the Eastern Counties. It is the toe of Essex. A bleak, flat, almost treeless island, lying between Thames and Crouch, the North Sea forever frothing in curdled, muddy spume on its eastern shores.

On all that 6,000 acres of dyke-seamed farmland and cattle marsh, winding reed-bordered fleets and girdling prairies of saltings, purple with sea-lavender in September, there are birds. Swans and wild geese, duck and waders, herons and plover, partridges and pipits. Sea-swallows flash and scream above the shining creeks. The tides suck and flow on shoal and fairway where brent geese sit in black armadas.

A place in summer, of hot, baking levels, where cattle switch their tails on exposed marshes, where the corn stands straight and golden in a lambent, lilting, clearness of light, that light which is all sunshine and blue sea and blue sky, reflected from the sea, cast down again upon earth by the sky, a light so clear that a man may walk on air.

In winter, a place of bitter winds, of drifting fogs and menacing tides. If the great hairy sea-walls that march like huge, bleached snakes between the saltings and the marshes were to 'blow', almost all the island would go under the tide. It did in the 'Great Tide'.

Scarce more than 40 miles from London, yet, they said, before the 1914 War not an islander had ever seen a soldier in uniform, scarcely one had been in a train. London was a distant mystery, brooding far up the sea-ways of Thames. No buses ran on the island's roads. There was no road to the mainland, save a track across the sands and mudflats, which ran for miles from Wakering Stairs on the mainland to the islands of Havengore, New England and Foulness. A road that went under the sea at every tide, its course marked only by the thin, scrawny tops of the 'brooms' which stuck up above the sliding waters like witches' fingers. Many an island farmer, homing from market, in his hard-sprung cart, has been trapped by the tide on a night of fog. More than one has been drowned.

Do you wonder that an island, so remote, bleak, bare, cold and cut off should have bred a race apart? Farmers and fishermen, smugglers and wreckers, unlettered and superstitious, defiant and independent, the Islanders have always been, and still are, a rum lot. Did they not breed those great prize fighters of the 18th century, John Bennewith; Minter, the fighting king of the bargees; Rippengale, the marsh waller, and that trinity of Foulness 'pugs', deliciously known as The Infant, The Giant, and Bullocks' Bones.

King of all the local characters was Hard Apple Blyth, the Paglesham smuggler, who, a devout churchwarden on Sundays, drank 'Damnation to all Revenue Laws and Officers' on week-days. He boarded a King's cutter on one epic occasion and took its cargo of spirits which the Excisemen seized from another smuggler. He killed a bull bare-handed with a club, and, when he died in 1830, asked for the Lord's Prayer to be repeated by his bedside. When it was finished he said quietly: 'Now I am ready for the launch,' turned his face to the wall and slipped his moorings on the last tide.

Little wonder that the best parson they ever had, in the old days, to rule that rough spiritual kingdom, was old

Tom Archer. In his blue frock-coat, white corduroy breeches, grey woollen stockings and red night-cap, he rode everywhere over the island on a raking great hunter, jumped stiles and dykes, smoked a clay pipe as he walked up the churchyard path on Sundays and left it in a niche in the porch, ready for the fusee to be struck the moment he came out of service.

Parson Tom was a bare-knuckle fighter himself and if any of his smuggler-pugs gave trouble he set about them in the way they understood. Yet he was a man of good classical education, who wrote excellent verse under the pen-name of Calliope.

This fine old man of God, whom Kingsley would have loved, broke his leg trying to jump the churchyard stile. He died soon after, in February, 1832, at the age of 82, and lies in Foulness Church, where still his dead ears may hear:

> . . . the lone notes falling,
> Where the long grey tides are crawling,
> Through the shouting west wind's buffets or
> the dripping fog's chill blanket,
> As the wild geese come shoreward from the sea.

Today, Foulness is connected to the mainland by a military road, but if you want to get there you will be held up by a policeman or a sentry, your pass demanded, and you will probably, be turned firmly backwards on your tracks. The road, a ribbon of concrete, strides across the creeks and saltings of Havengore and New England and strikes like a sword to the heart of Foulness, where the old church stands by the weather-boarded inn, amid its few wind-twisted elms and holly bushes, where the blackbirds roost.

Whatever way you look at it, Foulness is still a rum sort of old place. There always have been, and probably always will be, rum sorts of goings-on there and thereabouts.

You might, for example, meet the ghost of Turtle, the 'pug' who was killed in a fight in that lane they call Turtle's Walk near the church; or meet the spectre of Bullocks' Bones, the giant prize-fighter, coming lowering, up a rutted road under the moon; or see old Hard Apple storming over the sea-wall on a wild night of moon, waving a ghostly cutlass and roaring on the sharp wind his death-defying oath of 'Body and Bones'.

THE MARSH LARNS THE PLANNERS

ALL IS not well on the Marsh. That seclusive place of oysters and mudflats, where curlew whistle in the dawn and sheep graze on green miles within the sea-wall, is agog.

Certain persons on the Council, upstart foreigners, resident on the Marsh for a mere tittle of a dozen years, elected, doubtless, by blackmail, bribery and underground corruptions, have dared to talk of Town Planning. Ideas that smell of treason.

Car Parks. Street Lamps. A Dance Hall. The final impudence was the suggestion that 'Cattle Crossing' signs should be put up where the muddy track from Beelzebub Farm crosses the main road, just on the bend by the high hedge, full of spindleberries and honeysuckle, into the field which run down to the sea-wall.

The result is revolution. Cloak-and-dagger talk goes on in the *Nelson's Eye*, that haunt of infamy. You recollect that it was there, little more than a hundred years ago, that they planned the murder of the Revenue men, 24 of them. They were found next morning, washing back and forth in their long-boat, in what is now Dead Man's Creek. 'All the hull lot on 'em dead as hogs, wi' their throats cut from ear to ear. An' nobody niver knowed who done it. That was a head masterpiece.'

Today, history repeats itself. Someone is going to suffer. The Romans lost a feather or two from the eagles when they tackled the Marshmen. The Danes could not put to sea because someone pinched their oars and set fire to their cordage. The Normans, wisely, stayed on the upland. England was a hard enough nut by itself. Why add to the hornets' nest? As for Napoleon, so many Marshmen looted so many of his merchantmen and slew so many of his sailors that it is confidently reported that when drawing up his plans for the invasion of Britain he decided to give the Marsh a miss.

When Hitler dropped an errant bomb at a venture, destroyed a derelict barn and carved out a crater 15 feet deep, the simple Marsh farmer promptly killed all his flukey, maggot-ridden sheep - they were a poor lot anyway - added a couple of tuberculous old cows and distributed the lot round the lip of the crater. Killed by blast, of course. He then claimed, and got, £5,000 in War Damage. The fact that this sum was precisely what he had paid for the entire farm, when land values were at the bottom of the bucket, was a limpid coincidence.

It will be realised therefore that these presumptuous foreigners, with their pratings about Town Planning, were taking on more than they knew. Let the story proceed in the words of the Councillor.

He is long, thin and eagle-nosed, with bright spy - eyes and the general look of a weasel on the war-path. A higgler by trade, he deals in anything from dogs to donkeys, from ships' anchors to heifers, old bedsteads to bottles. He is also a farm contractor with a hideous fleet of antediluvian tractors and ploughs at his behest. On the Council he is the Galahad of local rights.

'Gas lamps! What on airth do we want they for?' he challenged. 'Allus a-flickerin' an' a-flarin'. A man can't see what he's up to nights an' there's times when he don't want as others *should* see. Come a gile o' wind and out they lamps goo. Then the gas blows up when ye lights 'em ag'in. They're like to kill a man or set a woman a-fire. And it's all on the rates.

'Ile's the boy.' He warmed to the subject. 'Paraffin 'll niver let ye down. Tarn it out when ye don't want it. Cook on it. Warm your fitten at it. Light your house with it and it'll light your road home in a hand-lamp. All for two-and-thruppence a gallon. If ivery man and woman on this here Marsh on'y had a little owd ile lantern, we shouldn't want no street lamps and the owd rates'd goo down like lightnin'. Gas lamps! - We'll larn 'em.'

The fact that the Councillor's missus runs the village shop which sells not only bacon, shoe-laces, butter, china unmentionables, water-boots, tea, oil-skins, hair-pins, sugar but also oil and oil-lamps, is by the way. We veered to the matter of the Car Park.

'Car Park!' he snorted. 'Git one o' they and this here Marsh'd be like that owd place, East-End-on-Sea, where they rob ye soon as look at ye. They got rig'ments o' min all dressed up like sojers, wantin' a tanner for this and a bob for that. All ye git is a little owd ticket and a place to set your car where ye can't git out when ye want to.

'If visitors comes here, there's allus a medder where they can park their cars for a tanner a day and no tickets to clutter 'em up.'

The fact that the meadow belongs to the Councillor's son, who is not unknown to demand double fees, because unsuspecting foreigners have no ticket to prove they have already paid once to his grubby minion, is a small point. What is of more Christian importance is that after rain or much usage, when cars are bogged, the Councillor inevitably appears with his 'little owd tractor which happened to be handy-like', and tows the frenzied victims out for sums ranging from five shillings to as much as a pound. As he rightly points out, it is no burden on the ratepayers and calls for the employment of no parasites in shining uniform.

As for the impertinent proposal to put up 'Cattle Crossing' signs at Beelzebub Farm gates, this impudence was squashed at birth. Not for nothing has Bungo Bull, the owner of Beelzebub's thistly acres, been on the Council all his life and his father, granddad and great-granddad before him, unto the uttermost roots. His wife's sister's husband's cousin, young Ada Mary Matilda, married that ginger-headed sailor, Nipper, who is a 'nevvy' of the Councillor. Nor must we overlook the fact that Owd Plum Duff, the landlord of the *Nelson's Eye* was a cash customer for unlimited illicit pig-meat in the dark, gilt-edged days of war. Who shall say that such friends may not be needed again in these crazy days of science let loose?

Then gentle old Zebedee Hamstring, the white-haired minister of that peculiar sect, 'The Ranters', who weekly make the Sabbath hideous with lamentation, confession, laudation and an American hand-organ, is not only Bungo's pilot for uncharted seas above, but first-cousin to Mrs. Bungo. Moreoever, her sister, Hepzibath married Skin o' Worms, that attenuated vendor of old cow-beef and doubtful sausages. All are either on the Council or in a position to disseminate views or offer guidance. No wonder the Romans went back to Rome and the Normans gave up.

As the Councillor put it gently: 'That little owd

crossin' out o' Bungo's stockyard, acrost the road into his top medder, can allus piy. When a car comes acrost the Marsh ye ken see it a-comin' miles away. Happen that's a furriner-like, and ye gotter an owd cow what ain't fit to send to market, ye jist *urge the owd gal* acrost the road jist as the car gits on the bend by the high hedge.

'Ten to one he won't hit the owd cow if he's a right good driver. If he ain't - well, he didn't orter drive, did he now? If he do hit the owd cow, he gotter piy heavy. He can't kill hisself 'cos he dussn't take that owd corner fast. So there ain't no danger-like. That'll just larn him to drive more careful like in future. So that does the public a bit o' good in the long run and helps owd Bungo. A dead cow's allus worth 20 pund, even if she's skin and bone.'

'Suppose he doesn't hit the cow,' I asked innocently. 'How does that help Bungo?'

'Ah! Jesso,' said the Councillor, magniloquently. 'Ginerally he don't hit it, 'cos Bungo keep an owd cow special. She's a reg'lar owd point-to-pointer. She kin lep like a hunter. Yew could run that owd cow in the Grand National and she'd allus win ye money back.

'When Bungo turns that owd cow on to the road and gi'es her a stroke across the backside with a hedge-stake, she *knows* there's a car a-comin'. Soon as that whizzes round the corner, she leps across the road, through the gate and down the medder like mad. Then Bungo goes to the car, what's pulled up half in the ditch, and ses, stern as an owd magistrit:

' "There goo my best pedigree cow. In calf, too. She'll slip that calf, sure as harvest, arter the ungodly way ye near kilt her. That'll cost me a mint o' money. I shan't on'y lose the calf but the owd cow might die too.

' "I'll hev to take ye to court, Mister - dangerous drivin' and damage to my vallyable stock, though I don't want to. But a pore owd farmer like me can't lose a calf like that for nawthen." '

'What happens then?' I asked, an innocent at sea.

'They allus piy up,' the Councillor said firmly. 'That owd cow's arned £50 between June and August afore now when they furriners is allus abroad in they motorcars. Arter all, a pore owd farmer gotter look both ways if he's goin' to scratch a livin', in these hard owd times.'

Do you wonder that the 'Cattle Crossing' signs are

still a planner's dream?

As for the Dance Hall, once a boat-builder's shed, it is almost a reality. I say almost, because although the dance floor is laid, the band platform raised, the bar an empty reality and the cloakroom a gaunt vestry of cloakless pegs, the basins and lavatories which would add the final touch of civilisation are without water. Light also is lacking.

The dual tragedy arose from the conflict of Councillors Art Bugg and Cackle. Councillor Bugg is, of course, our old friend, Sir Galahad. Councillor Cackle is a recent comer to the Marsh, a builder by trade. He made his presence first felt by erecting a hideous villa of breeze blocks, white concrete, glittering glass, yellow tiles and scarlet doors. This he dumped in a grass field whence it dominates the far-flung vision of shining creeks and sea-ways, opal mudflats and hazy marshland. Fortunately, he surrounded this architectural blot with a screen of privet which, in the beatitude of Nature, promises soon to enfold it in a green obscurity.

His election to the Council, prejudiced slightly by the broadcast appeal to 'Vote for Cackle', has earned the undying enmity of Councillor Bugg. He holds, rightly, that no man should be eligible unless his forbears were on the Marsh not later than 'them days when Owd Boney was about'.

Unfortunately, Councillor Cackle got the contract for converting boat-shed into Dance Hall. Having carried out the work at considerable expense, he proceeded to envisage a trench across the main road. Through this trench he proposed to connect both electricity and water. He reckoned without Councillor Bugg.

The latter has an uncanny knowledge of the lay-out of every pipe, drain, sewer, wire and underground cable on the entire Marsh. He knew - but Councillor Cackle did not - that the locally generated electric light cables ran under the road, in the path of the trench planned by the Cackle outfit. Moreover, Councillor Bugg's own water supply, of which he makes but sparing personal use, is conveyed under the same road, in a pipe which he laid himself, in far-off days of freedom, before Inspectors became too fond of poking their bureaucratic noses into other people's affairs.

Thus, armed with inside knowledge, he addressed

Councillor Cackle on the morning of the proposed trench digging with honeyed words.

'Ye got a rare job on, owd mate, diggin' that there road up,' he confided. 'That'll cost ye a mint o' money. I've knowed that owd road this 60 year or more. Time ye git under that owd tarmac that's all solid rock and stones what them owd Romans left behind, time they built their fort back o' the church. That'll need a rigment o' min to dig through that lot. There ain't a road like it for a hunderd mile round. That'll cost ye more in wages than you'll ever make in profit on the whole job. Take ye a fortnit or more, that will.'

Councillor Cackle blanched. He is well aware that the foundations of the Roman fort lie 'back o' the church'. Moreover, he likes to do a job quickly, cheaply - with the emphasis on the latter word.

'What would you advise?' he asked with urban pomposity.

'Advise?' Councillor Art Bugg replied gently. 'I ain't no chap to advise a London gent like you, what's bin a-buildin' housen all his life. I'm only a poor little owd dealer an' agricultural contractor. But I'll tell you what I'll do, mate, seein' as we're both brothers on the Council now. I'll lend ye, for a pound or two, me trench-digger, what'll goo threw them owd Roman bricks as sweet as a knife threw butter. That'll cut a trench five foot deep afore ye can wink. Do ye borrer me big owd tractor, set the owd gal t'other side o' the road, hitch a steel cable on the trench-digger, start her up and away she'll goo. Everything'll be up in no time.'

He spoke profound truth.

Next morning Councillor Bugg's heavy tractor, with Councillor Bugg's trench-digger, arrived. They deployed on either side of the road and barred all traffic by the expedient of hitching a steel hawser to either machine. Work started. Not, however, before 10 one-pound notes had passed from Councillor Cackle to Councillor Bugg, together with a receipt, 'all writ out like', whereby Councillor Cackle accepted responsibility for the machinery and all its works whilst on hire.

The trench-digger started at the ditch-side. It dug deep, like some gigantic rabbit, into the soft earth.

Then, getting the bit, so to speak, between its teeth,

it whirred, clanked and rattled remorselessly forward, ploughing up the tarmac like seas thrown up by the bows of a great liner. Over the other side of the road, the tractor wheezed, snorted and coughed. Smoothly, beautifully, the trench-digger burrowed forward across the road. By some odd miscalculation on the part of Councillor Bugg, who is elderly and perhaps failing in memory, it encountered no Roman bricks. Instead, as he had promised, it went forward 'as sweet as a knife through butter'. Equally as he had promised, everything came up.

First, there was a blue, blinding electric flash. The earth sizzled and crackled. Bikini took a back seat. Christmas Island was not in it.

The next instant, before the imprecations of Councillor Cackle, who was guiding the trench-digger, had died away, a Niagara of water - a foaming torrent - shot skyward from the trench and drenched the Cackle gang from head to foot. Councillor Bugg's water supply had gone for six. The richer Marsh-dwellers are still cut off from electric light at the moment of writing. Older and wiser ones stick to paraffin.

At that instant the funeral arrived. Councillor Cackle, too new to the Marsh to realise when decent folk are being buried, was ignorant of the fact that old Polly Rebecca Cantilow from the Oase End Farm, down at the bottom of the Chase that leads to Titterels Marsh, was being buried that day. Poor Becky had had a good run for her money. Well into her 97th, she might have gone on a bit longer had not the wheel come off the gig when she was going into market with her boy Joe. Joe, a mere youngster of 73, broke a leg, but the old lady fractured two ribs and, lingering just long enough to distribute her worldly goods with minute care, 'died kind'.

Since the Cantilows and the Pewters - she was a Pewter, who are cousins of the Musketts, the Rumbellows, the Tantrums, the Greenchilds, the D'Ponts (who came over with the Huguenots) - are also related to the Trivetts, who left Brittany 200 years ago, and a dozen other Marsh families, the cortège was considerable. Councillor Cackle got the benefit of the lot. He heard things not commonly said at funerals.

Planks were fetched. The coffin was edged gingerly out of the hearse and carried over the trench on the shoulders of four stout bearers. Each cast glances of murderous scorn on the luckless Cackle as they passed him with their solemn burden. Then the mourners filed over the trench with leaden tread and withering glance.

It is rumoured that heavy claims are to be made. It is whispered that a certain business may soon be in the market. Whatever the truth may be, Town Planning on the Marsh has oozed to a gentle stop.

REGATTA DAY

IT BEGAN, far away and long ago, on a sunny day when gaff-rigged Victorian cutters sailed the shining Main - that deliciously Elizabethan word which still means the North Sea. There were hoys carrying coal up the long creeks to villages with Saxon names. Thames and Medway barges, red sailed, with great leeboards like huge fins, brought the beer, hundreds of noble barrels, from Gravesend. They flew little red burgees, a white shrimp dancing gaily in the wind upon each.

The beer went by creek and estuary to ancient stranded inns, sitting snugly among their ducks and geese at the seaward end of dusty lanes where dog-roses bloomed. Or they were dumped, those rotund barrels, upon quiet little coastal towns, smelling of fish.

The oyster and shrimping fleets from the Island, from Brittlesea, from the Crouch and the Roach, from Tollesbury and Maldon, made a brave show of sail upon the satin seas of those quiet yesterdays. There were hundreds of smacks. Today you see a few dozen.

Out of all this was born the Town Regatta. Every town on that long, enchanted coastline has its regatta, so it is not a mite of use, as they say, for you to try and sort out which one this was. It just happened.

It was hatched jointly from the brains of a few old-fashioned, deep-sea going, Victorian yachtsmen, with their great cutters and beamy yawls, their schooner rigs and bluff ketches, plus the bearded, blue-jerseyed fathers of the fishing fleet.

Regatta Day became, and still is, the high day of the year. In those days there were races for big yachts and little ones, for sailing dinghies and, above all, for oyster smacks. There was a barge race and a punt sailing race. In the latter, local gunners and wildfowlers sailed their long, grey, narrow craft over a five-mile course of open sea and twisting creeks, past Tempesty Corner where any puff of wind kicks up a short sea, round a couple of mud islands, inhabited by curlew and redshank and so up past Porpoise Point, where, under any Hunters' Moon, you can be pretty sure that porpoises will be slapping their tails in the night hours, like barn doors falling down.

There were starting guns going off all day, fireworks exploding at night, bonfires blazing in the dark. Dancing on the village green, fiddlers fiddling, flags flying, bunting fluttering, beer flowing and jollity supreme.

It has not changed much. True, some of 'them chaps at the Club', suburbanly nautical in brass buttons, blue reefers, white tops and sedulously preserved military ranks, born of a temporary war, but now rooted permanently, are apt to give themselves airs.

They regard such men as the Councillor who, naturally, is on the Regatta Committee, with faint condescension. The Councillor, for his part, sweeps them all into the wastepaper basket of his disdain with one phrase of fine scorn - 'butterfly sailors, allus a stickin' sideways in the mud.'

Old Ephraim, who, you will recollect, is small, withered, with sharp black eyes, cheeks like winter apples, a Breton name, and a far-off foot in Dutch waters, is another object of patronizing amusement. At least, he was. Things have changed a bit since last Regatta Day. Eph is now an object of fear, loathing, scorn and hatred by 'them chaps at the Club'.

It all began with Maggie. Maggie stands 15 hands two, is a dark bay, with a white blaze down one side of her face, a wall-eye, four white socks and a tail like a rat. Her breeding is unknown. Her makeup is wire, fire and whipcord. The Councillor bought her from old Mel - short for Melchizedek - down at the Wick Farm on Lapwater Marsh. He paid a five-pound-note, a second-hand chain harrow, a crate of old hens and a bottle of Dutch gin 'what ain't never paid a farden to nobody' for Maggie. It was a good buy.

True, she bared her yellow teeth on first sight of the Councillor and made a venomous dart at the seat of his trousers, when he incautiously turned his back. A serious mischief might have been done to the champion of the people's rights. Luckily old Mel brought the stable fork smartly down on Maggie's quarters in an instant of shrewd timing. The Councillor bore no ill-will.

'That show she hev sperret,' he remarked sagely. 'I like a animal what hev sperret. Do they don't, they'll like as not drop dead on ye.'

He drove Maggie home in the Trap. The Trap is as well-known about the Marsh country as the State Coach at Coronation time.

In it, for uncounted years, the Councillor has trotted, sucking his pipe, cracking his whip, from marsh farm to marshland inn, from weed-hung hythe to red-shingled cottages, whose wavy roofs crouch far inland under the bosom of dusky woods. He travels the old green barge roads across the marsh. His wheels have rattled over every-shell-strewn 'hard' on 40 miles of coastline. They have rustled secretly through the leafy ruts of woodland ways where a hamper full of lead-heavy pheasants, concealed by a top layer of dead and ancient farmyard 'boilers', is occasionally consigned to him after a windy moonlight night.

Maggie has been his partner in all these business jaunts. No cargo surprises her. Squealing piglets, a couple of secondhand bicycles, crates of vociferous hens, geese, snaky in sacks, an old bedstead or a haltered donkey trotting behind the tailboard, are all the same to her.

The trap bears the illuminating information that it is the property of:

Councillor Art Bugg
General Dealer
Families supplied daily

The semi-obliteration of the last business item was forced upon the Councillor by unfeeling jibes at his inexhaustible fertility. The matter is no longer funny.

And now we come back to Regatta Day. It began, fine and sunny, the sea well polished; The Club efflorescent with pink gins and brassy blondes. *The Fisherman's.* which is quite another sort of Club, social and seductive, renowned for Lucullan cooking, was bursting with blue-jerseyed, thigh booted mariners of a more robust sort. They smelt insistently of mud and winkles. The Coast road was jammed with girls in shorts, yachtsmen in self-importance, dogs in fights and the 'Admiral' in a quandary. He is Commodore of *The Fisherman's.* And, as the oldest man for miles around - 'damn near a hunderd' - he bears, like Atlas, an empyrean aura of transcendant responsibility on this of all days. For the fishermen, rough, simple and untutored, totally lacking in the social graces of Stamford Hill or Dulwich, somehow have an odd knack of winning most of the races. Sad, but true.

The fact that many of them have sailed with, or are related to, the Sycamores, Heards, Leavetts, Souths, Barbrooks and other great yacht skippers of the mighty years between Lord Dunraven's *Valkyrie* and the 'J' Class may have something to do with it. They do not, however, sport brass buttons, wear white tops or drink pink gins. These regrettable lapses from the accepted 'ton' of the rest of the yachting world are tolerantly overlooked on Regatta Day. The 'Admiral' steers a firm but tactful course between the two worlds.

Yachtsmen have even been known to look in at the *Nelson's Eye* for a pint of mild and bitter, just to prove that there is no class distinction. Even the Major, more nautical than Allcard, has been seen to accept 'a quiet snifter' - inevitably a double Scotch - from one or other of the tarry band who prey upon the oyster.

This, it is admitted, is democracy at its finest.

On the morning in question, the Councillor, no mean business man, had secured the night before, from Bungo Blow, landlord of the *Nelson's Eye* a firm order for 'an owdacious lot of bakin' apples', to be translated into baked dumplings for the merry-makers, who, later, would feast within the inn and dance upon its fairy-lit lawn.

Precisely at 10.15 a.m. the Councillor, having loaded the Trap with crates of apples advanced upon the stable door, head-stall in hand, and unlatched it.

He forgot that Maggie had not been abroad for three days. During that period she had fed exclusively on oats. She was, therefore, full of beans.

'I lifts the latch, hulls open the door and out shot owd Maggie like a rocket,' he confided later.

'She knocked me in the swill bucket, what stood ready for the pigs. She went through me owd hins, like a roarin' lion, and shot round the owd pond like the wrath o' the Lord. Me owd cat flew up the pear-tree. Me owd sow bolted atween the Missus's legs an' oover she went into the killer (wooden clothes tub), kivered o' suds from head to foot. The ducks flew off the pond. Toby, me dawg, knocked over a crate o' eggs and bruk the lot - six dozen at fower-and-nine a dozen - and there stud owd Maggie in the pond, lashin' her tail and grinnin' like a cat.

'"I'll gie you oats, you orkard owd muck," I sez an' starts for her. That tuk me 20 minutes to round her up - and best part o' tew punsworth o' damage done.

'Well, I gits her in the shafts, harnesses her up, and orf we starts nice and steady, weavin' through the folks along the coast road, till we gets to the Club.' Then the fun began.

The Club mounts a formidable little brass cannon upon its lawn. This is fixed with a shattering detonation a few minutes prior to the start of a race, and later to start the race. It can be heard, on a fine day, six miles away. Gulls abominate it. Old ladies fear it. Small boys adore it. Little girls peer at it. Members of the Club puff with pride when it goes off. It gives them the Nelson touch.

On that far-off Regatta Day, Maggie, sensitive animal, picking her way, cat-like, through the gay long-shore sailors and their bright beauties, with a cluster of 14 foot Internationals jockeying for place in the blue waters of the channel, was thinking of oats. The Councillor, reins in hand, was thinking of the money he would shortly make from Regatta folks avid for his cargo of apples. Both master and mare were full of high emprise. It only needed the spark. It came. The cannon, glinting brassily in the sun, its black mouth not 20 feet from Maggie's left ear, went off. A shattering roar. Acrid smoke. The earth trembled. Maggie left the earth.

Her neck went down. Her head shot out. Her heels went up. The bottom boards of the trap flew out. And off she went.

That is a poor description. The launching of the sputnik had nothing on Maggie. The trap flew up in the air. So did the Councillor. Horse, wheels, man, trap and apples, charged up the Coast Road at thunderous speed. Brass buttons and brassy blondes fell screaming into oyster pits. They tripped over rusty anchors. They climbed up railings. They leapt for the over-hanging bowsprits of yachts on stilts in the shipyards. The road emptied like a flash. Like a rocket Maggie fled up it. The trap rocked, bumped, jolted, now on one wheel, now on the other. At moments it left earth altogether. It was the biggest thing since Boadicea in her chariot, with scythed wheels, went that way.

The Councillor, pale and determined, crouched in his seat. The reins were gripped tightly between bony fists. Ben Hur was not in it. Cecil B. de Mille faded to a mere period-piece.

'I was a-comin' down the Coast Road, thinkin' of a nice plate o' winkles and a quart o' beer, when Art Bugg's owd mare shot past like a chariot o' fire,' deposed Bob South.

'That owd hoss went past like a flash out o' a gun. And the owd Councillor had smoke a-comin' out o' his backside.'

Apples flew from this meteoric chariot like cannon balls at Trafalgar. One, weighing a pound or more, clipped the Major under the ear. That, it was felt, was an act of God. Another got the Captain (late Army Pay Corps) smack in the third brass button on the portside. Others, with a fine impartiality, peppered blondes and brunettes and were manna to small children. The lot, a hundred-weight or more, littered the road from the Club to the *Nelson's Eye.*

Miraculously, Maggie, who had set off with the apparent intention of getting to York quicker than Turpin, pulled up at the *Nelson's Eye.* She swept in to the yard with all four legs apparently off the ground, whilst the Trap maintained a precarious connection with it, through the starboard wheel alone. Maggie pulled up in a shower of gravel, a cascade of squawking hens and a flurry of ducks. The Councillor shot from his seat, landed on a grey gander, and swore.

'Sich langwidge I never did hear,' said Mrs. Bungo Blow sorrowfully. 'Comin' from a man on the Council too.'

Within the bar, witness of this cataclysmic entry, sat Ephraim. He was partly hidden by a quart pot. His function on Regatta Day is to fire the starting gun for the afternoon races. Behannon of the Club starts the morning races. He, to his sulphuric shame, had launched Maggie on her path of flame.

Ephraim listened to the Councillor's humiliation with just anger.

'Thass time them chaps at the Club had a reef or tew tuk in their pants,' he remarked sharply. 'Tew smart be half. That's wholly a shime what they put on yew, Art, me boy. Come 'sarternoon, I'll larn 'em.'

The rest is history. Precisely at two, Ephraim departed for the Club Commodore's steam yacht lying out in the deeps. There, the six metres start their races and eventually cross the finishing line. The Gun is fired from the deck of the Commodore's yacht.

'I don't want yew muckin' about along o' mey,' Ephraim remarked sternly to Bohannon when the latter had brought him alongside the steam yacht in the Club motor launch. He added, unkindly: 'Do yew hop off back to yar owd boozin' Club and keep all on a-ladlin' out the gin for them butterfly sailors o' yourn. I was layin' and firin' a naval gun again owd Kruger an' the Boers, afore you was pupped.'

Bohannon, who comes from the sylvan glades of Stoke Newington, emitted a rude noise. He placed his thumb to his nose and departed shorewards at high speed, a plume of foam and a stream of curses following him.

Ephraim nipped smartly down the companion-way into the Commodore's saloon. He opened a locker. It contained a bottle of whisky. He opened the bottle. Shortly, it contained little whisky. Ephraim explored further. He found a Service revolver and a box of cartridges. As 'a bit of a gunner', fire-arms hold a fearful fascination for him. He loaded the weapon and popped it in his pocket. Then, a little unsteadily, he mounted the companion-way. Salt air, a glittering sea, a flotilla of white yachts, crossing and re-crossing a good half-mile up-channel from the starting line, greeted him. The Gun glinted brassily on the foredeck. It was a wicked glint.

'Uppish lot o' mucks,' Ephraim grunted to a passing gull. 'I'll larn 'em.'

He took a brass shell, loaded to the bung with deafening explosives, slipped it into the breech - and fired.

The report thundered across the glittering waters. Consternation seized the skippers of 16 competing yachts. Each glanced at his watch. Each was convinced that it was 20 minutes fast. Yet the preliminary gun had gone and they were still half a mile from the starting line. Madly they manoeuvred for place. They whistled for the wind. It was the merest caress.

'Bang!' went the Gun again. And a minute later - 'Bang!' A puff of wind, sent by a power with a sense of humour, quickened that disorderly flotilla into the semblance of a start.

They crossed the starting line in more ragged disorder than ever was shown when the last of the Light Brigade rode back from Balaclava.

And as they reached away for the Backsea Beacon, miles out to sea, shot after shot thundered from the Commodore's cannon. It is said that the barrel became red-hot.

Ashore, the Commodore, downing a quick one in the Club bar, was red with fury. He raved. Committee men turned puce. Nautical gentlemen from Balham and Tooting looked precisely as members of the Squadron might look had the guardship loosed off a broadside just as *Britannia, Velsheda, Evaine and Endeavour* were drifting it out between them somewhere off Keyhaven.

'Go out at once, Bohannon, and stop that madman,' stormed the Commodore. 'Order him off my yacht and take over the Gun yourself for the rest of the races.'

Bohannon trotted off down the hard, sprang into the launch and departed for the steam yacht at high speed. When 50 yards astern of her, a bullet sang past his ear. It smacked into the mast of an anchored yacht and erupted an outraged gull from the top of it. Bohannon, storming along at top speed, had no time to throttle down, before he was almost under the stern of the steam yacht. Another bullet smacked into the water beside him, sending up a vicious spurt of foam. An empty whisky bottle whistled through the air and nearly brained him.

Leaning over the stern-rail, revolver in hand, Ephraim addressed him sternly:

'Them's on'y practice shots. Now hop it. I've kilt scorpions wi' one shot, out in the bush. Look.'

The revolver barked again. The whisky bottle, bobbing on the waves, 10 feet from the launch, shattered into a thousand pieces.

Bohannon swung the launch and opened her out for shore. As he did so, Ephraim, swung the black muzzle of the Gun. A shattering roar blasted Bohannon's ear-drums out of his head at 20 feet range.

'That'll larn yew to frit the owd Councillor's hoss,' floated on the wind.

TALL TALES OF THE TIDELINE

THE TIDE ebbed slowly with the slow rustle of silk. The mud-flats bared to the sun in stippled silver. Gulls quarrelled lazily. A 'May bird' or titterel, which is Essex for that grey ballet dancer the whimbrel, fluted his wild, lucent note up the fairway. Oyster smacks and spratters, brown nets drying in the wind, dozed lazily at anchor. Not a day for work.

Winter lay behind with all its memories of bitter winds and blinding snows, or marsh farms cut off for days on end, power cables down, telephones dead and cows unmilked in the long bales solely because the electricity had been cut off and young men on the farm no longer know how to milk with their fingers. Such is progress.

Then suddenly, like a dream, Spring came. Dressed in light and shining green, such as Algernon Newton would paint, land and sea, cattle marsh and cornfield, lit by high skies and the bright sun. Youth was rekindled in ancient bosoms. Old memories stirred like primroses in frosty soil.

They were all there, sitting on spars and a pile of oyster baskets by the side of the oyster pits, below the scarp of the Coast Road, where the tamarisk grows and oyster sheds make a warm corner to hold the sun. The Councillor lean and avid as ever. The 'Admiral', now in his 93, but still unbloodied and unbowed. According to calculations, mathematically based and vouched for by responsible men, the 'Admiral' has now passed the high-water mark of beer consumption, to wit 20,000 barrels of good Essex ale, swallowed as a man should swallow, over the years since good Queen Victoria was young upon her throne.

'I count that'd float a tidy-sized smack,' the 'Admiral' is wont to confide.

Then, just behind him, there was Ephraim, crab-like, with Chinese eyes and Oriental guile. He would out-think a fox. Academically, Ephraim is a full-fledged graduate, a Master of Artfulness in the University of Long-Shore Sharp

Dealing.

Lesser fry of dimmer wits sat, lounged, spat and reminisced. Titus the Gunner, Skin o' Worms, Long Harry and Atlantic Bob. The latter has crossed the herring pond in sail no less than 17 times. He wears an R.Y.S. blue Guernsey, sad relic of the great days of the 'J' Class. They were talking of ships that go by wind and steam and and not by oil.

'Blow! I was in a blow once, comin' round the North Foreland,' remarked Atlantic Bob, 'when the sea was all spume and spray so as you couldn't see a wave-top. It was all white water and wind a-flyin'.

'Roll! My heart, did we roll! There was a coaster on the port-hand what rolled that much that I looked right down the funnels and saw the stokers at work.' He paused for brief effect.

'Ah, jesso,' remarked Ephraim, magnanimously. 'You young chaps warn't pupped in the days when I sailed in owd Lord Dunraven's gret owd yacht *Valkyrie*. Her what raced the owd German Kayser's yacht and larnt him his manners.

'We was comin' round Flamborough Head, under bare poles takin' it green from stem to starn, every seventh wave, when she hit a beam sea. She rolled right over. The yards went under an', Lor' Bless yer, when the yacht rolled back again on an even keel, they yards was all hung with seaweed. Reg'lar blankets of the stuff. And the owd crabs was a-droppin' on the deck like grape shot.'

A moment of Buddhistic silence, punctuated only by the swift expectorations of Skin o' Worms, as he scored a direct hit on a crab about to enter the oyster pit, was followed by a slow sigh from the Councillor.

'I ain't a sea-farin' man, nit fishing nor yachting, as ye well know,' he confided. 'But me owd Uncle Tuddy, what was the headest gunner about these parts, was in an owd square-rigged barque time he was a lad, way back in the 70's. He was a-doin' his trick at the wheel one night off Yarmouth Roads, when that blowed up suffin' fierce, right easterly. The seas come at 'em like mountains. The Scroby Sands was all hissing white and boiling up like hell let loose.

'That blowed every stitch o' canvas out o' her with cracks like guns goin' off. She run for them sands like a hoss gone wild. She struck the tail end on 'em. The mast snapped off like matches. The yards, spars, riggin' and gear went overboard in a huddle, like the imps o' Hell. The men was a-hackin' and a-choppin' with the seas breakin' o'er 'em and half drownin' 'em.

'That was the marcy of the good God that me Uncle Tuddy was at the helm. He luffed that ship, knowin' the scour of the tide and the drag of all that gear overboard, so that she just scraped past the tail o' the Sands into deep water.

'Away went the gear, mast, spars, sails and riggin', takin' the bulwarks, scuppers, davits and boats along wi' 'em. The bawsprit snapped short off and got snarled up with the fore-foot. The hatches was stove in. The ship bore up, broadside on - and a wave as high as the Nelson Monument slapped right down on her. Down she went like a stone. Men washed overboard like flies. None on 'em nivver seen again.'

'What happened to your Uncle Tuddy then?' asked an unsuspected, unsuspecting innocent.

'He wore left, holdin' just two spokes o' the wheel in his hand,' the Councillor replied majestically. 'All the rest o' the ship an' crew had gone. Me uncle steered hisself into port, holdin' on to them two spokes of the wheel.'

The 'Admiral' regarded him gravely. 'Liars I've knowd in me time,' he remarked gently. 'Big 'uns too. Out East. Lick the Yanks any day. Men I could listen to wi' respect. But b--- longshore liars I nivver could abide.'

'That minds me o' the man what was out a-hand-linin' for codlin' orf Nass End, with another owd boy in a boat,' said Atlantic Bob.

'That was bitter cold weather, middle o' winter, hunderds o' geese flyin' backards and for-ards on the Main and widgeon in rafts what covered acres of the sea. You never seed so many birds in all your life.

'But wild, you couldn't get nigh on 'em. Them tew owd boys was out in their punt day arter day and never touched a feather. Every time they drawed up the ducks or geese, the birds was up and orf afore they was in a hunderd yards on 'em.'

'Then on the Thursday night, the wind went round to the nor'ard and that started. Fust that snew. Then that blew. Then that fruz. Then that snew and blew and fruz again. That went on for 48 hours. The sea fruz for miles. Icicles was hangin' from the mast and spars six foot long. The ship was fast in the ice. Gunners Creek, where they laid, was like the North Pole. Only a trickle o' water a-runnin' down the middle o' the channel. But lor' when these tew owd boys digs their way out o' the cabin, where they'd been fruz in, what did they see?

'Hunderds o' widgeon a-settin' a quarter-of-a-mile up the channel, thick as bees. The shore was black with 'em. Acres o' birds.

' "Blast! There sets our week's rent - ah! more like a month's rent,' they sez.

'Away they goes, creepin' up the creek in their punt, one on 'em lie flat on his belly at the lanyard of the big gun and the other one, lyin' flat behind him, sculling the punt along with the hand-pads. If you'd been a duck you couldn't a seen nothin' comin' but a low, owd punt, what look like a spar o' wood a-floatin' on the water.

'Well, you knows the game, sir. Soon as a punt gits within 70 or 80 yards o' a bunch o' ducks, the man in the starn, what's sculling the punt along, bangs the scull against the side o' the punt, or rattles his boots on the floor-boards to make the birds raise their heads and spring up in the air. You can kill twice as many when they are just jumping off the water than you would if you shot at a long line on 'em settin' asleep on the water with their heads under their wings.

'Well these tew owd boys draws up to 70 yards and then ducks. The gunner tips the big gun for a flyin' shot. The steersman rattles his scull against the punt and thumps his sea-boots on the floor-boards. They ducks never moved an inch.

'So he bangs the side o' the boat again. He rattles his owd boots till the punt shivers. Not a duck moved. Not a feather shifted. Then the tew owd boys both let out a holler to see if that'd fright the birds. Nothin' happened. By this time they was within 30 yards of the birds.

' "We're too close for a shot mate and I reckon powder and shot'd be wasted on them birds anyway. Let's draw up to 'em and see what's a-matter."

'They paddled right up to the edge of the flock. There set hundreds of ducks, mallard, widgeon, pin-tails, teal, dunbirds, bar-geese and a lot o' foreigners, what they'd never see'd afore. All that mass o' ducks jest set there, without movin', 'cept their heads. Their heads was a-swivelling about like snakes.

'Well the tew owd boys landed and walked right round that gret pack o' duck. One on 'em what had done a bit o' farmin' work, cast his owd optic over the lot on 'em and says: "Tew acres - there's tew acres of fowl here, mate, worth more than any tew acres of the best wheat in the land."

'Then they walks right threw them ducks. They had to tread careful like so as not to step on the pore things, and all them ducks did was to foller 'em with their eyes and swivel their heads about. They never flapped a wing among 'em.'

The speaker paused with that sense of slow drama inherent to the countryman. Obviously he waited for the fish to rise. Skin o' Worms, never very bright in the top storey, took the bait.

'Why wouldn't them owd ducks git up and fly away?' he asked innocently.

'They was fruz - fruz in the ice,' Atlantic Bob announced. 'And their wings was fruz to their sides. They couldn't run nor yit fly.

'Them tew owd boys had to go back, git their smack, borrer some dinghies, and then they only had enough cargo space to pack them birds aboard and take 'em back to the island. Time they'd marketed 'em, they'd made a mound o' gold, that kep' 'em comfortable all that winter and they done no work that summer.'

'But how did they git the birds out o' the ice?' enquired Skin o' Worms, now firmly hooked.

'Took a scythe, silly, and mowed 'em off by the legs,' Atlantic Bob replied. 'That took 'em two full days to harness that lot.'

'Talkin' o-gunnin',' remarked the 'Admiral', for the very good reason that no one had been talking o' gunning, ' 'minds me of the time when I woke up one mornin', looks out o' me winder and sees a covey o' partridges come over the sea-wall and light in owd Zebedee's dinghy what was a-lyin' on the mud with the pair o' oars with their blades a-cockin' up in the air, jist as he'd rammed 'em under the thwarts when he rowed home full o' beer the night before. Them blessed burds was a-perchin' on them oars, a-peckin' away at the insects on the wooden blades.

'So I hustles orf downstairs into me kitch-place, takes me owd muzzle loader down from over the fireplace, rams down a couple o' charges o' powder, tops 'em up with a bit o' *Daily Mail* for wadding and then grabs me shot-belt. Lawks, that was empty. Not a charge o' shot in the place.

'So I grabs an owd tin full o' tin-tacks, shoots a handful o' them down each barrel, tops 'em up with another bit o' *Daily Mail* and hopes for the best.

'I sneaks out o' me back door, down under the lee o' me boat shed and creeps up alongside of a smack what laid on the mud, till I gets right under her bows, not 30 yards from them partridges.

'I takes aim, pulls both triggers and orf the owd gal goes, with a row like a couple of housen a-fallin' down. That was all smoke and bits o' *Daily Mail* flamin' over the shore.'

'Did ye hit them partridges?' enquired the Councillor, no mean dealer in illicit game.

'Ah, I hit 'em but I den't git 'em,' the 'Admiral' replied.

' 'Not git 'em? How was that?'

'Well, yer see, them tin-tacks nailed them birds to the oars. They up and flew away with the pair on 'em - and damn nearly took the boat with 'em too.'

A herring gull barked derisively. Red shank took off from the tide edge with scandalised yelpings. Nature seemed affronted. Alone the bearded, wrinkled, salt-encrusted humans reminiscing by the square pool full of laden oyster baskets, pursued their prurient course.

' 'Minds me o' what happened to my owd muzzle gun,' Titus remarked gently. 'I'd stood the owd gal up in the washus corner all one summer with a charge in 'er. What the Missus a-bilin' up the copper tew days a week and the place full o' steam, the powder caked up. Hard as a brick.

'Come duck shootin' time, I goos over to Feldy in me punt, crawls up the wall and peeks through the grass on top to see what was on Sampson's Fleet, t'other side. There set a nice bunch of young ducks, not tharty yard away.

'I primes me owd gun with new priming powder, hops on a cap, squints down the barrel, sez me prayers - and -

pulls the trigger.'

'Did she goo orf?' Ephraim enquired professionally.

'Noo,' Titus replied. 'She give a hiss. Like a snake. Or a kettle.'

'What did ye do?'

'Hulled the owd gal right into the Fleet and bopped down behind the sea-wall quick,' Titus replied unashamedly. 'I warn't a-goin' to be blowed up. The owd gal was nigh on a hunderd year owd and the metal in the barrel had sugared. She warn't worth 10 bob.'

'So she wore a dead loss?' Ephraim enquired.

'Dead - but no loss,' Titus said firmly. 'She went off under water, just as she hit the bottom o' Sampson's Fleet and d'yew know mate, she blowed herself up and killed the nicest bunch o' eels I ever put in a sack. Tharty bobs-worth.'

On which note the company, seeing by the sun that it was opening time, wended its majestic way to the welcome arms of *The Victory*. Honour had been satisfied all round.

EPHRAIM'S LITTLE WAYS

'EFRUM' is like a walnut. Small, brown, wrinkled, weathered by wind and rain, and a rare hard nut to crack. But full of meat. No man on two legs contains more monkey-like guile or unlettered wisdom. And, like most East Coast men, he is an epigrammatist. His sayings are pointed. His wit, unlike that of the conscious town wit, is never repeated for the mere sake of effect. It is spontaneous - born of the moment.

Efrum has dwelt on the head-waters of our estuary for uncounted years. He may be anything between 55 and 80. Always the same bent, tight-muscled, little figure, nipping along the Hard, with quick, crab-like steps; sharp, darting little eyes; hands that are never empty; a mind that is always 'contriving'. He is smacksman, winkler, eel-netter, punt-gunner, flight-shooter, rabbiter, dealer in illicit or licit wildfowl. He is up to anything. Had he been born a century ago he would have been a smuggler. His grandfather was. Two centuries back and he would have been a pirate. His great-grandfather was. Three centuries back and he would have been a privateersman. His great-great-grandfather fought at the battle of Sole Bay. Efrum carried on the family tradition and earned local glory and War Office wrath by discharging his immense muzzle-loading 8-bore at a wounded Zeppelin, which limped low over him, on its homeward track to Germany on a dark night during the Kaiser's War.

'He'd bin a-bombin' on 'em up in London, so when he come back over me right low I give him one up the back-side, jest to larn him,' Efrum explained. 'Our gunners had put a shot in his locker and my old hand-gun jest about reached him. I heerd the shot rattle on his owd hide. But, Lor! The gunnery officer come down to see me and didn't half give me a flea in my owd lug. Sez as how that owd Zeppeleen might ha' dropped a bomb on the town jest to spite us.

"Well," sez I. "If you sojers daresn't shoot at him -

or mebbe you can't hit him if you do shoot - then an' owd feller like me is just a-goin' to let them Germans know as how us river gunners *can* sting 'em up." '

That was Efrum's major contribution to the First World War. In the more recent conflict he lassoed an aerial torpedo. It fell on a grass marsh at the head of a tidal creek which goes snaking inland from the wide estuary.

'That was same as this way. That there owd torpeeder come down on Brickhouse Marsh 'bout two o'clock one winter mornin'. That never went orf. Jest laid there. Jest a-fore light, along comes the looker (marsh farm bailiff) seeking a sick horse. He sees this here owd torpeeder a-layin' in the rough stuff and thinks that's his owd Dobbin.

' "Git up, hoss," he say. And he give that a stub with his boot. That made his owd corns holler. Then he tuk a look, sees what that was an', Lawk A Mussy! he shruk out like an owd owl and lit out for the farm like a long dog. That scat him. He's chicken-hearted, that one.

'So I no more to do but rove a cable round that owd torpeeder and me an' my little owd boy, we lugged that down to the creek an' dropped it in 10 foot o' water. Best place too. Can't hev them owd contraptions layin' about.'

Politically Efrum has made his mark. It happened last Harvest Sunday. Efrum's wife is a God-fearing, psalm-singing dame, a prop and pillar of the church, the apple of the Rector's eye. Not so Efrum. Church and he are hardly on nodding terms. Mrs. Efrum strives mightily to remedy this pagan state. She represented forcibly in nasal, minatory terms, that it was high time that Efrum should pay his respects to the Lord, his obeisance to the Rector and his thanks for the Harvest. She pointed out that all right-forward men went to church, if not to confess their sins, at least to support in public esteem their hard-working down-trodden wives who, throughout the week, work themselves to the bone, in order to provide callous spouses with good meals and warm beds.

'Chu'ch! Nit for me,' announce Efrum firmly. 'A man h'aint gotter goo to chu'ch ne more than three times in his life. That's a-plenty. Fust time he goo, they hull a lot o' water in his face. Second time he goo, they clap an owd woman on his back - jest like you, me owd mate -

and that take him all the rest of his life to get riddy o' she. Third time he goo, they chuck him in a hole and hull a cartload o' dirt on top of him. Thass all there is to this here chu'ch-goin'.' He spat firmly in the kitchen fire.

'You wicked owd davvle,' shrilled the sorely put-upon companion of his bosom. 'May the Lord strike you dead. What about the good harvest, what the good Lord send ye? Don't you give no thanks for that?'

'T'aint my harvest,' retorted Efrum majestically. 'Thass the owd farmers' harvest. Let 'em goo an' give thanks on their bended knees. They got forever o' money and bottles o' whisky in the cupboard. Let 'em goo an' praise the Lord, 'cos I don't doubt he'll trounce 'em when he get 'em up aloft later on.'

'What about your harvest money and your harvest beer and all them eels you drawed out o' the farmers' fleets, and your fishin' and your gunnin' - don't you give no thanks for them? Do you come a-Sunday',' persisted she whom he describes privily as 'me owd tarmagant'.

'Awright! Awright!' replied Efrum, weakening. 'Howd your clapper, I'll make a bargain wi' ye. If that rain I'll goo to chu'ch. If thass fine, I'm gooin' a-rabbiting.'

Peace descended. But, lo, when Harvest Sunday dawned, the heavens opened, the rain descended. Rabbiting was out of the question. Efrum sulkily donned his best greeny-black broad-cloth, rammed on his old hat and departed, grumpily, to church.

Recapitulating events later, he said: 'Cor! Blast! That rined so I had to goo. So, thinks I, I'll hev a front seat and make the best on it. So I gits right up in the front row, under the owd Parson. Lumme, the singing was lovely. They hollered out like a lot o' mavishes (thrushes). I sung out wi' the best on 'em - allus keepin' a-jump or two ahead on 'em. Then that come to sarmon time. The owd Parson he clawed his way up into the pulpit, stuck his owd glasses on his snout, poked his owd snout into a lot o' papers, peeked at us like an owd owl and sez:

' "Now, bretheren, I'm agoin' to give you a little discourse about the time when our good Lord fed the multitude on five loaves and tew little fishes."

'Lor! I hops up quick in me front seat an', bein' a good owd Tory, I sings out sharp: "Cor! Blast! Master, you don't mean to tell us they got a Labour Guv'mint in them days?" '

A decent veil has, by common consent, been drawn over the decorous uproar which followed. Efrum, capped his political pronouncement a month later, when the old Squire was taken mortally ill. Between that benevolent, rural overlord and Efrum, there existed a mutual bond of love and respect - a bond born of many days together in small boats with the gun on salt waters. So, at the point of death, the Squire sent for Efrum, who departed for the Hall, with lagging steps and sad mien. He was shown in by the butler, and ushered upstairs to the sick man's bedroom. A feeble voice bade him enter. What transpired is best told in Efrum's own words.

'There laid the pore owd Squire, gashly white. Wonderful shrunk he was. As good an owd gennleman as ever rode a hoss or cocked a gun. A rare good owd pal to me too, an' all on 'em that worked on the estate. One of the rale owd gintry. He cocked his owd optic at me and he say, wonderful weak: "Well, Efrum, boy. I ain't long for this here world. I'm goin' aloft, or down below. Don't know which, till I git there. But I wanted to say goodbye. We've allus bin good friends Efrum."

' "Ha! Man an' boy, Squire," I says, "You've bin a topper, sir. What you want now is a drop o' rum. That'll hev you on your hindlegs quick. Nelson's blood. That'd make a mouse bite a dog."

' "No, no," says the Squire, "I'm a gonner. But look here, Efrum. I want you to do one last thing for me - one last wish."

' "Anything you say, sir, shall be done. Double-quick, too."

' "Well," says the Squire. "When I'm dead I don' t want to be buried up in that chu'chyard. I ain't a-goin' to be no worms' breakfast. I want to be cremated and when I'm cremated do you git the h'ashes and put 'em in a h'urn and put that little owd h'urn in a box, and put a little note in the box with it and post that little owd box up to that owd Chancellor o' th' Exchequer. And in that little owd note you write these words: "Now, you owd miser. You've got the d---- lot' ".'

'But there,' Efrum recounts with unction. 'I warn't a-havin' none o' that lark. I fetched the owd gennleman up a bottle o' rum an' the owd butler and me shot a few tots o' that into him and he ain't in the chu'chyard yit and he ain't in no box. He's a-gettin' about, strong as a hoss. Too good to lose, too fierce to die. Thass our owd Squire.'

THE RACING DONKEY

EPHRAIM'S NEPHEW, Art Bugg, is on the Council. A potent fact. Ephraim, who is small and cunning, full of sin, ancient and tough as old wire nails, thinks small beer of his nephew. That is understandable. For Ephraim is a man of salt water. His life is spent going down to the sea in small ships, hauling on trawls, gunning for the wild geese under the white moons of winter, winkling on the bitter mud flats where the November 'easterly' cuts like a knife and netting eels, on illicit forays, from private marshes. In short, Ephraim is a man of action.

Had he lived in the days of Good Queen Bess, he would have been a robber, a buccaneer, a slitter of Spanish throats. As it is, he is merely a smacksman, with an eye for the main chance and a foot in every hatchable plot. Ephraim is no fool. Flies which light upon him spring skyward with hot feet.

So when Ephraim button-holed me in the Captains' Bar of the *King's Head,* which stands in the village square opposite the lock-up and the church, whose tower flies that bold copper vane of a smack under full sail, I paid attention.

'Look here, Master,' said Ephraim, jabbing me with his blackened clay. 'Yew know my nevvy Art, him what's on the Council. Him what's a higgler, an owd hen-dealer. Him what would send his own mother to market if she had feathers on, the artful young muck. Yew know him?'

'I've known him 25 years or more, Ephraim. You know that.'

'Ah! I dessay. But yew don't know that young muck as I dew. You only know him when he's got a clean collar on. Artful! He's sharper than Cleopatra's needle.' This, coming from such a red-hot practitioner in cunning as Ephraim, is no mean tribute to the artfulness of Art.

'Well, Ephraim,' I said mildly. 'What's on your mind?'

'T'ain't on my mind, Master, but that'll be on yourn

afore the night's out. I want you to put a piece in the papers about that there young Art. The publick orter be warned. Dew they ain't, he'll ketch 'em, sure as harvest.'

'What's he been up to, Ephraim?'

'Tradin' in donkeys - damn nearly traded in death.'

I sought elucidation. Art, the hen-dealing Councillor, who will buy and sell anything from a pig to a pram and who travels the tortuous marshland lanes in bone-shaking discomfort on a rust-eaten bicycle of antique vintage, this earning ribald comment from streetcorner wits, had been to a Sale.

The sale was at Scrivener's Farm, an old place lying in a moat at the head of a creek full of white ducks. Art bought 'forever o' things'. A set of chain harrows, four bedsteads, a dozen chairs, 30 hens, a tumble-cart for 30 shillings, some bee hives, a stuffed fox, an old drill which fetched five shillings only, a set of Herd Books for a shilling, a muzzle-loading gun - and the donkey. The donkey was in a pig-sty.

The sale was on Friday. Art removed the hens on Saturday plus several trusses of hay which he had neither bought nor paid for. He spent Sunday collecting the chairs and beds which he put into the Monday junk auction in the market town. Tuesday, Wednesday and Thursday were spent selling the stuffed fox for half-a-crown to a small-holder, fobbing off the chain harrows on a farm foreman when his master was known to be away for the day and selling the bee-hives, for which he had paid three and six-pence to an old lady for a pound.

On Friday he called for the Herd Books and gun on his bicycle, having sold the tumble-cart the night before for five pounds 10 shillings. As he was loading the Herd Books into his carrier he heard dull, thudding explosions from the pigsty, followed by a heart-rending bray, which soared to a sky-shattering plaint of unalloyed agony.

'Cor! Blast! Thass me owd donkey,' ejaculated Art. 'I'd wholly forgot the owd muck. He'll kick that sty ter bits.' He went to the pig-sty, unlatched the door and let the moke out.

That is a bald description of an unforgettable eruption. For the donkey, bereft of food for days, shot out of the pig-sty like a cannon-ball from a medieval arbalast and catapulted itself round the stockyard at a rate which would have made Robert the Devil look silly. *En passage* it rent the welkin with ear-splitting brays.

Art, leaning contemplatively on his bicycle, appraised his performance with a glint in his eyes.

'Cor! Thass a proper racin' donkey,' he muttered. 'A real Newmarketer! He'd win the dam Derby if yew kep' him short o' grub fer a fortnit. Here, come on, mate.'

Thus addressed, the donkey, mellowing on his 14th lap, sidled up to Art who, catching it by the head-stall, led it into a stable, where a morsel of unrobbed hay had survived his raid.

'That on't dew to let yew stuff yar guts right out, me owd mate,' he remarked to the donkey, 'seein' as how yew've been short o' grub for a week. What's more I want yew to come up to Parson's. He bin talking o' gittin' a donkey for his little owd trap. So I'll hop on the bike and yew can give me a tow up-street.'

Mounting his bicycle, Art gave the donkey a longish rope and was towed at a smart trot up the village street and past the Rectory, where he knew the Rector would be working in his herbaceous border. The smart clack of hooves caused the Reverend's eyebrows to raise themselves from Mother Earth and swivel with bushy inquisitiveness towards the road.

'Ah, Bugg, a donkey I see,' remarked the Rector, straightening himself. 'A very smart trotter, too. Is he good in a trap?'

'Mild as milk, smart as paint and set up and say his prayers if you ast him,' lied Art cheerfully. 'He bin the the friend and comfort of a pore lady wot passed over ne more'n a fortnit ago,' he added knowing full well that the Rector had never ventured on to the lower marshes of Scrivener's Farm where the donkey had pursued his vagabond existence.

'I'm takin' him up to me sister, wot want a little owd donkey to go in a little owd cart. I bin lookin' out special for suffin for her.'

'That's a pity,' the Rector observed. 'I wanted just such a donkey as that to go in my trap. What with the price of petrol and the chances of it going on the ration again, I feel a donkey would be an admirable compromise. Easier to feed than a pony too. And the children could ride it. But, there, your sister comes first naturally.'

'That she don't,' said Art with finality. 'She's away for a week and I gotter keep this old donkey till she comes back. Bein' I'm a busy man, an' all me Council work as well, I jes' as soon get riddy of this here owd donkey to a gennleman like you as I would have that roamin' round me backyard for a week. Five pun, me sister said she'd gimme.'

'Indeed,' said the Rector, who has private means and believes the best of his fellow-men. 'Then, if I were to offer you five pound 10 shillings, perhaps you would be able to find your sister another donkey to suit her needs.'

'That I could, right smart,' Art replied, 'but 'haps not as smart a donkey as this here. But there y'are, sir, he's yourn, and I'm right glad he's gone into the Chu'ch.'

The donkey meanwhile, released on the Rector's lawn, had just smartly tossed his nine-year old daughter over its head. Art observed this out of the tail-end of his watchful eye. The Rector, his back turned to his rueful offspring, now sitting up and rubbing her head silently, not daring to admit her unlawful experiment with the Councillor's steed, had seen nothing.

'Is the animal good with children?' he enquired mildly.

'That will be! Time that git into their ways,' Art said hastily, 'That on'y need a bit of knowing. Yew can larn that donkey anythin,' adding under his breath 'with a hedge-stake'.

'But there you are, Sir, I mus' be gittin along, so if yew like to gimme five pun 10 we'll call that awright.'

'Certainly, certainly,' said the Rector, digging out his notecase. 'Here we are. And I cannot thank you enough, my dear Bugg.'

Art, who had pouched the five pounds 10, wanted no thanks but merely to remove himself as quickly as possible to his own parish, five miles away, leaving the Rector's children to the tender mercies of the Newmarketer.

A week passed. Then news travelled by marshland tom-tom to the effect that the donkey had kicked the bottom boards out of the Rector's trap, thrown the eldest daughter into a dyke, jumped into a cold frame, damaging the frame but not himself, and had gone for the Curate with its teeth bared and its tail out as straight as a poker. Things in the parish of Saltcoat-cum-Salting were fairly humming.

Art reflected that he had done well to buy the donkey

for 30 bob without seeing it and sell such a bombard of trouble for five pound 10 - until the Rector's car drew up with a rattle at his gate and the Rector's eyebrows shot themselves accusingly at him.

'That donkey, Bugg,' he began:

'Same as me poor little owd donkey,' said Art mournfully. 'I count he bin a-pinin'-like. He never bin away from home afore. I doubt he's a dolourin'.' He regarded the Rector with a benign and humanitarian eye.

'The donkey has nearly killed my daughter,' the Rector said severely. 'He has kicked the bottom out of my trap and he went for my Curate as though he was going to bite him.'

'Ha, thass 'cos he bin all his life along o' that pore owd lady what passed over,' Art explained. 'He ain't used to young folk and I dessay your trap rattled. He allus went in a little owd basket carriage afore. If he heerd an owd trap a-rattlin' behind him, he might lay into it with his heels. Tain't only human, arter all. Ain't it?'

'But why did he go for my Curate?' the Rector demanded.

'That all depend on what your young Rarverand say to him,' Art observed judicially. 'If he giv that owd donkey the rough edge o' his tongue when that owd donkey ain't had nothin' but soft words all his life from this pore lady wot passed over, that ain't only natural as he should go for the young Rarverand. 'Haps he ain't as kindly spoke as you are, Sir.'

The Rector ignored the artful thrust.

'What I want to know is what we are going to do about it,' he replied. 'I must get rid of the animal. Are you prepared to take it back?'

"Nit at five pun 10," declared Art firmly. 'All thru' obligin' of you, I've lorst a sale to me sister, for when she heerd as how I'd sold this here donkey, what allus took to wimmenkind wonderful well, she up and bought another one herself - the owd cackler. Even if I 'blige you by takin' that donkey orf your hands for 50 bob, I might hev him hangin' round my yard, eatin' his head off, for months. And being a busy man like, with all me Council work as well, I can't git cluttered up with no donkeys.'

'Come and get the beastly thing,' said the Rector testily. 'It's a menace to life and limb. Take it away tonight and you can have it for 50 shillings and good riddance.' Saying which he let in the clutch and rattled off, bristling with most unecclesiastical choler.

Art waited until the Rector would be at Evensong. Then he appeared in the Rectory stableyard, collected a bottle of beer from the maidservant, assuring her that all such deals were celebrated at the vendor's expense, hitched the donkey to his bicycle and calmly pedalled away with the unpredictable beast trotting alongside him as gently as a lamb. It seemed to like bicycles.

This gave Art an idea. He bicycled a mile and a half out of his homeward way in order to pass through the long and straggling village of Layer-de-la-Tregoz, one of those charming Norman-French place names which are scattered through the marshlands.

Over a pint and a deal in hens at the *Donkey in Buskins* the night before, Art had heard that a new inhabitant, a young Londoner, had come to the Norman-French village and had bought the local milk round. He had the round, the milk float - but no pony. Art pedalled quietly past the front of the dairyman's house, guessing rightly that he would be busy in the garden. The donkey looked as though milk would never curdle in his mouth, trotting prettily beside the bicycle, swishing its tail daintily. The milkman looked up with an appraising eye. Art waved with grave magnanimity.

'Welcome to our little owd place, Sir,' he said genially. 'I knowed Alf Cant wot had this round afore yew, all me born days and I on'y hope yew do as well as he did. Thass a good little owd bizness, if yew don't mind the rough owd roads and narrer little lanes. The're cruel on a motycar. Run yew into forever o' money. But I dessay Alf warned yew.'

'Yes, it's a scattered round,' said the young dairyman politely. 'Some very out-of-the-way spots - but very quaint. It must be a bit bleak in winter.'

'Up to yer backside in slud,' declared Art with indelicate forthrightness. 'That'd swaller a motycar. You want a good strong animal - suffin what'll live rough, lay rough, travel rough and never let yer down.'

The dairyman cast an enquiring eye at the donkey. It stood by its master's bicycle, the picture of sleek strength and docile obedience. Somehow, Art has a way with him.

'That's a handy looking donkey,' he remarked. 'I suppose he'd pull anything and go anywhere.

'He bin a-pullin' beer barrels most o' his life,' said Art casually. 'Me brother wot worked for a brewery used this here donkey for pullin' a little owd cart wot they used in the narrer lanes in Marshport. He's pulled enough beer to drown'd a hunderd strong men.'

'Then he'd be just right for my milk float,' said the dairyman.

'Right. He'd knock on the doors for yew and count out the change,' said Art. 'That donkey bin brought up on these here marshes. I'm a takin' him over now, this minnit, to a man at Layer Britton, wot want to give me five pun 10 for him.'

'Well I'll give yer six pounds here and now,' said the dairyman, fascinated by the mildness in the donkey's eye. The animal changed hands quicker than a bookmaker changing a cheque the morning after Race Day.

We will draw a decent veil over the events of the subsequent fortnight. The donkey is creditably reported to have bolted with the float full of milk bottles, scattering their shattered fragments over a mile of rutted road. It is said to have bitten a customer's pig for no apparent reason other than that the pig 'sidled up'. It reared up on its hind legs in the dairyman's yard and planted both fore feet firmly in the midst of tray upon tray of eggs of doubtful origin, thereby, no doubt, doing a public benefit. Finally, it kicked the dairyman himself. Some say in the stomach and others in the cowshed. Appeals to Art fell on deaf ears. He maintains that the smell of milk curdled the temper of an upright and forthright donkey heretofore nurtured on the manlier smell of malt and hops. As for taking it back, he is known to have declared:

'The right place for that there donkey is Newmarket. He's a racin' donkey - wasted in these here parts.'

And I, true to Ephraim's trust, have now warned the public.

EHPRAIM ON FISH

'SAME AS FISH,' remarked Ephraim. 'They're rum owd pups. You'll think a fish warn't nothin' more'n a fish wouldn't you? But Lor! Some on 'em is artful as foxes. Now look at them owd roker.'

We were sitting on the tarred and salty deck of the smack in the mouth of Lalling Creek. She swung at her anchor on an ebbing tide. Up-river the immense estuary was Mediterranean blue. Seventeen miles long and three miles wide, our river is of no mean sort. A river of wide sea-scapes, of saltings and shining muds that melt into the far horizon of low up-land, where the corn stubbles were harvest gold, between ramparts of tall Essex elms.

'Look at them owd roker,' Ephraim went on remorselessly, slewing his cock-sparrow eyes which have weathered more than 70 winters of nor-easterly blows. I forbore to look, for though we had taken 23 great roker, which is Essex for skate, in our peter-nets, the night before in that creek, now not a fish. Not even a dab. Not a smell of a scale. It might almost have been as if no fish had ever been there at all.

'It's a mystery,' I said. 'Where have they gone?'

'Thass a rum 'un. I'd swear to any man as there was 300 owd roker in this here crick last night. Big, ugly owd davvles, too. Yit we ne more than ketched under tew dozen on 'em, afore losing their bosses like, t'othershave all gone off into the main river to look for new gov'ners. Thass the nature on 'em.'

Now Ephraim may, or may not, be right, but he is a wise man in the ways of fish, especially of that ugly, horny-backed, irritating, sometimes exciting and always extremely edible fish, the skate.

Whether skate follow their leader or not we cannot tell, for they keep fairly close to the bottom of the channel, but certainly grey mullet will follow a leader like a flock of sheep. More than once, when netting them, if one mullet jumped the net, the rest of the shoal invariably followed, flying out of the water like trout. I reminded Ephraim of this. He grinned cunningly.

'Ha! But you can best 'em. Allus set a second net below the fust one. They'll jump the fust one, but they'll never jump a second one.' The point is worth remembering.

These mullet nets, which are used on various east coast estuaries and formerly employed on Breydon Water, near Yarmouth, are known as poke or purse nets. The main net consists of light, small meshes, on either side of which are larger, loose-fitting nets.

'When them owd mullet strike the outside net,' announced Ephraim, with oracular finality, 'bein' bull-headed-like they blunders on into the little owd light net and pushes that through the meshes of the bigger net. So each owd fish sort of pockets hisself. That's what comes of bein' bull-headed.'

'But, Lor',' he went on, 'if you'd have wanted to see a bull-headed owd booy you should ha' seen that owd conger what I took a month back on the Stumble. Weighed 27 poinds he did and went at me like a dawg.' I awaited details.

'I wore out on the flats arly one mornin' jest arter the tide had drawed off, lookin' for winkles. I finds me beauty stranded in a little owd fleet. As long as an oar and as thick as my thigh, with a head on him like a dawg and eyes as wicked as me owd dad's when he's had a skinful.'

Since Ephraim's dad, to digress, is well on in his 90's and given to Saturday night brawling, and once earned local fame by declaring, when asked, at a Coroner's inquest why he had not cut down a poor suicide whom he found hanging in a cart-shed early one morning: 'What I cut him down? Not me. He warn't dead yit' - I reflected that the conger must indeed have been the epitome of all wickedness.

Moreover, since he was as long as an oar, he must have been rather longer than Ephraim, who is short, bent and infinitely guileful.

'I ha'n't got no axe, nor yet no hammer,' Ephraim went on, 'and you allus want an owd axe handy, or a dam gret hammer, when you happen on an owd conger. He'll bite through your foot as soon as look at ye. Cunnin' as an owd farmer-whilk (spider-crab). And he'd out-think a fox.

'Well, I has no more with me than an owd 'tater sack for me winkles and me two bare hands. How was I to git that there owd conger in that there owd bag?'

'Blowed if I know. How did you?'

'I charmed him in! Fust of all I puts the bag in front of his owd snout and clouts him on the tail with a bit of an owd spar, what I found on the mud. Lor! He whipped round like a flash, chucked up the water all over me and dam near had me by the leg. I hopped as high as the church spire.

'Right, me beauty, thinks I, if you won't go for'ard we'll see if you'll go backwards. So I howds me owd bag open behind him with one hand and clouts him on the snout with me spar with the other. Lor! He barked like an owd dawg and his eyes glared at me like the davvle. Ooh! He looked hell, fire and murder, did that owd eel. But he drawed back into me bag awright, a good foot-and-a-half on him.

'So I drops the bag on him, draws back a yard or two and then comes creepin' up on him like an owd fox, sayin', sort o' low and fierce-like; "Yew owd davvle! You'd eat a dead sailor, would ye! I'll tan ye!" An' I aims another clout at his snout.

'Lawks a-mercy! He reared up like an owd boa-constrictor and thinks I, "Efrum, he'll hev ye!" So I hulls me bit of spar at him. He drawed back awright - another foot on him. Still drawing into me bag. I keeps this here caper up and in the end I got him in me bag, tied up the neck and humps him on me shoulders. I carried him across the flats, best part of a mile to the sea-wall, and then I gets a bit o' rock and stove his owd head in.

'But, Lor! He twisted and scrapped round in that bag all the way back to me cottage, like a mad thing. Very nigh chucked me off me owd bike. Then I didn't get ne more'n a pound for him from the shop I sold him to. That done me for ketching congers for that place. I'll send you the next one, bag an' all.'

'What's the worst customer you've ever had out of the river?' I asked the old man.

'Six-foot shark in the nets one day. Had to shoot him with me owd cripple-stopper. Then I had an octopus years agoo - got suckers on him two or three foot long - and jest afore the war I found an owd swordfish, half-dead, up in a gut in the salts. He was nine foot long and had a sword on him three-and-a-half-foot long. A gent comes down from the British Museum arter him.

'But, Lor! I wish I had that owd swordfish now. I'd take him right up to that owd London, smuggle him into that owd Parlymint and let him gie one or two on 'em a good owd poke with his snout. That'd larn 'em to ruin Foulness and tax the beer and 'bacca. Lor! I'd give that owd swordy a pension if he'd do that little job.'

'What's the biggest crab you've ever caught?' I asked.

'A six-and-a-half pounder, that I caught off the Kentish Knock about a fortnit ago. He had claws on him like a money-lender. He'd a done well up in Parlymint, too. There's two or three on 'em what I could've pointed out to him. Me owd mate had a seven-pounder a year or two back.'

'They got a 14 pounder at Mersea in the middle of the war,' I said. 'Took him off Harwich. I've got one of the claws as a paper weight, nine inches long and four inches wide. How's that?'

'Ha! they Mersea men allus was liars - born that way,' Ephraim observed judicially.

I reminded Ephraim that C. J. Cornish had recorded a crab of 16 pounds, and that the late Arthur Patterson, that painstaking Norfolk naturalist, had a record of a crab caught off Penzance which was said to weigh between 20 and 23 pounds.

'In January, 1912,' I added, 'Patterson found, in a picture framer's shop in Yarmouth, what he at first thought to be a pair of mal-formed fallow deer's antlers, but which turned out to be the pincer claws of an enormous crab, sent from Portugal, which was said to have provided a meal for five hands on board the fishing boat.

'He measured the claws from pointed end to socket and found them to be exactly 16 inches in length. When he compared the measurements with those of an eight ounce crab proportionately, he reckoned that the big Portuguese crab had not run to more than 14 pounds, which hardly agrees with the nine-inch claw, of my 14 pound, crab from Harwich.'

'Yis, yis,' agreed Ephraim. 'There's rum owd things come out o' the sea and there's some rum owd booys ought to goo into it - with bricks tied round their necks. I could find a few on 'em up in that owd London if I was to hop on me bike and goo up there and hev a peek round. A wicked owd hole. Allus was - allus will be.'

On which sociological note we cranked up the anchor, shook out the sails and voyaged up-river to the untainted innocence of Ephraim's home town, where every prospect pleases and only visiting politicians are *de trop*.

ON POACHERS

THE SALMON poachers are up to their dirty tricks under the moon. Within weeks the grouse poachers will set their nets across narrow corries to catch the coveys flying low to their feeding grounds. Soon the motorised wide-boys will move in on pheasants and partridges. The poaching season is just beginning.

There are two sorts of poachers - the cold-blooded mass killers who take game for the market and the village poacher who does it for sheer devilry and to get his Sunday dinner. I have several old chums who belong to the latter class. Even the game-keeper, a very human chap, usually has a soft spot for the local hedge-bandit.

No one has sympathy for salmon poachers. If you were in the Highlands tonight in a lonely glen, you might see, as I have seen in Western Ross, dark figures moving stealthily on both banks of a tumbling salmon river. They cast something into the river just where it swirls into a deep pool. Below that pool it runs over shallows. There, the three men, knee-deep, wait for their prey.

Suddenly the pool is convulsed by the agonised plunges of great salmon fighting for their lives. Some leap straight out of the water on to the bank and lie there gasping. Others swirl belly-upwards, gleaming whitely, into the shallows, and are scooped up in landing nets by the waiting poachers.

This is Cymag poisoning. Chuck it into a river and within seconds the fish cannot breathe. That is why they throw themselves bodily out of the water on to the bank, victims of silent, calculated murder. Minutes later a van parked on the rough hill road is loaded up with silvery corpses and driven off into the moorland night. In the morning, hotels and boarding houses, full of tourists, have a back-door caller offering fresh-caught salmon at cut prices. Wise hoteliers say 'No' and slam the door. Those less scrupulous - or naive - snap up the 'bargains'. They do so at their peril. A fish poisoned by Cymag carries the deadly threat of cyanide poisoning for those who eat it. That is why salmon poachers go to jail for a long stretch.

I prefer the ancient ways of my old mate, Jake, the marshman. When he plods homeward at dusk he puts down his 'yokes' - copper-wire snares - and picks them up at dawn.

'I set 'em one fist high for a rabbit, two fists high for a hare' says Jake. 'Always 10 yards out from the hedge, 'cos when a rabbit comes out of his hole, he sniffs the wind, hops a few yards and then, generally, sets off at a fair trot. That's when he sticks his neck into my yoke. If I set it close to the hedge, he'd see it or feel it. I never set 'em where sheep are. If they get their legs tangled up it causes a lot of damage and too many enquiries.'

Jake has a rough half-bred lurcher called Nick. 'Cunning as the Devil hisself,' he confides. 'I set long gate-nets trailing loose from the bottom of the field gates. Then I set yokes in the 'smeuses' - or holes in the hedge - where hares go through regular, if they don't go under the gate. Soon as that's dark I send Nick into the field where the hares feed. He rounds 'em up like sheep, quiet as a mouse. Them hares rush to the gate and the hedge. They go straight into my gate-net and get bundled up in the loose end. If they go through the smeuses, my yokes catch 'em. And I'm waiting in the lane with a sack over me shoulder. I might get half a dozen in a night - one for the missus and me, one for my old mum and the rest for me mates. Arter all, two hares eat as much as a sheep, so the farmer orter give me a medal for ketchin' 'em.'

Later, when cock pheasants come out to feed at dusk they may find brown cardboard cups like inverted ice-cream cones planted neatly in tiny holes. Each cone is baited with wheat. The rims are smeared inside with sticky bird-lime. In goes the cock-pheasant's beak. The cone snaps smartly over his eyes and sticks like glue. Blinded, he flaps helplessly about. And Nick, the creeping shadow, has him in a flash. Jake never takes more than a brace or two of pheasants that way. 'I like one for me Sunday dinner,' he assures me. 'But if I sold 'em there'd soon be somebody yapping his head off and I'd be up to court quick.' Country common-sense.

Jake has a love-hate alliance with George the gamekeeper. Each year he tells George of isolated partridge or pheasants' nests by roadside or field paths. The keeper takes the eggs and hatches them under hens. Jake is in favour.

He does George even greater service when he takes the number of a motor car from London which, driving slowly along a country lane, pulls up suddenly. A gun or an air-rifle is poked out of the window. A shot follows. In an instant the car poacher's dog streaks across the field to collect a dead pheasant. This motorised poaching is carefully planned. Sometimes motorbike scouts ride ahead of the car or behind it, warning the poacher by horn-signal of an approaching police patrol car.

Any car-poacher risks a heavy fine and the loss of his gun and motor car. So Jake's careful note of the car number from a ditch-bottom where he is ferreting an illicit rabbit is an invaluable aid to game-preservation. Who could grudge him his Sunday dinner? George turns a Nelson's eye to Jake's little ways.

Not all poachers are so human or endearing as Jake. I have no time for the boastful fellow - most of us know him in Essex - who proudly proclaims that he has been prosecuted and convicted umpteen times and still goes on shooting other people's pheasants - which is plain thieving - and basking in the reflected glory of continued newspaper publicity. That sort of man is a mere swashbuckler and not a humble village sportsman.

Nor has one any time or sympathy for the old villain in a Broadland parish where the reed-beds were infested with pheasants. He cut a swathe through a bed of reeds, made himself a reed-hide at one end and then proceeded to set out three or four long fishing lines, the hooks baited with raisins. Previously he had baited the swathe for a day or two with a handful or so of raisins each day. He bought up a consignment of fruit which had gone musty from the village grocer for a shilling or so. So his operating costs were not high.

Within a few minutes of settling down in his hide a snakey head with a pair of beedy eyes poked eagerly out of the wall of reeds on the right-hand side of the swathe. The eyes swivelled sideways up and down the swathe. Not a man in sight. So gingerly a cock-pheasant, in the full splendour of plummage, stepped out, made for the nearest baited hook and snapped up the raisin. The poacher promptly pulled the fishing line. The hook stuck in the bird's throat. Up it flew with a mighty hooroosh of flapping wings and then came down thump as the old reprobate pulled on the line. He rung its neck within seconds. Thus he collected a bag-full of pheasants - and no sympathy from anyone when he was convicted.

The days have gone when large, organised gangs of poachers came out from the towns at night to raid the coverts and frequently engage in bloody battles with the keepers. Sometimes the motive was profit and not sport. Old game books and estate records sometimes have vivid tales to tell of the gangs of men who swept the stubble fields at night with silken drag-nets for jugging (roosting close together) partridges or stormed the coverts, shooting the pheasants at roost and sometimes shooting the keepers who attempted to apprehend them.

Old Israel Buckle, who was Head Keeper at Merton until shortly before his death in 1873, had many battles with really desperate men. Israel was small and active and very quick on his feet. One day he chased a poacher across a stubble field. The man, carrying his gun over his shoulder, suddenly sloped the barrels backwards and downwards, pulled the trigger and blew the brim off Buckle's hat. Buckle dived between the man's legs, brought him to earth and sat on his head until the other keepers came up.

That was before my time; but such stories of murderous men linger on most great estates. The late Tom Turner was for many years head keeper at Elveden and has told me hair-raising tales of the gangs who, up to 1914, regularly raided the coverts and partridge manors. In the North and Midlands, where large estates adjoin mining areas or great manufacturing towns, the gangs were often organised to the hilt and would stick at nothing.

Small wonder that game preservers set man-traps and spring-guns and that keepers wore hard bowler hats, which acted as helmets, against bludgeons. At home we had two typical bludgeons, which hung in the harness room. One was a square bar of iron with a rounded grip and the other was a hard oaken cudgel about 15 inches long, with the thick end loaded with a core of lead.

Man-traps were set, not only to catch poachers, but more particularly to guard lonely country houses against desperadoes who would think little of committing murder. The average man-trap was about four feet long and shaped like a gigantic rabbit-trap. If you put your foot on the plate the jaws sprang up and gripped you just below the knee. Once you were caught a man had to stand on the spring before the jaws could be released. Most mantraps had saw teeth, which meant, almost inevitably, that whoever was caught lost his leg in the long run. I have one of a more or less 'humane' variety, in as much as the jaws have no teeth but are plain bars of iron. Even so, any leg caught in it would almost certainly be broken. Desperate men called for desperate remedies.

Man-traps have been illegal for very many years, but I know a keeper in East Norfolk who actually set one and caught his man not much more than 30 years ago. The poacher, a desperate village ruffian, had been repeatedly caught and fined. Finally, he threatened to murder the keeper if he ever tried to catch him again. One night they met in a wood.

'He upped with his gun an' let drive at me not more'n 15 yards off,' the keeper told me. 'The shot ripped through me jacket an' missed me hip by about an inch. Then he bolted.

'After that I made up me mind to get him. There was an owd man-trap in the coach-house up at Mautby Hall, all rusted up. I got that down to me shed, oiled it up and got it working. Then I watched for me man. I reckoned he'd be workin' a little owd wood of about seven acres down on the edge o' the marsh. That wore full o' pheasants. A dyke runned right round it. So I knowed he'd go in at one corner where there was a bridge an' a gate. I soon found his marks and two nights arterwards I set me trap.

'I went round arly next morning afore that wore light and there wore me man, gripped fast. He laid there like an owd rabbit, a-moanin' and a-blarin'. I tuk his gun and I looked down at him and I said: "Now, me owd mate, we're square. Yu tried to shute me and I've ketched yu. If I let yu out o' this, yu gotta lay off me coverts." He looked up at me, nodded his owd head and I stood on the spring o' the trap. He crawled out but he couldn't stand yet awhile so I helped him to the road and there I left him to git home as best he could.'

'What happened?' I asked. 'Did he ever say a word about it?'

'Nit a word. He's got a wooden leg nowadays. Cor, his owd woman reckons he's a changed man. He's bin a good husband to her ever since and thass a dam' sight more than he wos afore. That owd trap cured him.'

This extraordinary tale is true. I knew the keeper well. The poacher knew that had he complained the keeper would have charged him with attempted murder. Both kept their secret.

SAGA OF A HIGGLER

HE WAS small, black-eyed and shrewish, with jutting eyebrows, a weasel face, a sidelong gait and an air of suspicion.

He came, in days far away, from the cobbled rat-runs of the East End, when farmers and market gardeners sent their corn and greenstuff by horsedrawn wagons to the markets of the metropolis and cattle-drovers walked their herds, iron-shod, to the slaughter houses of the capital city.

Some dormant yearning for green fields drew the weasel-faced cockney boy, with the boot-button eyes, from his slum lair to join a gang of cattle-drovers returning to the bright pastures and sea-going rivers of Essex.

There, in a weather-boarded old farmhouse that leant crookedly with the wind on the top of a little hill they call Oak Hill, young 'Cobber' Cobbett found hard work, hard dealing and fresh air. His 'guvnor' was a higgler, one of that timeless pack of human mongrels who hang on the skirts of dealers in cattle, horses, pigs and sheep, the men who nod in hundreds and sign their cheques for thousands. Always at their heels are the sly higglers, snappers-up of unconsidered trifles. Thus was 'Cobber' tutored.

He grew into a foxy middle-age, retired, badger-like, into a night walking old age, and finally was buried in an atmosphere sanctified by an alcoholic send-off which would have turned the mourners at an Irish Wake emerald with envy.

Now Cobber, being of the Horse and Trap Age, never took kindly to motor-cars. Horses understood him. Pigs he was at home with. Cattle did his bidding. Hens, ducks, rabbits, geese and ferrets were the everyday familiars of his kitchen. But the internal combustion engine and Cobber were eternally at loggerheads.

Nonetheless, being a man of business, he bought himself a van from one of those roadside dealers who sprang up overnight when the great arterial road to Pillage-on-Sea was driven through the placid countryside. Wolves in human form lie there in wait for the unsuspecting. Cobber was neither unsuspecting, nor scared of wolves. Which is why he got a bargain. It was 18 h.p. with sliding seats, tin body and handy doors at the back that would admit anything from half-a-dozen crates of chickens to a couple of black-market heifers. He paid £60 in £1 notes, plus a second-hand Hoover, a large piece of bacon cut from a post-war pig that had committed suicide, as post-war pigs so often did; a case of eggs and a bottle of Scotch. They were all things hard to come by in those sere days of austerity. But the van went.

It went without let or hindrance, without oil or care, with no more than a fill-up with petrol, with no better garage than a tumbledown cart-shed, whose tiled roof sagged drunkenly. Hens roosted on it. Pigs rootled under it. Dogs baptised it. Cows rubbed their warbled flanks against it. The lean greyhounds which infested the muddy yard sniffed it inquisitively. But it went.

True, there were no brakes. What matter? Cobber always drove soberly and quietly to market and returned thence, like the angler, 'smelling of strong drink, and the truth was not in him'. He drove then on the horn.

His going forth on market morning was a triumph of simplicity. The open door of the cart-shed points out of the yard gate, down the steep slope of Oak Hill. At the bottom of it, a side-road leads to the main road. The fields on each side were Cobber's. So he made his own Rule of the Road.

Since, without brakes, the van could lurch out of the cart-shed by the sheer pull of gravity and plunge downhill to destruction, he rammed a churn-lid under each of the back tyres. This held the juggernaut fast.

Came the dawn and, stuffed with one pound notes, Cobber, attended by a gangling, straw-chewing youth, would mount the driving seat, grip the wheel with granite purpose and yell: 'Kick 'em art, Bert.' Out flew the churn-lids. A shove from Bert and the van rattled forward. It gathered speed, lurched out of the muddy gateway, scattered ducks, geese and piglings, and then plunged, clanking, down the dizzy hill. With luck, it coughed twice, wheezed stertorously, gave a sort of mechanical shriek and burst into self-propulsion. After that it was plain sailing.

There were odd mornings when the fog got in the

throttle, or rain into the petrol tank, or a hen into the bonnet and the thing refused to start. Once it landed in the ditch. Cobber was flung blasphemously into the hedge. On such occasions, Bert came with a phlegmatic carthorse which towed it to the top of the hill again. Once it stopped half-way down the hill. So they hitched up the horse. Bert gave him a cut across the quarters with a hedge-stake, and Punch strained at the tow-rope. Lo! The car started. It plunged forward, bunted Punch under the tail, wheezed, clanked, and surged remorselessly downward. Punch broke into an elephantine gallop. No National winner ever travelled faster over a deadlier hundred yards.

Heaven knows what ghastly immolation might not have overtaken horse, man and motorvan, had not Punch jinked violently, like a Kadir Cup boar, at the gateway into a side-road when a boy sprang out of the ditch yelling 'Gone Away!' with a scream that Tom Firr would have envied.

The van struck the gate-post. Cobber struck the wheel, windscreen and roof simultaneously. He lost three teeth, most of his wind and a lot of bad language. The tow-rope snapped. Punch went through the hedge and across three fields. He was never the same horse again. Course men have offered to run him at Punchestown.

The epic day came when Cobber, having bought, sold and drunk, loaded up at market with assorted crates of ducks, geese, hens and rabbits, plus a few tray of duck's eggs, a loft of cooing pigeons and a wooden, perforated box. It contained six stinking ferrets, four whites and a brace of polecats. The lid was held by a leather thong looped over a nail.

He had just loaded it into the van and was showing its pink-eyed inhabitants to a sporting friend, with a promise of Saturday rabbiting, when two bowler-hatted gentlemen with note-books caught his eye. They were examining the next car closely, jotting down suspicious details with stubby pencils.

'Ker-rist! Ministry o' Transport snoopers, arter cars wiv no brakes or lights.' grunted Cobber. 'I'm orf!' He slammed down the ferret-box lid, forgot to fasten it, jumped into the driving seat, clanged the doors shut and shot into the crowded High Street. His horn blared. Farmers' wives, gaping yokels and straggling children scattered. A policeman turned his head. Then, bang in front of the Town Hall, the van stopped. It had run out of petrol. The ferret box lid flew open.

A second later the back of the van resembled Noah's Ark hit by a torpedo below the water-line. The ferrets got to work. Rabbits squeaked their last squeak. Ducks quacked. Geese broke loose. A crate of hens fell down and the hens flew out. Eggs, pulverised and glutinous, wrapped themselves round a brace of Belgian hares. A policeman appeared.

Traffic piled up for a hundred yards. It looked like half a mile.

''Ere, what's all this?' demanded the Law.

'Give me a perishin' shove and stop yapping,' Cobber demanded with the righteous rage of a consistently-summonsed ratepayer. 'Shove me to the gerridge. I'm out o' juice. You're 'olding' up the traffic. Shove!'

Obedient to the voice of authority, the policeman shoved. A couple of drovers added their weight. The van lurched into the dark safety of the garage portals.

And, since the devil looks after his own, the policeman vouchsafing no enquiry but merely flinging over his shoulder the parting kick of: 'Don't let this 'ere 'appen agin!' went back to his point-duty.

Cobber got home with six dead rabbits, four mauled ducks, five escaped hens and half-a-dozen ferrets puffed up with blood.

There was, however, the kinder day when he bought a bunch of bullocks and a bull, a vast Friesian who weighed about a ton. He drove them home and put them in his stockyard. Now the cattlesheds surrounding the yard are like gruyère cheese - full of holes. The bullocks were athletes. The bull was an individual. Cobber chained him up in a converted cart-bay.

Next day, I went over with Frank Love, the dealer, to make a bid for some of the stock. Churns full of milk stood in a yard inches deep in muck. Pigs, lean as greyhounds, rushed, grunting furiously, out of henhouses, cartsheds, horse-stalls and the kitchen-door. Five or six greyhounds were eating a dead calf on the 'muck-dungle'.

As we poked our noses over the stockyard-gate, the bullocks, wild as hawks, with tossing horns and flourishing tails, jumped one after the other through gaping holes in the brick walls. Cobber, a man and two dogs, went into the field to round them up.

The yelling of men, barking dogs and bellowing cattle roused the bull. He took charge. Throwing up his head he jerked out the staple in the manger to which his chain was attached. Then, like a thunder-bolt, he went, head-down, through the wooden cartshed wall and shot into the field with half the shed hanging to his shoulders and clattering at his heels!

Lesser men would have fled. Not Cobber. Seizing a pitch-fork, he leapt on to a tractor and charged after the bull. Don Quixote on a mechanised Rozinante. Before the astounded bull knew what was happening he was stabbed in the rear with the fork, scooped up by the tractor, bundled into a horse-stall, blindfolded with a sack, lassooed with a cart rope and penned in a concrete bull-box that would have held a dinosaur.

'That'll larn 'im,' said Cobber, spitting on his hands.

Then he went on with the deal - the usual taradiddle of offer and counter-offer, the production of grimy wads of notes, pretences at indignant withdrawal from the whole business, ending, finally, with a settlement for £57 in cash, a second-hand Ford van, a set of old plough tackle and a bottle of sloe gin.

Cobber wanted the £57 in pound notes. The dealer insisted on paying by cheque. He demanded Cobber's Christian name.

'John,' said Cobber. 'But what's the good of a bit o' paper to me? I can't read or write. I carry it all in me 'ead.'

Thereupon the dealer, with sudden irony, wrote out a cheque to Sir John Cobber. Cobber pocketed it, having first scrutinised it with sullen suspicion.

Recent financial intelligence confirms that it took Cobber half-an-hour of sulphuric language to explain things at the bank, sign his newly-minted title, and draw the money.

Titles remind one that, soon after the Coronation, the local Lord was induced to display his robes to his farm bailiff and estate workers. It was a strictly private view in the estate office up at the Hall. Cobber was a privileged outsider.

Whilst the rest gaped in suitable awe, he, full of

shrewd curiosity, approached the patient peer, fingered the ermine and asked:

'What's them there skin, m'Lord?'

'Ermine. Very valuable,' smiled His Lordship.

'Vallyable? Not them,' said Cobber stoutly, his dealer's blood alight. 'I wouldn't bid yer fourpence for 'em, m'Lord. They're only damn owd stoats.'

THE GREAT ISLAND RACE

'SHARP ON TEN, Harry'll fire the owd gun - and off yer goo. 'Smart walkin' pace, no runnin', stick to the sea-wall, all the way round the owd island. Halt for five minutes at the Stone down East. The owd coastguards'll be down there wi' a donkey and cart and a barrel o' beer. Reckon yew chaps'll need a drink by then. On'y five minutes though. Then orf ye goo again. Fust man home gits a gallon o' beer and a gret owd plate o' sausages. There'll be sausages and beer for all, come to that. There ain't no prizes - jist honour and glory. All right, mates?'

The speaker, blue-jerseyed, sea-booted, his face graven with the fine lines of wind and salt-spray, gazed round the smoke-filled bar of the *Nelson's Eye.* A rattle of pewter pots and a chorus of grunts, like bar-geese on the muds outside, signified approval.

Thus the Great Island Walking Race was born. It all happened, long ago and far away, in the gay days between the wars.

The Island is five or six miles long, a mile or so wide and 16 miles round if you go by the sea-wall, which winds and twists like a great hairy snake, the blue fleets and green cattle marshes on one side, with the bright swelling barley stubbles beyond on the backbone of the Isle. On the other side lie the rich amethyst and purple acres of sea-lavender on saltings, a lace-work of little shining creeks, where terns drop like bullets in the flashing tide. To the landward or England-side, broad creeks and shining muds cut off the elect of the Isle from the dull mass of main-landers.

They are a rare breed, these Islanders. Viking, pirate, smuggler, Elizabethan seaman, Napoleonic privateer, smacksman, wild-fowler, oyster dredger, winkler, poacher, yacht-skipper and deckhand, with a fine smattering of deep-sea merchant seamen have made them a self-contained humble aristocracy of the tide-line. Not that there is any-thing humble about any of them. They will fight the first man who asks for it. They want no charity. They own their own smacks and oyster pits. They till their own farms, but there is not a dull Hodge among them. Even the men of the farms have one foot in a furrow and one in a boat. Which is why you will find an inn called *The Plough and Sail* and another *The Anchor and Hope,* and a third *The Dog and Pheasant*, a fourth *The Old Victory* and a fifth *The Whalebone,* scattered about those creeks and marshes that are a land unto themselves.

'Them Islanders 'ud shute their own mothers if they had feathers on,' a man 'over in England' remarked to me with bitter envy. 'They're the headest lot for devilment as ever sailed the seas.'

Do you wonder that with these wild strains of Dane and Jutlander, Dutchman and Huguenot, singing in their veins, that the islanders are forever up to all manner of larks? Such as the Great Walking Race. It has the true 18th century flavour.

Our Islanders had no big money at stake. Money is too hardly won by trawl and dredge, by punt-gun and plough to be wasted on a mere walk. Their 'long trot' was for the fun of the thing with bushels of brown and sizzling pork sausages and gallons of beer as the shining prize - the ultimate laurels.

At 10 sharp outside the *Nelson's Eye* 50 stout sons of plough and sail assembled. There was Titus the gunner, and Sooty the oyster-man; 'Duck', the wildfowler, and Owd Swan, the punt-gunner, who was once plastered with half-a-pound of duck-shot by his nephew, who mistook his white beard in the moonlight for a wild swan. 'Gunner' Cook turned up in his red stocking skull-cap with 'the owd Admiral', that bearded boatwright, in peaked seaman's cap and long water-boots, astride an old grey donkey to see fair play.

Here indeed were the cream, the élite of this characterful corner of the world. There was Bungo, who had sailed the Atlantic, and Dasher, who had raced in the great days of the deep-sea giants, and Harry Boy who is the 'headest man with an eel shear' for uncounted miles, and Nipper, cunning with ferrets. There was Becky, the eel-catcher, with gold ear-rings in his ears; Owd Plum Duff, who was in sail on the Australia run; Ted, the bull-tamer and adder catcher; Tarpot from the ship-yard and young

Chippy, the ship's carpenter with Dick-by-the-Pond and Skin o' Worms, who was born hungry; young Rammel-net, the 'coyman and gentle, silent Uncle Clarke, who is tall and other-worldly, with the face of an old-fashioned nobleman and tales of the China seas. Then there was 'the Councillor' and others of lesser note and long strides.

They all lined up, talking and laughing. Harry Boy raised his 'owd muzzle-gun' to his shoulder. A circling gull peered at it indignantly. 'Bang!' The smoke bellied in the sunlit air. The gull squarked and back-pedalled. They were off.

Bungo, who is long and thin, got off to a flying start, with Dasher in yellow ducks, lying close to the rails - I mean the tamarisk hedge - and creeping up fast. Nipper, in orange slop and yacht-hand's white, linen hat, Becky, young Chippy, smelling of shavings, Tar-pot and Titus, all quoted at 100-8 in half pints, were bunched together, 'Yappin' their blessed hids off,' but, for all that, looking like stayers.

The field tailed out along the sea-wall, with silent Uncle Clarke coming up with that stealing action, which marks your thorough-bred racer. Sooty, in a blue R.Y.S. guernsey, who, by all accounts, had had a skinful before leaving his stable at the *Nelson's Eye* showed signs of roaring over the first furlong. He was known, however, to have a powerful second wind.

Owd Plum Duff, round and moon-faced, rolling along like a square rigged barque in a long swell, looked like being a stayer; but it was doubtful if he could concede the quart he had already swallowed to the Sardine and Gunner Cook, whose red-knitted skull cap was bobbing steadily along, hard on the heels of the leaders.

Way back, the long, lean, Tin-Ribs form of 'the Councillor', a runner of no blood and unknown breeding, but a dark horse for all that, was just distinguishable in the ruck of the runners-up.

A word concerning 'the Councillor'. Foaled Charlie Pigg from an unknown stable in Suffolk he is eagle-nosed, hawk-eyed and greyhound-built.

Let this chronicler now hand over the narration of the Race to the skilled tongue of 'the Councillor':

'I warn't a-pressin' meself fust goo off,' he confided. "Let them race as can race," sez I. 'That there Bungo and

Dasher went off like race-hosses for a mile or two. When they gits to Fen Creek, Bungo starts a-swearin' and Dasher is a-hobblin'. Seems as though their own fitten (feet) had turned on 'em. Buth on 'em takes their shoes off an' starts a-cussin'. Sech langwidge! I reckon they must a' bin a-bargin' up London River time they was nippers. Seems as though they had nails a-workin' through the soles o' their shoes. Reg'lar crippled 'em.'

The fact that the shoe maker is first cousin to Charles' missus and had promised the night before to put 'reg'lar runnin' spokes' in the shoes of the two hot favourites, need not be laboured, except by the most evil-minded.

'I soon overhauls Gunner Cook and Owd Plum Duff, who was argufyin' about who'd catched the most eels,' he went on. 'Then I passes Owd Sooty, what had his trousers down behind a bush and comes up on old Uncle Clarke. I gits a-'talkin' to him about some young cockrels he wants ter sell. So what with offerin' a bob or two more nor what he expected, I soon draws ahead. Nipper were on the marsh takin' a rabbit out of a yoke what he set the night afore. That put he back.

'Young Chippy, Titus, Tar Pot and that lot were all a-blowin' ahead like they had their spinnakers set in a fair wind, but I sees the two owd coastguards trottin' across the marsh, towards the Stone, down at East Point, with a barrel o' beer in the back o' the cart, and a crate or two o' bottles.

'Ah, me hearty young cocks,' thinks I to meself, 'You'll all be a-settin' down soon and layin' an egg or two, if I knows yer.

'They no sooner sees the beer-cart, than they cracks on all sails and draws ahead o' me by a knot or two. They come on that beer cart like a pack o' hounds on an owd dog fox. Down come all their canvas with a run - mainsail, jib, fores'l, spinnakers, stuns'l, mizzens and every stitch. There they was buzzin' round that owd donkey and cart like a swarm o' bees.

'I stops the five minits, says "no" to the beer - you had to pay for it there, but it was free if you won - sucks an owd gob-stopper and smart on the five minits I wus off.

'Blast, if owd Uncle Clarke didn't pass me. That owd man hev got a stride like an hoss. Then Nipper, Becky, Tar-Pot and the rest on 'em, comes roarin' up behind like young bulls. We was all on the wall, back o' East Hall. Owd Shruk Owlett lives there, as you know. Rum owd booey. Lives all alone. Don't shave, don't wash. Niver goes up to the pub. 'ont hev a womankind on the place. Got a shorthorned bull as bad as hisself. Out he comes, sees me and hollers out: "Too many damn foreigners about here."

'"Ha! booey, they're blarin' like yar owd bull," I sez. "There's a rare pack on 'em ahead o' me."

'"I'll give 'em bull," he hollers. He runs off to the barn, throws open the door, grabs a muck fork, stubs the old bull up the backside and out the bull come like a cannon-ball. He sees that lot ahead o' me and goos for 'em like a rocket. They scatters all over the marsh, with young Tar Pot clearin' the dyke like a long-dawg. The bull wuz hard arter him. Cor! They was disqualified right away.

'Owd Uncle Clarke nips down 'tother side of the sea-wall and kep' on all steady, where the bull couldn't see him. So did I, quarter mile behind. Meanwhile the owd bull was a-sortin' the rest on 'em out. I bides me time, and a mile from home, I ketches up with Uncle Clarke. He was elderish-like, but a-goin' steady.

'"Well, mate," he say, "we might as well finish together. That'll make comp'ny-like;" so I chats away pleasant to the old man, 'til we gits within a gun-shot o' *The Nelson's Eye*. Then I says: "Well cheerio mate! Can't stop now. I gotter 'pintment with a bushel o' sausages."

'I cracks on all canvas and blows in over the line, right into the bar and fetches up all-standin' with Uncle Clark a good 50 yards astern.

'We'd ate half a bushel o' sausages a'tween us and swallered two gallon o' beer, afore the rest o' the fleet come into harbour.

'Lor', Master, then we had a night on it. Titus was a-singin' "Forty-Ginger-Headed Sailors", Tarpot was a-bangin' the peehanner, Owd Plum Duff was doin' a horn pipe, and the rest on 'em was a-stampin' and hollerin' like owd Owlet's bull.

'We never went home until half arter mid-night. The copper was in the back was-hus, washin' up the plates and glasses, his owd face as red as a harvest moon. We had gaiety in them days.'

ART BUGG GOES FOWLING

'ANYBODY what was a man 'ud be out in his punt arter ducks on a night like this. Thass on'y a mouse what 'ud set a hottin' up beer in a little owd saucepan by the fire on sech a night,' observed Ephraim, gazing fixedly at the stuffed otter above the fireplace. He removed his clay from the leathern slit which does duty as his mouth, bared a ragged row of blackened teeth and spat viciously at the fire of chopped-up barge timbers on the great brick hearth.

The shot, judged shrewdly as you would expect by such a master-gunner as Ephraim, landed neatly, with a decisive plop, in the saucepan of beer which his nephew, Art Bugg, had placed, as is his evening wont, to warm in the embers.

Nephew Art, crouching like a broody hen over the fire, a full half of which he and his villainous fox-coloured mongrel managed to obscure from the rest of the company, shot up with a thin snort of protest.

Art Bugg is a thin sort of man. His nose is long and sharp. His eyes close-set under bushy little brows, swivel from side to side with the speed of ferrets. His shoulders are hunched, and his cheeks are pinched. His cloth cap, which he refers to as 'me flat 'at', is drawn down over eyes, eyebrows and beaky nose until it, too, looks like a larger, upper beak. Whereby you would say that Art Bugg resembles a hen. This is not surprising as he deals in hens - and anything else that pays a quick non-taxable turnover.

Ready money, preferably in pound notes, is the key to Art's heart. He will buy and sell ducks, geese, turkeys, ladders, corrugated iron, perambulators, or even boats, trawl nets, oars, job lots of standing riggin, fished-up anchors, or anything else of a sea-going nature, which he can fob off on the unsuspecting yachtsmen who descend like white-capped butterflies upon our coastal village in the finer months of the year.

To Ephraim, that sea-going, evil-eyed son of the

House of Belial, Nephew Art is a puzzle, an object of grudging wonderment, and a spittoon for withering contempt.

Ephraim, for all his sin, has lived hardly for near on 80 years by punt-gun and fish-trawl, by oyster dredging and winkling, by craft and hardihood.

But Nephew Art scarce wets his feet in salt water. For him the pleasant byways of marshland lanes provide ample fields for quiet deals. Moonlit hedgerows and reedy ditches are his hunting-ground when sport is afoot. His long, single-barrelled muzzle-loader, jutting over the reed-walled lip of many a marsh dyke, with the ferret eyes of the Bugg glinting craftily down the barrel, has spelt death to many a browsing hare and squatting rabbit. His toll of pigeons and peewits is notched high in these account books which the Tax Collector never sees. And when a pheasant, that rarity of the marshes, is smuggled in at the back door of the inn, you may be sure that it emerges unruffled from the big hare pocket in Art's tattered coat. For, as he sagely remarked: 'We don't let nawthin' big git away here.'

But this ditch-gunning and hedge prowling is small beer to Uncle Ephraim, that midget of wickedness, whom his nephew once described, at a careful distance, as 'Two chamber-pots high and as full o' artfulness as a hutchful o' ferrets'. Uncle Ephraim may be small in stature, but his great swivel-gun is nine feet long and shoots a pound of shot, with the same uncanny accuracy as that with which Ephraim spat into his nephew's cherished panful of beer.

'You ain't no call ter spit in me beer, Uncle,' protested Art shrilly. 'That ain't a right-forard thing to dew. Yew've spilt me beer.'

'That'll gie a bit o' body to it,' grunted Ephraim, replacing that short black pipe which would bolt a badger or asphyxiate a fox. 'Now, pay yew 'tention ter what I'm a-goin' ter say.'

Art spooned the avuncular missile from his pan of warm beer and poured the untainted remainder carefully into his pint pot. He is a careful man. Moreover, Uncle Ephraim owns a smack, a punt and big gun, an oyster 'lay', and a pair of weather-boarded cottages. Art counts on 'expectations'. He cocked a bird-like ear and slewed bright and bird-like eyes upon the hunched and wrinkled figure of the senior member of his family.

'Yew may lay rightforrard a-dealin' in them owd hins o' yourn and sich,' he remarked gravely, fixing the stuffed stoat above the bar with unwinking eye: 'But yew ain't a right Bugg. All us Buggs hev been gunnin', fishin' and short-sea tradin' fer hundreds o' years. Yar the fust wot iver tarned into an owd hin. Thass time yew went afloat. The fust wigeon are in, the tides is right and there's me punt and me big gun, all loaden and me got the screwmatics. An' wigeon fetchin' ten bob a pair. An' ter think I carn't git afloat. Cor, blarst! An' here's me that's kilt tharty or more on 'em at one shot afore now. That'd be 15 pun' in ready money today. Them what wants to foller on arter me had better pull their britches up - an' right quick.' He spat again, this time into the fire.

Art, quick to take a hint, expostulated: 'Same as gunnin', Uncle? Whoy, I allus wanted to goo a-gunnin' but I ain't got no big gun and I daresen't borry yourn. You're the head gunner in our family.'

'Thass time you started. Me punt lays on the Hard, me gun's loaden in me backus, the tide's right tomorrer night and they wigeon is a-feedin' on the Nab Islands,' he announced. He knocked out his pipe and stumped out into the October moonlight. The fiat had gone forth.

Thus it came about that Art Bugg went fowling afloat.

And thus too, by one of those mischances that govern the destiny of men and winding streams, I also was afloat in my punt from a creek three miles away across the coastal marshes under the October moon the night following. With me there went my friend and fellow-puntsman, 'Too-Hoo' Cant, a sea-gunner in whom is blended all the wisdom of a far-flung fowling ancestry and all the seamanship of one who has been to Australia and back in sail.

The broad creek brimmed before the low sliding bows of our punt like a sheet of silver, full half a mile wide. Not a ripple stirred the silken flow of the incoming tide. Gannet strutted on the mudflats. A heron cried hoarsely as he flapped high over under the moon to some far fleet of eels in the misty bosom of the fresh marsh behind the low and glimmering rampart of the sea-wall.

Out in mid-channel a school of porpoises rolled and wallowed, slapping the water like doors falling down. As the punt glided like a knife through the water, one porpoise rolled right under us, causing the slim grey craft to rock dangerously and dip its scantling almost under. Too-Hoo grunted softly. 'If I hed me spear (flounder-spear) I'd jab that owd sea-hog right up the backside, jes' to larn him.'

Ahead the low, whaleback outline of the two Nab Islands, Big and Little Nab, showed flatly black against the moon-shimmer on the tide. Curlew were whistling on Big Nab, giving that comfortable, bubbling, feeding call, which means that they are happy and unsuspecting. The thin 'Wheoh, Wheoh' of wigeon came from the seaward point of the little mud isle, and the low purring of others. They, too, were on the feed on a patch of *Zos* grass. Too-Hoo listened intently while he sent the punt gliding forward with smooth, noiseless, under-water strokes of the hand-paddles. I lay forward of him at the lanyard of the big gun, its seven-foot, grey painted barrel poking venomously over the fore-deck. At my right side, lay the long single-barrelled, muzzle-loading four-bore which shoots a quarter pound of shot, and has been known to down half a score of birds, when they were packed tight enough.

'There ain't above half-a-dozen wigeon in that bunch I'll lay,' Too-Hoo whispered. 'I see'd 'em here las' night. They ain't hardly wu'th the big gun. Give 'em the big showder gun if you can.'

That was the counsel of prudence of one who counts the cost of powder and shot in these days of rocketing prices. I nodded silently.

The punt slid on, a grey gliding ghost in the moon haze. We were alone in the immense, salty silence of the sea-marshes, the village a mile and a half behind on its elm-crowned upland. To port and starboard the tide glittered silverly. Beyond it lay the embanked marshes, where bullocks moved stiffly in the mist, blowing clouds of glittering steam, and ducks spattered in reedy fleets. Ahead gleamed the vast bosom of the North Sea and over the starboard bow of our tiny craft, with its bare six inches of freeboard, there winked in the far distance the few scattered shoreward lights of the island village where Nephew Art and all other law-abiding men would be 'a-gofflin' their beer' prior to turning in to righteous rest beneath the shingled, wavy roofs of that little huddle of black, tarred cottages.

It was good to feel that one was out and alone on that watery wilderness, with none but the strident curlew and the wigeon from the cold north to keep company with the sleepy quarrel of gulls and the thin threnody of redshank flitting on scarlet legs along the white lip of the tide. The punt glided with a silken ripple along the island shore. To a bird's eye, it must have seemed a mere sliding shadow, a grey blur on the water under the Hunter's Moon.

A hundred yards ahead a great herd of curlew moved in a forest of legs on the point of the mud. A cock and a hen wigeon constantly called and answered each other. Obviously, the curlew, stubble-fed and fresh off the harvest field and therefore, for once in their fishy lives, eatable, were the quarry. I was not going to waste a shot from the big gun on them. Cautiously the four-bore was fished up from the fore-deck, carefully capped, cocked and laid in the cradle beside the big gun. Too-Hoo's hand paddles, touching the mud in the shallows, stole softly alongside the punt like water-mice. Softly, oh, so softly, the punt slid nearer and nearer that feeding, whistling, gabbling, long-legged herd of curlew. I do not usually shoot curlew, for I love their wild whistle too well, but a mob of young birds, full-fed from the harvest field, is too good a quarry for the fowler to miss. Eighty yards, 70, 60 yards - they were well within range. Another five yards would do it beautifully.

I raised myself cautiously to my knees on the half-filled sack of straw which is the punt-gunner's carpet and, even as the big gun touched the shoulder, that great herd of curlew, 150 strong, sprang on wing in a clamour of wild whistles.

'Booo-oomp!-oomp!' A yard-long flame seared the moon-haze, a cloud of grey smoke bellied over the mud, and the dull boom and echo of that thunderous discharge of black powder thudded heavily over the creek and the mist-drowned marshes. Birds fell like sacks of wheat, and, even as Too-Hoo reached for the cripple-stopper and fired two quick barrels at runners on the mud, there came an agonised yell and a storm of oaths from the other side of the mudhorse.

'What the hell! Yew've b—— well shot me! Cor, blarst! I'm killed . . . ' and in a rattle of oars and scurry of water an unseen craft receded into the misty vastness of the North Sea, raising the welkin with fearful imprecations. The anthem of his woe faded seaward.

Too-Hoo, who was out on the mud in a flash, and had already stopped two more cripples, came back to the punt, sliding over the mud in his water-boots with those curious, long, skater-like strides which is the only proper way to walk on mud without splatchers. He carried a bundle of eight curlew, the total of the shot, threw them into the punt, grinned slowly, and remarked cheerfully:

'Yew warmed his backside awright, I reckon. But that don't s'inify. He ain't dead yit. He's on'y one of them Island men. They'd shoot their own mothers if they had wings to flap.'

Saying which, he stepped carefully aboard, pushed off, and we departed in search of worthier fowl for the big gun.

But alack, the sequel came three-quarters of an hour later in the snug bar of the Island inn, where Uncle Ephraim sat toasting his rheumaticky toes in front of the fire, a noggin of hot rum, lemon and sugar clasped firmly in the brown claw of his right hand.

To him there entered, wild of eye and ashen of face, Nephew Art, gibbering.

Five minutes earlier a punt-gun had gone off with a shattering roar, not a hundred yards down the beach, causing the window panes to chatter, and the inn spaniel to jump to his feet, hair on end.

Ephraim slewed a suspicious eye upon his shivering nephew.

'What yew bin up to, yew young muck?' he demanded.

'I bin shot, Uncle,' gasped Nephew Art. 'I lay in me little owd punt a-creepin' up to a rare gret owd herd of curlews on the Big Nab, and was jes' a-goin' to pull the trigger when a gret gun goos off right in me face. There was a yard o' blew flame come out of the b—— and a pound of shot roun' me earns and a pair of ladies knickers and a whole *Daily Mail* a-flarin' and a-flamin' all roun' me head. Gawd, I'm lucky to be alive.'

'Yer mother 'ud a-bin luckier if yewd' bin stillborn,' grunted Ephraim ungraciously.

'What was that big gun that went orf jes' now?'

'That wore yourn, Uncle,' admitted his nephew with

the nearest approach to a shamed face he has ever been known to wear. 'I wore a-rowin' me punt up to the Hard, a-settin' up with me backside right up agin the butt o' the big gun, when I rowed right slap into a dingy. The gun were cocked, and when the bows hit the dinghy, that jarred her orf. Lor'! that lefted me like a balloon. My backside is that sore I can't set down for a week.'

'Yew on't when I've done wi' yer, yew young muck,' said Ephraim, rising threateningly to his full five feet five inches. 'Whose dinghy wore it?.'

'Owd Skin o' Worm's,' said Art, naming by his ungracious nickname a man even thinner than himself. 'That blowed the top strake right orf and set the boat afire - jes like a little owd boy's Christmas tree. That'll cost me a couple o' quid to put a new strake in and paint the topside,' he added mournfully. 'Thass been a bad day for me.'

'That wore a bad day when you wore born,' said Ephraim, succinctly. 'I never 'spected nothin' on yew and now yew're wuss'n I ever 'spected.' And out he stumped.

Ephraim is still alive. Nephew Art is still 'expecting'. Time, the great healer, he trusts fervently, may yet work miracles. But the rest of us have our doubts.

GUN-RUNNERS

HE WAS PINK and in 'The Tins'. His little ginger moustache bristled with infant ferocity. His blue eyes flashed as though on parade. He smelt strongly of new leather.

He arrived importantly in a little, low, red, smelly car. It snorted to a stop outside the *Nelson's Eye*.

Leather, brand new and shining, was decanted. Bright brown guncase. Bright brown boots. Bright brown cartridge bag and bright brown binocular case.

The elect regarded him cautiously through the fly-glazed panes of the Captain's Bar. They were all there. Yacht skippers, smacksmen, oyster dredgers, winklers, with their faint, eternal reek of the mud, wildflowers and the rest of the long-shore community, including, of course, the Councillor. His is the smoothest tongue and slyest eye in all that company of guile.

'Young orficer,' remarked Titus the Gunner, thoughtfully. 'Come a gunnin' no doubt. 'Haps he'll need a hand to larn him where to goo.'

'Reckon he'll need a punt to git there in,' said the Admiral, who builds them.

'Dessay he'll need a big gun to goo in it,' added Owd Swan. 'I've got a tidy piece what'd suit he right well.' Shocked eyes are turned upon the old man. Age and a failing mind alone could excuse the fact that he had spoken aloud the predatory thoughts common to them all. Not a man in that lot lacked a death dealing weapon ready for sale.

Meanwhile, the 'young orficer' retired to his bedroom, unpacked his bright brown bags, put out his monogrammed hairbrushes, stowed his bright brown gun-case under the bed and was now poring over a brand-new map. It depicted faithfully the estuaries, creeks, rills, gutters, mud-flats, saltings, mud-horses, sand-banks, Red-Hills, sea-walls, fleets, dykes, deeps, swatchways, shoals and sea-ways which compose that sea-picture of which the Island is the bright jewel. The only thing it does not tell is how the tides run and where the birds feed.

Presently, the young man folded the map and fingered lovingly the bright pages of one of those glossy volumes, which, illustrated in the best Bond Street mode of wildfowling, paint Elysian visions of opalescent dawns and green-gold eves, stippled by the wings of countless wildfowl. It is a picture which never fails to charm under the arduous conditions of watching it on T.V., the screen which cannot lie.

Reassured by this best-seller, the young man paused before the looking-glass and gave the little ginger moustache a confident upward quirk. Then he strode downstairs towards the bar. There, the wit and wisdom of the foreshore awaited him. He entered.

A blue haze of nigger-head and stale slops stunned nose and eye. A ginger-brown mongrel tripped him up. A chorus of hearty voices greeted him with rustic welcome.

'Don't yew mind the little owd dorg, Sir. He 'on't hut ye.'

'That's only me little owd Napoleon, Sir. Do ye give him the toe o' ye boot.'

'Come in, Sir, come in - that does me right good to see a sportin' gent walk in among us pore simple owd fellers.' This from the Councillor, never backward in the drive for trade. 'I can see you're a gunner, Sir. Plenty o' fowl about. Plenty o' fowl about, Sir.'

Thus encouraged, Pink Face advanced to the bar. A score of eyes followed the production of his wallet.

'What'll it be, Sir?' asked Bungo Blow, the landlord, sweeping his eyes round the poor simple old fellows, with a compelling glance. Pink Face capitulated. Stronger men than he have fallen for the embracing order.

'Er, what'll these gentlemen have?' he asked with a parade ground voice that had barely broken.

'Drop o' Nelson's Blood, Sir. Hope they flies your way, Sir.'

'Mine's a double rum, Sir. Bes' respex to you, Sir.'

'Drop o' Scotch wi' a gent like yew, Sir. Pint o' mild and bitter - best make it a quart Bungo. Dog's nose wi' a double gine in it, Sir, bein' as I've gotter cowd.'

The orders flew fast as snowflakes on a January gale . Little change was left from three pounds.

'I see you're a proper wildfowler, Sir,' began the Councillor easily. 'We had that Master Peter Pict, what paint the pictchers, down here a year agoo. Rare nice young gennleman, Sir. Jes' like you, Sir. He larnt us poor simple owd fellers a rare lot what we didn't know. Us chaps still talk about he. Dessay you can larn us chaps a thing or tew afore you're done wi' us.'

'Oh, I don't know about that, I'm sure,' Pink Face demurred. 'I shall have to know the lie of the land first. However, I've got my charts. Seems plain enough. They tell me the Oyster Fleet is good for widgeon and the Oaze End is the place for geese.'

Thus welcomed and financially bled, Pink Face retired to bed to dream of tons of geese.

Within a week he had been sold a secondhand punt, its leaking seams puttied the night before by the Councillor. He had placed an order for a new double punt, which would make £200 look silly. He had been sold a muzzle-loading punt gun, which had done honourable duty as a garden fence post for uncounted years before being re-suscitated, painted and oiled. He spent a week afloat with Titus at five shillings an hour, plus £1 for every bird killed. A day or two aboard Bungo's smack taught him the depth of the channels and the shallowness of a £10 note. Every-one was happy.

Then came the night when Pink Face took to the tideways alone. Under the moon his punt glided down the immemorial sea-way of the Danes. Somewhere ahead in the moonhaze, the geese 'cronked'. On the Shore Ends widgeon mewed and purred like cats.

We shall never know precisely what befell Pink Face on that night of moon and bird calls. The voiceless tides and Uncle Swan alone know the truth. The latter is economical.

'There was me, a-sprittin' along in me little owd punt when all of a sudden, I sees a black patch on the water ahid on me - just like a bunch of widgeon. So I sets up to 'em wi' me big guns, loaden wi' half a pound o' shot, as big as backache pills. Seventy yard. Sixty - now, me beauties, I thinks, I'll hev ye. An' I pulls.'

'What did you get, Swan?' I asked.

'Biggest bag o' me life,' he answered simply. 'That wore a *man* - that young orficer.'

'Seems like he couldn't rightly manage his punt. Got athort the tide. Was a-driftin' sideways. An' bein' a ammiture his backside was a-stickin' up.'

'Did you get him?' I asked.

'Git him' That I did. Riglar riddled that owd punt. That sunk under him. An' one o' me pellets ketched him right acrorst his backside - cut a furrow what you could lay a finger in.

'Pore young feller! He looked like a hot cross bun for a month afterwards.

'No, Sir, he ain't bin back - and I doubt he will. There's many miss their free beer.'

ISLE OF BIRDS AND BONES

IT LIES in the wash of the tides between two great walled marshes. Eastward the island shoals into the North Sea, a glittering mud-flat where curlew stalk. Behind it, into the sunset, lie miles of shining creeks and saltings, purple with sea-lavender, green-yellow with samphire and sea-pinks. The broad creeks on either hand are empty of man and boat. A few smacks, tarred and salt-stained, swing at rusty anchor chains far up-channel. A place of sea-silence and stippled tides. Lanes of sea-silver, between the spindly 'brooms', mark the oyster layings on either shore.

The island is long and narrow. A mere score, unnoticed acres of coarse grass and sea-lavender, with green spikes of samphire lucent in the mud-gulleys; suaeda bushes and a tuft of wind-twisted tamarisk on the 'Red Hill' in the centre. There, they say, the Romans had a salt-pan a thousand years or more ago. Red Samian pottery lies in broken testimony. There are others who will tell you that the little 'hill', a few yards in circumference, is the last foundation of a pre-Roman pile dwelling, the sea-shore equivalent of those lake huts, built on stilts, whose remains were found in Wretham Mere in Norfolk and amid the Somerset Fens, not so many years ago.

So you see, the island has a whisper of history as well as lonely beauty. But, alas, it is not always there. When spring tides flood up-channel and brim against the sea-walls, the isle goes under except for the bushes on the little 'Red Hill'. There I have lain hidden on many a winter day when grey herds of curlew are skirling up the creek, wigeon go over in high packs and Brent geese come scything over the yeasty seas, like black witches askew in the gale.

There is, praise God, no house nor yacht nor bungalow, nor any sign of man on all these lonely miles of creek and sea- wall and misty cattle marsh. The shoaling muds and endless menace of the tides see to that. A few years ago, all those marching miles of sea-walls and luminous marsh went under the sea. Fishing smacks sailed where drowned cattle bobbed above their vanished pastures. That was the final answer to those who had cast greedy Cockney eyes on 'desirable building sites'. Mud and the sea are the salvation of the island and of the saltings and cattle-dappled marshes which are its picture frame.

You would say, at first sight, that is is not worth a £5 note for the lot.

So, as we came down-channel, under a blue sky and a rag of sail, on a June morning, in the big fowling punt, I remarked to 'The Boy':

'Let's go ashore on the island. I haven't been on it for two or three years.'

'Ha! You 'ont know it now,' he answered. 'Thass populated.'

'Yis! Yis! Hund'eds of inhabitants. The gulls hev set up house an' the tukies (redshanks) an' terns and ringed plovers, till you can't set a foot down without smashin' an egg. They only come there a season or two ago - arter they left your owd marsh, I reckon.'

Years earlier, on a great marsh over the creek, which I rented for enchanted years, there had been a screaming, quarrelling gullery. An aerial circus of wings. A cheerful waterside slum of slap-dash nests and broken eggs, of white-splashed droppings and sprawling chicks. There the black-headed gulls had reared their young each summer, far down the sunny years, long before the Dutchmen's guns thundered off Sole Bay or Napoleon was a menace beyond the sea horizon. The German bombs fell on the marsh. The gulls took wing and never came back. For years we never found an egg on all the lonely miles of that half-land of the sea.

The punt nosed ashore, her sharp bows cutting like a knife into the mud. Instantly, the air was alight with a frenzy of wings, an aerial fantasy of white and screaming birds against the Delft-blue of a June sky. The noise was deafening. Scream of gulls, the rusty creaking of terns, pipe of ringed plover and the shrieking of redshank. A file of black-headed gulls rose from a shingle bank out in the channel, solemn, as though outraged by the back-alley racket on the island, and went out to sea, great pirate ships in line. An oyster-catcher, which we call an 'olive' on those waters, since he was the favourite bird of St. Olaf, the Saxon saint, piped his thin, clear whistle over the mud and was away.

We stepped ashore, gulls swooping and diving about our ears. Terns glided overhead in fork-tailed grace. The stippled glitter of the sea, the silver flash of a mile of bared mud, dazzled the eyes.

It was top of the tide, but the lap of wavelets was miles below normal high-water mark.

'These are the Bird Tides, ye see,' The Boy remarked.

He has never grown up, despite the fact that he is 42, sails the world in deep-sea traders and is father of a family.

'You 'on't find 'em in the tide-tables nor yit in the Sailin' Directions but there allus hev been Bird Tides at the end o' May and beginnin' o' June, ever since tides fust flowed at the pull o' the moon. They're the lowest tides o' the year - so that the salts on't be overflowed and the nests flooded out. The Birds knows when the Bird Tides are a-comin' and they hatches out accordin'.'

Beyond the tide-line wrack a little beach of oyster and limpet shells shimmered whitely in the hot sun. A cock ringed-plover, balanced delicately on a stone, regarded us with distaste. Gulls screamed abuse. White droppings splashed the sun-baked mud-hummocks. Everywhere were nests, some not a yard apart. Tiny platforms of dead-grasses, withered sea-lavender and tide-line drift, each with one or two brown and yellowish mottled chicks or a pair or two of parti-coloured eggs. In a scrape among the white shells lay four ringed plovers eggs, cream coloured with black scribblings, points inwards.

'That means they're a-goin' to hatch pretty soon,' said the Boy.

Beyond the ringed plovers' austere abode was a common tern's nest. Two of the three eggs were buff with darker brown blotches, but the third was almost pale blue with dark brown markings. All over the island the variations in colour and markings among the eggs of gulls and tern would have defeated an avine Sherlock Holmes.

We walked the length of the island, near half-a-mile. Almost every square yard had its nest.

At the far end, where the opal muds go shoaling out and a great whaleback of shingle has newly risen from the sea, we squatted on a bed of shells. A wild flurry of curlew rose, shrieking like witches. Forerunners of the Autumn thousands which later make musical these lonely creeks. They went beating out in a purposeful phalanx high over the blue sea, glittering to the horizon.

On the skyline a fresco of yachts sailed in superb beauty. White clouds marbled the sky. A great gaff-rigged cutter with foresail, jib, mainsail and gaff topsail all full and drawing, was reaching away for the Rays'n. An Edwardian picture come to life. A tall ocean racer, two-masted, under full canvas, came standing in from the sea, a white queen among the scattered snowflakes of lesser sails. Red-sailed, a Thames barge, her gunwale almost awash , with 'a bone in her teeth', went thrashing up the fairway a mile to starboard. There was not a smudge of smoke in the sky. The last days of sail are not yet played out.

'I reckon that ocean-goin' yacht don't pay a penny in tax for her 'bacca or her liquor,' remarked The Boy tersely. He has a practical, piratical mind. 'See how they yachts stand out sharp agin the sky. See how the loom o' the land stands out - miles away. That's allus the same when the wind blows easterly. That sharpens the light.'

He turned and surveyed the island, sun-drenched beneath a flickering fantasy of white wings. Birds were settling down on their nests.

'Looks a bit different from that day, jest afore the end o' the war, when that plane come down in the mud, jest over there,' he remarked. 'I were home on leave from mine-sweeping. She were loaded wi' machine guns, automatics, bombs and other gear for the Resistance chaps over in France.

'I come down channel in me smack, arter the sojers had took the poor pilot's corpse away, and I done a bit o' salvage. I worked most all night - and two nights arterwards. I had all the good metal out of her, with compasses, batteries, pressure gauges, mileometers and all the rest wuth salvaging. I had pounds worth o' stuff out o' her. That *made* me leave-pay. Set the old woman up right comfortable in the Post Office bank. Arter all, salvage is thicker 'an regulations, ain't it? Dad's folks was a-salvagin' up this coast for hundreds o' years.'

'What about the weapons aboard?' I asked.

'Ha! The kids had them,' he grinned cheerfully. 'All the little owd boys up in the village come a-swarmin' down here in boats and loaded theyselves up wi' pistols, grenades and Gawd knows what. That's a wonder they didn't blow theyselves sky-high. Well, the news got about and the copper and the School Inspector goes up to the owd school one mornin', shuts the doors and sarches all the kids. Do ye know, 14 had pistols on 'em, and two little mucks had hand-grenades in their pockets.'

This sidelight on our East Coast backslidings of war is, let me add, incontestably true.

'You've had some rum salvage one way and another up these creeks,' I remarked.

'Jesso,' he agreed. 'The rummest I had was a skull. I was stow-boatin' with me owd mate, Nipper. He allus reckons he ought to hev been born a pirate or one of they owd Vikings.

'"Gimme a skull," he used to rear. "And I'll drink me beer or owd Hitler's blood out on it."'

'Well, I dredges up this skull in me trawl one day. That was nigh-black, wonderful thick in the bone and covered o' barnacles. I scrapes 'em off, polishes the owd skull up with sand, rams it full o' ashes and cinders and polishes it up inside, and then I gives it a wash. That looked right smart.

'So I brews up a kettle o' tea, pours it into the owd skull and whops it down in front o' Nipper.

'"There y'are, mate," I says. "There's yer tea cup what you wanted special." Blast! He fell back'ards.

'A doctor chap had that skull orf o' me. Said it was ten thousand year owd. He took it up to some larned Society in London an' I never heerd no more of it - or of him. Reckon he towd 'em *he* found it.

'But there, that warn't nothin' to what happened when we landed on Dead Man's Island, over in Kent, one day afore the War. They buried a lot o' French prisoners o' war there, time owd Boney was about. One of the coffins had heaved up out o' the ground, because of extry high tides, and when we trots across the Island in the moonlight, owd Nipper goes ass-over-tip into this here coffin, smack on top o' the skeleton. Lord! He up and runned.'

The Boy considered the picture for a moment with silent relish. Then he slewed a quizzical eye upon me.

'Did you hear of how our owd village copper was bit

by a skull on this Island?' he asked.

'*Bitten* by a skull?'

'Yis! Yis! There was a skellington laid in the mud off the East Point for months, jist arter the War ended. The fishin' chaps seed it fust. No one on 'em was a-goin' to say a word, 'cos they knowed if they had done, it would hev meant a Crowner's Inquest and that means knockin' a day off your work. Thinks they, the skellington's been there long enough a'ready, so he's quite happy. He don't want to move. Why should we worry.

'Then some yachtin' chap sees it an' tells the copper. Down he comes in a motor-boat, silver buttons, helmet an' all, settin' up like an admiral, same as if he was lord o' the sea.

'He was new to these here parts and reckoned he was goin' to larn us chaps a thing or two. These owd marshes allus tames 'em in the end.

'Well, the launch-man runs her bows up the mud, the copper blunders out in his long boots and nearly goos flat in the mud and then he spots the skellington a yard or two away.

'"Ha! I'll hev to look into this here matter," he says to the launch-man, what was owd Bill Puddock, orf the *Teazer*. "Why hevn't this here matter been reported to me afore? I hear this here hunidentified skellington has been a-lying in the mud here for weeks, without the Law bein' made knowledgeable and cognisant of the fact."

'"They ain't my bones, mate," says owd Bill. "And I dedn't put 'em there. You'd better inwestigate."

'Well, the copper he blunders up the mud, gits to the skellington, damn nearly falls right on top of it and then pokes his great hand into the jaws of the skull, so as to lift it up fust and cart it away.

'*That bit him*! Lor! He let out a bellow like an owd bull and fell ass-over-back'ards into the mud. The skull was a-hangin' on to his fingers - and *still* bitin' him.'

'How on earth did that happen?'

'Gret owd crab inside,' said The Boy succintly. 'That hung on like a bulldog. That owd copper ain't been salvaging along these shores since then. That larnt him.'

A whistle, like falling swords, cut the sunlit air. Startled we looked skyward. A score of whimbrel, 'titterels' in the old and lovely language of the marsh, swooped and dived overhead like scimitars, grey-white underparts flashing. They fled up the channel.

'Half-jacks - jest come in from overseas,' remarked The Boy placidly.

'We've seen a mort o' birds this mornin'. But you niver know'd there was hundreds o' nest and eggs on this here island, as well as Roman bones and skulls what bite coppers, did you?

'Don't you say a word to anybody, Master. Do (if) ye do, we'll hev the egg-collectors here, snatching 'em up for the market, an' the bird watchers, them week-end gull-worriers, traipsin' round and scarin' all the birds off the nests.

'I likes to see 'em settin' about, all peaceful and quiet. They're a better sight than our owd copper.'

THE MISSUS GOES TO SEA

EPHRAIM has ploughed the green alleys of the Essex seas for more years than the mind of man runneth. The estuary, to him, is mapped as plain as any London street to a Cockney. Its 'hills' and 'lows' are as familiar to his sea-sense, as potent of meaning, as charged with news as village lamp-posts are to Mr. Soapy Sponge, that dog of dogs.

Why, then, should Ephraim take his wife to the sea-shore? Mrs. Ephraim had never seen the sea. Born in the fishing town at the head of our estuary, she has never been aboard her spouse's smack nor ventured the dozen salty miles to the bounding main.

It cannot be pretended that Ephraim laments the distressing landlubberism of the mate of his bosom. Far from it. He does not hold with marine misses. Indeed, his comments on the week-end blondes of the yachting resort of Ditchcrawl-at-the-Bar are pointed.

'All hair, an' teeth an' trousers. Brass-faced hussies. Brass hair too, the half on 'em. I wouldn't gie ye a pint of winkles for the best on 'em.'

No, the truth is that Ephraim's decision to take his wife to Yarmouth, away up in the foreign parts of Norfolk, was due to no laudable desire to inculcate in her hammock-like bosom a love of the sea. Business, hard business, was at the root of it. Money.

For Mrs. Ephraim's sister, married to a prosperous fish-curer in that windy town of bloater, beer and skittles, had 'up and died'. She had bequeathed Mrs. Ephraim 'a piece o' money'. Also a 'mite o' chattels an' sich'. Ephraim rightly decided to give his over-worked bedfellow, cook and handmaiden a holiday. 'Same as yew an' mey, owd mate, hev bin rubbin' along tidy-like for 50 year an' I reck'n thass toime that I tuk yew to the seaside for a piece o' gaiety.'

So to the railway station the twain proceeded, she in decent black, bedizened with glittering jet, he in greeny-black broad-cloth and Sunday shirt, topped by his peaked fisherman's cap. Now Mrs. Ephraim is a woman of weight. She is, according to Ephraim, 'rigged on barge lines'. But Ephraim is small, active and incredibly ancient. He is no man with whom to trifle.

Rapping smartly on the ticket window counter which his nutmeg - brown face just topped, he smacked down a couple of hard-earned pound notes and demanded of the gangling railway clerk:

'Tew tickets an' look dam slippy about it.'

'Right,' said the clerk, who knows his Ephraim. 'Where to?'

'None o' yar dam business where I'm a-gooin',' snapped Ephraim.

'Shut yar trap an' gie me they tew tickets.'

Eventually by the threat that no tickets would be issued unless the destination was notified, Ephraim capiulated with the one word 'Yarmouth'.

Little is known of the journey into foreign parts other than that Ephraim's opinion of Suffolk was that all Suffolkers were 'sorft and silly' but Norfolk, with which he does great traffic in eels, earned his approbation. 'A rightforward lot o' indipindent min - sharp as needles, cunnin' as weasels as best ye as soon as look at ye. Good owd booeys.' Thus the accolade from the master of sharp dealing.

Arrived at Yarmouth, Ephraim escorted his wife to the beach. They walked along it for a while, then sat down among the dunes and stared out through the marram grass.

'There she be,' he announced. 'There she be an' some rum owd games she get up tew. She takes some tamin' when you git her running full belt on the Scroby. She's a handful up here, I can warrant ye.'

Dimly, one had the impression that a skittish mare was indicated. Ephraim's next words dispelled any such illusion.

'Thass th' owd sea, mate,' he announced. 'There she be an' a rum owd bitch she can be. I bin a-masterin' her all me born days an' she ain't got top side o' me yit. What yew reck'n on her, mate, now you've sin her?'

There was a pregnant pause. Mrs. Ephraim gazed fixedly at the North Sea, crested with occasional white caps. Then she spoke:

'That bin a-muddlin' in an' a-muddlin' out ever since we set down here half an hour agoo. That rightly don't seem to know where thass a-gooin'. I don't think nawthin' to it, that owd sea.'

Ephraim's righteous outburst was mercifully stillborn. Mermaidens intervened. They tripped by on naiad feet, clad in the briefest of brieferies. One, diving through a breaker, rose from its spume like Venus Anodyomene and shrilled, in the accent of Stratford-atte-Bow:

'Wotcher, me owd cock. Won'tcher old missus let yer come and paddle wiv us? Coo - let 'im orf the chain, missus.'

Now, Mrs. Ephraim, who is no shrew, except when Ephraim returns home markedly to windward on Saturday nights, melted to this artless girlishness.

'Ain't that suffin' cowd out there in that sea, dearie?' she enquired kindly. A chorus of Cockney voices informed her that the ocean was all that heart or feet could desire. In the midst of the girl's gossip a female of rustic roots sauntered down the beach, paused beside Mrs. Ephraim and divested herself of stout, mud-stained country shoes and uncompromisingly cotton stockings. This divulged the fact that her feet had not recently been on visiting terms with soap and water. Mrs. Ephraim, regarded them and their owner with slight acerbity.

'Cor! Yar fitten ain't half dutty,' she exclaimed with East Anglian frankness. 'Whatever yew bin an' gone an' tuk yar shoes an' stockin's orf for?'

'Cos I'm agooin' to paddle. Time I bin in that owd sea an' gin 'em a good owd rinse that'll ha' clent 'em.'

Mrs. Ephraim digested the information silently. Then a youthful look crept into her eye. The dormant spark of vanished girlhood flickered into new life. Her opinion of the sea was undergoing change. She rose majestically in embosomed majesty and, quivering jet at each massive undulation, stalked towards the kiss of ocean.

Pausing, she bent stertorously, fumbled beneath billows of skirts and unguessed inner battlements, unbuttoned her boots, unshipped her stout woollen stockings, tucked up her skirts and kicked off her boots. A second later she stood, like Boadicea defying Rome, her mien that of a British queen about to command the ocean.

Alas, the feet thus revealed matched almost the sable

colour of the black bombazine which billowed above them.

All would have been well, for in one moment those feet would have been laved by the creaming surge, bosomed softly in sand, cleansed by the sharp tide and none would have been wiser.

But alas, the younger paddler, smarting under Mrs. Ephraim's criticism had seen the worst. She proclaimed shrilly.

'Cor! Look at yar fitten. They're black. And what's more they stink. An' then you talk about mine.'

'That don't s'inify,' retorted Mrs. Ephraim, calmly, waddling majestically into the surge. "That don't s'inify if they are black. Lor bless yer. I'm tharty years older than yew.'

And that was that.

THE PIRATE

HIS GRANDFATHER had a beard like a brush, a nose like a beacon and eyes like blue flames. He sailed the narrow seas from Dungeness to the Orkneys in fishing smacks, coaling brigs, deep-sea trawlers and every sort of short-sea trader that went upon lawful, or otherwise, occasions.

His wit was barbed in a jovial, unlettered way. His boast was that he could get drunk on a penny. And he did.

'I've knowed me owd Dad git as tight as a fiddle on a penny - when a penny was a penny,' said Will, son of the deceased reprobate and father of my young marsh buccaneer, The Boy. 'He'd goo to me Mother an' ast her for twopence, when beer was twopence a pint. He'd gie me a penny on it and then hop orf up-street to the *King's Head*. He'd git in the Captain's Bar wi' all them owd skippers and young fellers, and there he'd stop.

'I'd goo by an hour arter-wards and hear 'em all roarin' out like bulls. Larfin' fit to bust. An' toppin' the lot 'ud be me owd Dad, tellin' them young fellers how he'd cum round Flambro' Head in a tempest, under bare poles, takin' it green. Lor' I knowed he ha'n't been *near* Flambro' for a year or more. But he'd git a pint frum every one on 'em.

'Then he'd cum rollin' home tew his dinner wi' his owd beard stickin' out like barbed wire, his snout as red as if that'd flew afire and his owd eyes nappin' like a sparrer-hawk's. He'd wallop down a skinful o' pigs trotters and Mum's duff and then be orf on the tide a-fishin' all night. Ooh! A rum owd pup, was me Dad. An' The Boy take arter him. He's the davvle's brekfuss.'

That was in the mellow days, between the wars, when Will and I sailed the shining Essex creeks in our double-handed duck-punt, shooting and fishing for whatever flew or swam. The Boy was then 10.

He was designer, shipwright, builder and skipper of a fearful hermaphroditic conveyance, known as 'me uptown schooner', a sort of sand-yacht, built like a boat, with a prow, rudder, a towering spar, a boom, a bowsprit, a jib and a gaff, which bore aloft a mighty spread of canvas.

This 'frightful contraption would whistle round the corners of narrow lanes, setting cattle afright, stampeding horses, gliding under the front wheels of village buses, which winced visibly in their tracks, as though they had been shot.

It poked its bowsprit in at the open doors of the pub and set the dogs barking like mad. It upset the pavement displays of the greengrocer and the general store dealer. They would pursue it, those props of Church and Chapel, roaring ungodly oaths.

And The Boy would let out a reef and, with a knotor two in hand, sweep up the street like a great bat, the envy and hero of other small boys, the whip and scorpion of his elders.

He learned to shoot when he was eight, or it may have been nine. Need I say it was a muzzle-loader, a double-barrel of peculiar bore, something like 13 or 14, with two hammers and a trigger guard, which alternately fell off when detonation was attempted.

Written on my heart, Will and The Boy returned from a day on the tide. Will loped ahead, with the slow stride of the marshman, up the side of a hedge, which ran from the sea-wall to his cottage back-garden. A place of bleak fields and bleached grasses. No place for pheasant.

Will, bowed under a pair of long smack oars, a dripping mountain of brown nets, a salty sackful of clammy, new-caught fish.

The Boy whistled cheerfully in the rear, burdened by nothing more embarassing than his conscience and that frightful gun. Will, short, stocky and leather faced, with all the tale of the sea graven finely in the wrinkles about his merry eyes, grunted: 'Yew young hound! Cum an' carry these oars. I'm loaded down like a hoss.'

'Not me, Dad,' chirped The Boy. 'Yew got the brekfuss. I got me gun ready to shoot the dinner.'

'You'll shute yar blessed-self if that damned thing goes orf,' grunted Will sourly. Then he stopped dead. There in the hedge, it sat, gorgeous in colours as a rajah, luxuriating in a dust bath in the September warmth of sun.

A cock pheasant, by St. Hubert! Who cares if it was September?

'There he set, a-buffin' hisself like an owd hen,' Will told me later. 'A-buffin' an' a-fluffin' an' not more'n a duzzen yards orf. I beckons The Boy. He sees it sune as I did. Ups wi' his gun, cocks both hammers - Lor' I shifted that owd net round in front of me phyzog quick, I tell yar, cos Gawd knows when she'd blow up or not - an' he pulls the trigger.

'The right hammer falls orf. True as I stan' here. He pulls the left. She snaps - misfires. He reaches down, picks up the right hammer, claps it on agin, wedges it wi' a bit o' matchstick and pulls buth triggers. An' b'lieve me, the left hammer falls orf, the trigger guard cums unshipped and the right barrel misfires.

'Cor! An' that owd pheasant still went on a-buffin'.

'The Boy picks a pin out o' his jacket lapel, pricks the right nipple, shutes a drop o' powder into it ou' o' his flask, wedges the trigger on ag'in and has another go. Orf she goes like a eight-bore - he allus overloads - an' the owd pheasant flops out. Dead as a hog.

'"There y'are, Dad," he sings out. "I tell't yer that 'd git the dinner. Now yew hop orf hum to Mum wi' them little owd fish for brekfuss, while I bring up some real grub."'

Will reminded me of that epic feat last Sunday when we stood in the hen-run-cum-pig's-court-cum-gun-room-cum-dog house, which is the ground floor of his sail loft and net store.

'Here The Boy cum up the yard,' he said. 'Jist back from foreign. He's fowty-two now and reg'lar scientific, but Ooh! still a proper young davvle.'

Striding up the yard in sea-boots, naval trousers fishermen's slop and khaki jacket, surmounted by a sun-wrinkled, grinning face and a mop of tight, curly hair, The Boy greeted me with a shy grin.

'Dad look a'right for a nipper,' he vouchsafed. 'Jist on his 70 and git about like a cat, don't yer, William?'

'Got tew, wi' yew about,' said William. 'Nothin's safe, sir. He pinches me cartridges, borrers me guns, uses me boats, wears me boots and he'd rob me o' me tools if he knowed where I hid 'em.'

'Hammer's under the peter-net, saw's back o' the tar

barrel, nails is in a bag in the pig's court and yer files and planes is in the kitch-place,' grinned The Boy. 'I used 'em las' night time yew was up-street wi' Mum.'

'Cor! Blast!' was all of which Will was capable.

THE ASTOUNDING DOCTOR SALTER

'THERE YOU ARE. That'll please you. You remember him. So do I. Most people have forgotten him - but what a man. They don't breed 'em like that nowadays.'

A gamekeeper with half a century of Essex wisdom of the fields and marshes thrust a book into my hands. It is 16 inches long, 9½ inches wide, 3¼ inches thick and it weighs five pounds. It is bound in brown leather and bears the simple inscription *Sporting Record - J.H. Salter.*

It is written, page after page, in a fine, clear hand which records the wild duck, snipe, teal, coots, moorhens, redshank, plover, grouse, hares, rabbits, golden plover, green plover, wild geese, pheasants, partridges, woodcock and 'various', shot between the years 1865 and 1929, by one of the most remarkable sporting characters that ever lived.

How many people today remember the late Dr. John Henry Salter, the village medico of that most elegantly named Essex village of Tolleshunt D'Arcy, which lies a little inland on the north shore of the great and shining estuary of the Blackwater?

Born in 1841, he died at the age of 90 in 1932. For 70 years of that long life he dwelt in the tiny village with the Norman French name and the rose-red cottages grouped around the Maypole, which lies in the salt-smell of the sea with its face to the glimmering marshes and its hands to the plough and the harvest fields.

During those years the village doctor became an honoured guest of the Czar of Russia, a close friend of the Grand Duke Nicholas, the projector of an expedition which discovered gold, coal, oil and other mineral wealth in Spitzbergen; the trainer of 23 runners for the Waterloo Cup; the breeder of several notable race horses; world-famous for his gun dogs, both pointers and retrievers, and a judge of dogs with a world-wide reputation. He became Provincial Grand Master of the Free Masons and Vice-President of the Kennel Club. He judged roses for the

Royal Horticultural Society and was awarded their highest honour, the Award of Merit, for producing the only blood-red alstroemeria in existence.

During his life-time he owned 2,696 dogs, of which he bred 2,123 himself. They were of 44 different breeds and produced six different breed champions, viz. pointers, retrievers, Sussex spaniels, Gordon setters, Irish setters and greyhounds. He won 611 prizes at dog shows, including 199 firsts and 30 silver cups. In 1925 he succeeded the Duke of Grafton as President of Crufts Dog Show. In addition, he won 1,400 prizes for fruit, flowers and vegetables.

This remarkable man was a giant mentally and in physical endurance. He thought nothing of walking 14 miles home from Colchester in his 70th year to get himself fit for the shooting season. He took out his first shooting licence in 1850 and, from 1865 to 1925, he shot 62,504 head of game and wildfowl, including 104 varieties. Eleven wolves, shot in Russia, were part of his bag.

Like all Victorian sportsmen he maintained a private museum of stuffed birds and animals, including many notable rarities. After his death they were presented to the Chelmsford Museum where the Doctor Salter Room was formally opened to the public by H.R.H. Prince George in May 1932. Despite the fact that he lost the sight of one eye at the age of 20, he was a dead shot, a remarkably fine boxer and a good horseman and motorist.

He began with a brilliant student's career at King's College Hospital, London, and was earmarked for a Staff appointment. Instead, he preferred his rural practice, his thousands of acres of shooting, his horses and dogs and the garden which he created out of a hayfield. When, in later years, the Governors of the Hospital asked him to return to them, he refused. Had he gone to London there was little doubt that he would have become an outstanding surgeon. Instead, his boast was that he had brought more than 10,000 Essex babies into the world.

This man who loved horses, dogs and flowers and whom I was fortunate to count as a friend, worked hard, travelled widely, read deeply, was elected to many important offices, always wore a buttonhole and was, as the late Lord Lonsdale said:

'A man of whom there are no detractors . . . . he stood

for all that is most admired in English sport and life.'

At the age of eight he began to keep a diary and kept it up until the day before his death on April 17th 1932. It filled many volumes.

It recorded the wars, public events and everyday doings of a life which had known the Indian Mutiny and the Crimean War; the Franco-Prussian War; the Boer War and the First World War. He lived through the days of General Gordon and Florence Nightingale, of Gladstone and Disraeli, of Tennyson, Darwin and Huxley, of Queen Victoria, Edward VII and George V.

I doubt if any village doctor has ever lived a fuller or more varied life. Yet, today, his name is forgotten outside East Essex.

The late Alderman J.O. Thompson rescued many of Doctor Salter's diaries and incorporated them in a book published by John Lane in 1933. In my view it deserves to rank with the diaries of Parson Woodforde, Gilbert White and Farington.

Salter went to Tolleshunt D'Arcy on October 29th 1864, where he dwelt in D'Arcy House, that pleasant red-brick, Georgian-fronted house, with the village street bang on the doorstep.

The record of his purchases for the new house 'a horse and trap, a cat (of the rough, heavy, brush-tailed Russian breed) a pug dog and a Newfoundland' plus 'a wedding ring of extraordinary thickness, a diamond guard for my bride and a gold pin for myself.' When the bridal couple reached the village they were 'received with great cheering' and practically the whole parish turned out to welcome them. From that day until his death, Salter became the friend and confidant of almost every man, woman and child for miles around. He records, on Sunday November 20th of that first year in the village, that:

'A farmer called after dinner, and nothing could move him any more. He sat and drank his wine till tea-time, and he sat and drank his whisky and water till supper-time, and then again the same process till past bed-time. One of the most eccentric and thorough specimens of an Essex farmer, I should say. However, just before 12 he took his leave.'

Coal was 19s. a ton and he burned a ton a week. He misses nothing. At Windsor, on June 23rd 1867, he records 'saw the Queen and "John Brown" starting out for a drive,' or a visit to that once famous pioneer of agriculture, Alderman Mechi, of whom he writes: 'Rode on horseback to Tiptree Hall and introduced to Alderman Mechi - very pleasant and hospitable. Looked over his outhouses, partook of his rum and water, and smoked one of his best cigars. I take him to be a shrewd, quick, intelligent, progressive man, somewhat proud - in fact, a trifle vain of his own success and acquirements - but ever ready, without ostentation, to take a new idea or discuss an old one with a novice.'

The shooting entries, particularly those concerning the wonderful Old Hall marshes, which I was fortunate enough to rent for a time after the old Doctor's death, are more than interesting. Here are a few entries:

> *September 23rd 1871: Two of us shot at Old Hall Marshes and made a brilliant show of 42 head at the end of a most enjoyable day.*
> *July 31st 1876: Down to the marshes eeling - 130 lbs. of eels, all good ones. Left by moonlight.*
> *November 20th: A rare day on the marshes. Killing, to my own gun, 138 head. Stayed for a flight, and got a couple of duck.*
> *October 12th 1881: Shot the marshes; broke cart with the weight of game.*
> *November 12th 1882: Started early and shot the marshes - 145 head.*
> *March 5th 1884: Aboard the Curlew, and off to the main, after geese. Fell in with plenty of black duck and saw thousands of wild geese. I shot a couple of pair of the black duck and knocked down two more, but they were such magnificent divers that they beat us after an exciting chase. The geese were unapproachable.*

On December 11th, 1885, he records that he bagged 16 duck with four barrels. Later he shot 12 duck with two barrels. At the age of 72 he shot 189 rabbits in three-quarters of an hour and, the next week, 'talked all day, got wet through, put 107 to the bag'.

If we grumble at rain, consider August 2nd 1888, when the railway line between Brentwood and London was 10 feet under water in some places and 'a man swam down the High Street at Brentwood and beer barrels were floating about in the road down the course of the valley towards the Thames'.

At 79 he was up at 4.30 a.m. on November 22nd 1920, shot 35 duck before breakfast, then did five hours in the garden and attended a public function in the evening. One month later, on the day before Christmas Day, he was up at 4 a.m., down on the flooded marsh, up to his knees in water 'with an east wind blowing strong and rain in torrents' and records that he fell into deep mud and water 'shooting under the worst circumstances of weather from 5 to 10 a.m., a walk of the beastliest description for 8 miles and then 50 miles patient-seeing afterwards . . . . a good wholesome day for a young man of 80.'

Then in 1926, in his 85th year, he records these epic entries:

> *August 9th 1926: First day of duck shooting. I walked about from 5 till 7.*
>
> *September 1st: St. Partridge Day once more, and I went out to keep up the old tradition. Came away very contented that I could keep going for 4½ hours. A man came out, and making himself known to me, said I brought him into the world 61 years ago.*
>
> *September 4th: A poacher called and insisted on seeing me. He said he had hired a shoot and asked me to have the first go there. It was very civil of the chap, seeing that I have sent him to gaol many times for poaching and other misdemeanours; he showed me his signed and stamped agreement, and his receipt for the money he had paid for it. He says it will pay for itself over and over again with the rabbits, of which he declares there are at least 3,000. He is not all bad! He always had a sneaking regard for me and (really) I for him. He wears my old hats and clothes, and is very proud of himself when so arrayed!*
>
> *September 6th: The promised day for the poacher's shoot, but the elements were against us - it rained hard and stopped it all. I went to 'the meet' of course.*
>
> *September 8th: The shoot 'came off'. We found a good lot of English coveys, and I did the walking well.'*

He also records that three ladies gave him a kiss after he had dined with them.

At the age of 85, on a bitter winter day, he put to sea from Mersea Island with two young fishermen and two enormous punt-guns in an open boat. A snow storm came on, the boat was driven out to sea off the Dengie Flats, and nearly sank but, at last, after six hours of driving snow, they made land. The 85-year-old doctor then put the two young fishermen to bed, as both were half dead, and then drove 10 miles home, had a hot bath, dined and was hard at work next morning.

Wolf hunting in Russia, he was 'kidnapped' by his sleigh driver who drove him into the forest out of sight of his companions after Salter had refused to give him money.

Thereupon Salter, unarmed, jumped from the back of the sleigh onto the driver, got him down, put his knee in his stomach, pinned him down with one hand, and seizing the reins with the other, turned the pony round and drove back to the shooting party.

At Gatschina, the Summer Palace of the Czar, Salter was entertained by Prince Galitzine who was Master of the Horse. He discovered that the Czar was fond of Cock-fighting so he sent the Czar the finest game-cocks he could find in England, and records 'they killed all the rest'. He notes that the Czar was a very good fly-fisherman and had a herd of 'buffalo' in Gatschina Forest - probably aurochs.

In 1901, staying with Prince Youssoupoff at the Palais Rouge, he records that the Prince's eldest son, 'a tall, nice-looking lad', was being tutored by a Suffolk squire, Cook of Polstead Hall. Little did he dream that the 'nice-looking lad' would become the slayer of the evil genius of Russia, the rascally monk Rasputin.

Another friend, the Tartar Prince Sharinsky, one of the richest men in Russia, went bear-hunting with a spear, cornered them single-handed and killed them. He had killed nearly a hundred in this fantastically dangerous fashion.

Thirty-one years later, when the old Doctor lay near death in his bed, I took Prince Nicholas Galatzine, the grand-nephew of his former friend, to call on him. He talked animatedly of his old days in Russia for the better part of the morning and the conversation is almost the last entry in his diary.

Ten weeks later I saw him lying in his coffin, a study in calm nobility. At the foot of the coffin two huge, grey wolves sat gazing glassily at the old hunter who had slain them more than 30 years before.

So passed one who epitomised all that is admirable in the character of the English country gentleman.

A SALT WATER MYSTERY

'WORK,' said Charlie. 'Work! I ain't no enemy of work. Work an' me allus got on well together so long as we kept a tidy bit apart. Work's good for a man - that keep his brine on the hop a-dodgin' of it. Why, a man 'ud get reg'lar like an owd woman, just settin' in a rut like an owd hen on a egg, if that warn't for work allus a-creepin' up on him. I *like* work - providin' that ain't *hard.'*

Charlie spat skillfully into the third eddy of the wake - a bull's eye - as the smack chugged softly under her engine past the little pier which juts into the estuary from the tiny, sandy beach of that island which the Danes called Oozey. It is still a place of ooze. A place of wild duck in the dawn, of black geese that cronk under the winter stars, of curlew that skirl above its saltings, aloft on autumn winds.

Its few bold, bleak fields, elm-bordered, girdle the old yellow-walled farmhouse, where, generation after generation, Essex yeoman have reigned as kings uncrowned of this salty isle. At the seaward end a long sandy spit goes shelving into the tide. The geese sit there sometimes in their black hundreds. Widgeon string out along the tide-edge in scattered scores. Curlew sleep there, like grey wraiths on stilts - if curlew ever do sleep. Many a punt gun has boomed its deadly message along that island spit under the cold moon. A place, indeed, hallowed in the unwritten annals of our local fowlers.

'Same as that spit to port,' said Charlie, suiting action to words, with beautiful precision.

'Many a man has earned his week's keep and filled his kids' bellies and shod his owd woman just by shootin' off his big gun into a bunch of birds a-settin' there. You wouldn't call that hard work. Thass pleasure.'

'There's plenty of hard work in getting a punt across a mile of this tide to the island,' said I. ''Specially if you've had to sprit half the way down the other shore before you crossed over. Why, you could get drowned here as easy as wink. And as for hard work, my back and shoulders have been sore for a week after being out in a punt half the night.'

'Ha! You're soft. Don't do enough on it reg'lar to get your back hardened up. These reg'lar owd gunners have got backs like bullicks. You could chop up a log o' wood on their owd shoulders and they wouldn't no more'n scratch theyselves thinking that was an owd louse a-tiddlin' 'em. Hard? They're as hard as ships'-bottoms. Wonder they don't grow barnacles on their backsides.

'But there. Talkin' o' *hard* work, would you say that was hard work if I told you as I knowed a man who made 90 quid - 90 quid, mark ye - on that owd spit only three Christmases agoo? Took him 10 minutes - thass all.'

I looked suitably receptive. Charlie gazed loftily at a wheeling gull and went on.

'You rec'lect that a London gennleman bought the owd island a year or two afore the war. Sort of speckylator. Reckoned he was goin' to build a holiday camp there or some sich dam' nonsense. The war scuppered that all right. He was left with the owd island on his hands at a top price. Sarve he right, too.

'So he start a-farmin' in a sort of way. Got a manager in. Put a lot o' them racing greyhounds round the place, kennels full on 'em, yapping an' bawling all night. Then he tarned a whole lot o' turkeys down. That's what done him.

'You know our owd gunners don't let nothin' *big* get away on this river. That warn't any more than a week afore Christmas, on a market day, when the owd manager and his Missus had gone across to the mainland to do a bit of Christmas shoppin', than who should tarn up off the island but owd Efrum in his owd punt. He'd got his big gun - Cor! Blast! She *is* a big 'un, too. Two-inch bore and shoot a pound and a half o' shot big as pills.

'Owd Efrum lays his punt up in a gut t'other side of the spit, gets ashore with a rare owd canvas side-bag, full o' *suffin* hung round him, and goes a-cropin' up the spit and half way into one o' the top fields, where these here owd tarkeys was out on the stubble.

'You'd have said, if you'd seen owd Efrum, as how he might have been lookin' for a wire (rabbit's snare) or two. Or p'raps just peckin' about for some o' them owd arrow-heads what tarn up now an' agin. Anyway, the owd boy draws back to the spit, takin' his time like, dippin' his owd fin in this here sidebag every now an' agin. Lord above only knowed why. He gets right out to the end of the spit, highwater mark, an' Cor! Blast! His owd bag was right empty then.

'That was a big tide, that market day, about three o' clock, an' a big tide cuts the end o' the spit right off, just like a little owd island. Of course when thass cut off like that you might say that that *is* a island. Sort o' No Man's Land.'

Charlie favoured me with a glance of forensic finality, rather as a King's Counsel might lift his eyes to the Judge to emphasise a point, as though mutely to say: 'A rib-binder, Me Lud.' Dimly I perceived the satanic drift of Charlie's mind and Efrum's rum little ways.

'Come three o'clock,' Charlie went on, putting the tiller over by habit as we passed the unseen, sunken wreck of a Spitfire fuselage, on which many a net has been torn to perdition. 'The tide was right across the end o' the spit an' on that little owd island there set a lovely bunch of geese. Geese! Well they *looked* like geese when owd Efrum come a-creepin' out of Death Crick in his little owd punt. Big 'uns, too. Bigger'n any owd geese as Efrum hed ever seen on this owd river. But there, ye know, there's times as when the owd grey geese or them owd Canadas tarn up here - both on 'em a dam sight bigger'n our owd black geese. Why, an owd Canada'll go 15 pound.'

'I had one two winters ago that weighed just that weight,' I remarked.

'Jesso. But these here owd geese they was *double* that weight. Great owd things big as - big as - well, big as you like.

'Owd Efrum drawed up to 'em in his owd punt, pretty-like. They was all bunched lovely. Hadn't got any more'n a yard or two of sand an' mud for the whole bunch on 'em to stand on. Cor! Packed like shrimps they was.

'Owd Efrum gets up to 80 yards range, squints down his owd barrel, draws up another 10 yard or two, thinks to hisself like: "I'll make sure on 'em - but I don't want to spoil their plumage." And then . . .'

Charlie paused. He spat with Oerlikon-like speed and accuracy at a floating patch of widgeon-grass and tide-scum. The effect was timed with that artistic crescendo of drama of which Charlie is a master unique.

'Owd Efrum,' he went on casually, 'has allus been a shortsighted man. That run in the family like. His owd Missus hev a pair of specs like binnacle lights. An' Cor! Blast! She needs sumthin' to kiver up that owd phizzog of hers. That'd start a dog fight on a black night if she peeked round the corner when the hounds was out.

'Owd Efrum must have been unconscious when he lugged that lot up to the altar - or drunk. Beer *wuz* beer in them days - tuppence a pint and that'd alter a man's wisdom.

'Well, owd Efrum, he squints down the barrel of his owd gun, he sees these here geese - rare *big* owd geese, a-settin' packed like owd women at a bunfight, on the end o' the spit. He pulls the lanyard of his big gun an' 'Boomp'.

'Off she goes with a row like a lot of housen a-fallin' down. The owd punt shoots back a yard or more in the water. The smoke goes up like a bomb abustin'. And the geese - they was laid out all-ways. Nigh all on 'em dead, but five or six flackers fell in the water, but couldn't rightly seem able to swim.

'"Thass a rum 'un," thinks owd Efrum to hisself. "Never seen the like o' that afore. Never seen a owd goose what couldn't swim."

'So, bein' inquisitive-like, he shoved his punt up to the spit - gettin' darkish by then so as he couldn't see too fur or *be seen* - jumps out, gets his birds, hulls 'em in the punt, and what do you think he'd got?

'Turkeys! Turkeys! Tharty lovely turkeys. Everyone on 'em worth three quid apiece and no questions asked. Ninety quid just by luck - luck an' good judgment.

'Of course, the man what had the turkeys, he couldn't say nothin' 'cos once they turkeys had strayed off that owd island o' his and got on that little owd island what warn't his, 'cos that was cut off by the tide like, well, they was wild birds, warn't they? Wild birds all alone by theyselves out in No Man's Land with the salt water a-lappin' their pore little owd feet.

'Then along comes owd Efrum. Allus was a shortsighted man. Pore hard-workin' owd feller, out with his gun, a-lookin' for suffin to stuff his kid's bellies for Christmas an' stop his owd Missus' jaw - well, there y'are, that all seemed to go together, de'nt it?

'What did owd Efrum do with they turkeys? Sold 'em - mighty quick, too. Plenty o' people up in London with their owd bellies a-hollerin' out for a bite o' Christmas turkey. Efrum had to think o' the likes o' they. Pore chaps.

'Allus was a Christian sort o' man, owd Efrum. No sooner got his 90 quid than he bought his kids new boots, his owd Missus a new hat - ought to have been a muzzle or or a mask - a new suit of sails for his smack and a bottle of Nelson's Blood to comfort his owd stummick-like.

'How did they owd turkeys get on that spit? Ah! Thass a mystery. Allus have been. Allus will be. Thass a mystery, too, what owd Efrum had in that little owd side-bag o' his. Might have been wheat. Might not. Thass a mystery.

'I happened on the Manager o' the owd island two days arterwards. Ast him if he'd a nice turkey to spare for Christmas. Told him I was a pore owd chap what ha'nt had a mite of turkey for a year or more.

'"Blast, Mate," he say: "If you'd have spoke up three days ago I could've sold ye a nice little owd turkey. But there's tharty on 'em gorn. Couldn't have been a fox 'cos we han't got no foxes. Couldn't have been a man 'cos we han't had no visitors. There warn't never a feather left nor yit a drop o' blood."

'"No, my owd booy," I thinks to meself. "There wouldn't be no feathers, ne yit no blood 'cos 10 minutes arter Efrum drawed away in his punt the tide, bein' extra big that day, kivered that little owd island right over."

'"Cor! Blast!" I say to the owd manager. "Thass a mystery."

'"You're right, booy," he say. "Thass a mystery. That allus will be."

'And seeing, sir, as how his owd head is as thick of wood as that owd tackle-block, that allus *will* be a mystery.'

On which we sailed into the sunset.

THE PRETTY LITTLE DEAR

The wind it sang in the pine-tops, it sang like a
humming harp;
The smell of the sun on the bracken was wonderful
sweet and sharp,
As sharp as the piney needles, as sweet as the gods
were good,
For the wind it sung of the old gods, as I came
through the wood.
(Patrick Chalmers)

THE HAY cutter missed him by less than a foot. No doubt the old gods had something to do with it. They have warded his kind for long enough. There he lay in the long grass 'most fairylike and elfinwise', light dappled, sandy-haired, leggy and helpless. A long ear cocked inquisitively as a bumble bee buzzed out of the fallen swathe like an indignant mayor from the ruins of his parlour.

Large, sloe-coloured eyes, a bluish bloom upon them, eyes as big as marbles, regarded the world, the men and the clanking hay-cutter with Olympian calm. Nothing, one felt, could possibly disturb the timeless trust born of a bare week's experience of this world.

He lay not more than four feet out from the wood's edge, warm in the sun.

'Well, there's a pretty little dear for you,' said Frank, who farms these fields and loves his woods as his forbears did a century ago.

He picked up the fawn, tenderly as a woman with a new baby. Its long legs dangled, little hoofs shining black as jet in the sun. A half-squeak, half-whimper. Then the infant nuzzled the coat sleeve with a wet, black nose and snuggled down. All was still well with this new world.

His coat, silk-smooth, was clean as air, scentless. After all if Nature provides a mother who drops one in a bracken brake or a bed of meadow grass and there leaves one for an hour or more in between milk sucks, it must provide at least an insurance for young and innocent things. Hence the scentlessness of the nesting pheasant, the sitting partridge and the fallow fawn.

Somewhere in that green tapestry of woodlands which climb the low Essex hills and clothe the little valleys, there walked his missing mother. There are 60 or more fallow deer in those woods, the very private secret of a very few of us.

Two hundred yards away lorries and buses thunder on the main road, motor cycles roar by on their trail of peril and Cockneys drink ghastly drinks from coloured bottles at roadside shacks. Beyond the road main line trains thunder north. Less than 18 miles from the green aisles of the old woodland are the smells and wickedness of London. And still the deer are secret.

The deer have been freemen of farms and woodland alike for 15 years. Ever since the park palings were torn down during the War and tanks and guns thundered under the stag-headed oaks whose fathers knew the deer, rufous red and glancing fallow, long before the Seven Kings of the Saxon Heptarchy met down the road not many miles away. That was 900 years ago or thereabouts. The ancestors of the little thing which regarded us, nose twitching and ear flicking, were old inhabitants then. When the palings went down his grandparents took to the woods. The family have been there ever since.

Like the rabbits, they have their friends. Quiet country people who like to see live things about.

'There's enough food for both of us on the land - I haven't starved yet, nor my father before me. So live and let live, I say.' That is the philosophy.

Occasionally a buck is shot. Sometimes venison is on the farmhouse dinner table. Usually, when someone takes too much of a fancy to the young apple trees in the orchard.

'Now isn't he a pretty little dear?' remarked Frank, tickling the little dear's ears. 'I see you coming out of the wood and was just going to holler, when my eye lit on this little dear lying in the grass. Another foot and the cutter would have had him. They never move when they're that young. Just lie there stock-still. Nature tells 'em to be quiet and then no one will see 'em. That's how we happened to cut the legs off just such a little 'un in this same field a year ago. I had to shoot the poor little dear. But not you, my beauty.'

The fawn turned blue-black eyes of faith upon him.

'Ate up a quarter acre of my young barley, your family did, t'other week,' Frank went on quizzically, rubbing the fawn's throat gently. 'But I shan't miss it. The pigeons and rats do more damage than all the rabbits and deer put together. Be a hard old world if a pretty little dear or two couldn't live in it, wouldn't it little 'un? I'm taking you home to my missus.'

He climbed into his truck, settled the fawn on his lap and started up that antediluvian chariot of war. It goes like a bomb and sounds like an air-raid. It rattled off, a cataract of mechanical thunder, bucketing over waves of grass pasture, visible relics of the days when the field was down to corn and ploughed on the seven furrow 'stetch'.

The fawn, cupped in one huge hand, whilst its new parent drove with the other, showed no fear. It merely opened those wide eyes a millimetre wider. Any well-behaved infant would do no less on its first motor car ride.

Charging over ridge and furrow like Boadicea about to assault Camulodunum, we crossed the main road and rattled up the 'chase' to the farmhouse.

In the kitchen, on the scrubbed table, beneath the eyes of foxmasks grinning, the fawn found his legs a little awkwardly.

A feeding bottle filled with warm milk was offered. He gave that half-whimper, half-squeak as the teat was pressed gently into his mouth. The first drop of milk touched his tongue. It was enough. He sucked eagerly. The pint bottle was emptied, the blue-black eyes narrowed - content. Feminine hands and voice petted him. He took it with superb grace. Fear was not in this world.

Three hours later, when the stable clock chimed nine, the fawn was fast in the back seat of the car for a seven mile drive. The stream of holiday traffic, lights, the ant-like pavements of a market town, the roar of a train at a level crossing, and the ecstasy of a 10-year-old daughter in a dressing gown were all accepted with the same bland poise which refused to be stampeded by the hay cutter or rattled by the battle-wagon.

When Tan, a minute Manchester terrier, erupted from

beneath a table with a volley of barks, the black nose gave no more than a moment's twitch.

The fawn was taken out of the truck, put in a loose box and bedded down on new hay. It settled down to sleep in the lee of a truss of hay as calmly as though the snort and stamp of a hunter in the next box and the smell of harness and horses were all part of the woodland world to which he should belong.

Morning sun on the dewy lawn and a cautious peep through the loose box window. She - for we now saw it was a female infant - had slept well and woken happy, for she was jumping the hay bales like a steeplechaser.

Then came the great experiment. Would a ewe suckle her? If so, could the fawn on its long stilts of legs get down low enough to reach the ewe's udder? We all know that a cow will suckle a fawn and that a nanny goat was Nature's own foster-mother, but although there are 400 head of cattle on the farm there are no goats. There were however, a score or so of ewes which had recently had lambs. The first five ewes refused point-blank - with that stoney-faced obstinacy of which sheep alone are capable - to have anything to do with the strange dappled child of the woods with the enormous eyes and ears and straddling stilts of legs. Indeed at least two sour-faced matrons showed every sign of being ready to murder the infant.

The sixth, a Kerry ewe, who had lambed in March, had still a little milk in her udder and kindliness in her heart. She regarded the fawn with startled decorum. When it skipped towards her she shied a little rather like a Vicar's wife at her first visit to 'The Crazy Gang'. The fawn, however, had a way with her. She was all feminine charm and grace and pretty witchery.

In no time she straddled her ridiculous legs, like altar candles, bent her head and was nuzzling the ewe's udder. In a minute or so all was well.

Today, a fortnight later, the foster mother and adopted daughter are doing far better than anyone ever expected. The ewe has an air of perpetually startled pride. Such a look, one surmises, as Queen Victoria would have worn had the lion and the unicorn suddenly come to life and dedicated themselves anew to her service. The fawn, on the other hand, accepts it all with the easy, airy grace of any bird-witted debutante who takes it for granted that Londonderry House was built specially for her own coming-out party.

Meanwhile Tan, who is knee-high to a fox, has adopted the fawn as his own especial pride and charge. Woe betide man or beast who threaten that pretty infant when he is about.

As for the farmer-owner of this strange trinity, he is the living quintessence of pure delight. Though lord of a thousand head of sheep and cattle, he had always cherished the dream that one day he would own a fallow fawn as a pet. Hence that 7 mile drive to his farm on the night when the hayfield gave up its secret.

That is why you will see a light in his eyes akin to bewitched enchantment. For old gods still cast their spells and who but Pan himself leaves those small hoof-marks in the farmyard mud by the duck-pond?

THE RAM, THE BISHOP AND THE SHEPHERD

'BULLS IS bad but rams is wuss,' remarked William, stuffing a slice of ham into his mouth. 'You kin see a bull a-comin' an' stand aside. But an owd ram - he waits till you're a-gooin' away, when you can't see *him* a-comin'. Then he come. Git an owd ram up your backside an' you'll fly over the hedge into the next parish. Owd davvles!'

'Ah!' said Tom, slicing the top off an egg with his knife, with the swordsmanship of Godfrey de Bouillon beheading a Saladin. 'I don't like none o' the both on 'em, but I have to deal with 'em, seein' as I deals *in* 'em. A mort o' trouble they've given me too, in my time.'

A period of champing ensued. Peace, broken only by mastication, reigned in the marsh farmhouse parlour. We were at tea. Sliced ham, pink and white. Boiled eggs, recumbent like the Rokeby Venus on beds of lettuce. Tinned salmon spilled into a glass bowl and laced with vinegar. Cold sausages, portly and self-contained, reclined, like prosperous Levantines, in a willow-pattern dish. A huge plum cake, full of eggs and fruit, flanked a decanter of port on the sideboard. That was to top up with.

Meanwhile, rock cakes, a jam roll, sausage rolls, sardines and home-made bread, with a mountain of butter fresh from the churn, flanked a teapot whose dimensions somehow reminded one of a woman chairman at a Party meeting. We were, indeed, at tea.

Tea at William's after a day's shooting on his lower marshes is always an event. You can shoot before it - but not after. No Olympian, ancient Greek or Parnassian hero could weather one of William's missus's teas and lift a gun after it.

So when Tom, who is farmer, cattle dealer, heavy-hunter judge, steeplechaser and fox-hunter, and I repair to shoot William's widgeon and marsh hares, we give luncheon a miss. The talk, like the tea, is fit for Pantagruel.

'Ah, rams,' resumed William, bolting the last of the

ham, much as an anaconda would dispose of a sizeable goat. 'Me dad an' me once went to Seadyke Show to buy a pair o' champion rams. Best in England, they was. One was a Cheviot an' t'other was a Border Leicester. They stood up there like reg'lar owd monarchs o' all they surveyed. Bone! Why their owd foreheads was *solid* bone.

'Dad had to bid to git 'em, too. Several was arter they rams. Cost him a tidy bit over a hundred pounds afore he'd got 'em into the wagon and all netted over in separate compartments.

'Drivin' home, Dad says: "Boy, those two owd rams'll make our fortunes. They'll straighten out some of our owd half-handy ewes an' give the flock a bit o' tone! Tone - that's what pays. Get your name big in the shows and you can ast big money. This time next year our lambs'll be worth solid gold. Two years from now we shall have a sideboard full o' silver cups."'

Alas, for rural dreams of Golconda. The warrior blood of the high Cheviots and the cavalier spirit of the fox-hunting Shires saw to that. Their souls were above money. Let the tale be told in the terse prose of William.

'Soon as we gits home, the owd guv'nor backs the wagon into the stockyard, opens the gate into the 10-acre piece and lets out both they owd rams together.

'Down they hops. Fust they shakes theyselves, then they glouts(glares) at each other.

'Then owd Master Cheviot trots off half-way up the field, whilst owd Border Leicester goes t'other way. When they'd got half a field between 'em, they wheels round like sojers on hossback. They gives one dirty look at each other, an' Lor! - they comes full tilt, like charging cavalry . Heads down, three almighty jumps and they hit head-on. Bang! They heard it in the next parish.'

'What did they do then?' I asked.

'Do? Dropped dead! Bruk their blessed necks. Snapped like candles. Bang went dad's hundred quid. That larnt he a lesson, though. He never let two owd rams out in one field arter that.'

William stretched a sun-burned fist for the tinned salmon, swallowed half a pound or so, wiped his mouth with the back of his hand and remarked blandly: 'There ain't no silver cups on the sideboard yit.'

'I bought an owd ram that looked as wise as a parson,'

Tom said, ingurgitating a brace of sausages like lightning, 'that'd stand and look at you like a bishop. Any minnit you'd expect that owd ram to go down on his knees and say his prayers. Milk and water warn't in it with the meek-and-mildness on that owd ram's face. I give 25 pun for him when money *was* money, and I reckoned he was worth it - till I turned me back.

'Then he give three jumps and a snort and I flew into the pigs-swill quicker than a squalling baby into the font.

'Time I'd picked meself out and looked round, that owd ram was half-way up the field, cropping grass, as meek as mice.

'"Right, me boy," thinks I. "I'll larn you."

'Next morning I goes into the field and when I'm 25 yards from the old ram, I turns me back and walks away, both ears a-flappin'. Right smart I hears thump, thump and I knowed His Lordship's a-coming. Round I whips, just as he lands on his third jump, head-down and going like the National winner. I jumps to one side and, as he thunders past, I lifts me boot - six rows o' nails and an iron toe-plate - and lands him one in his luggage-rack that sent him head over heels.

'"I'll larn you to try them back-door tricks on me, you owd beggar," I said. And I let into him with a hedge-stake, same as he'd never forget. That give him suffin' to think about.'

William swallowed half-a-pint of scalding tea with the nonchalance of Vulcan downing the Brigade of Guards with fixed bayonets, speared a sardine, plastered it on a slice of plum cake, and munched.

'Bishops! Rum owd pups. Allus arter your money. If that ain't the collectin' plate on a Sunday, that's a special appeal for proppin' up the parsonage, or half a quid for larnin' the black niggers how to read the Bible upside down - or tithes. They're hot on tithes. Sharp as the old fox is arter my hens.'

Having delivered himself of this anti-episcopal broadside, William, who at heart is a stout upholder of that indivisible trinity of rural pillars of faith, High Church High Farming and Old Port Forever, seized an egg, red-hot from the saucepan, since he likes them hot and soft-boiled. He tossed it in the air, as though discarding a wasp, caught it again, flicked off the top with a swoop of his knife, shot in the salt, rammed in a finger-piece of bread and butter, withdrew it, bathed in egg, and popped the lot into his mouth. Then he smacked his lips, swallowed another cauldron of scalding tea and repeated the egg-and-bread rite. Finally, having scooped out the last white of egg with a piece of crust, he threw the empty shell at the cat and relaxed.

'Ever hear o' what happened to the owd shepherd off the marsh and the Bishop of Seafleet?' he asked.

'This owd shepherd was a-goin' to Seadyke for the Show. He warn't much 'customed to trains, so he hops in fust-class, with his owd crook in his hand and his owd dog at his heels. Down he sits in a corner. Who should set opposite but the Bishop o' Seafleet. Got his owd glasses stuck on his snout and his owd head rammed in the *Church Times* like a terrier dawg down a rabbit-hole.

'Course, he'd got his breeches and gaiters on, frock-coat and top-hat wi' strings on. Shepherd hain't niver seen nawthen like this here afore. Bishops was new to he. Our owd parson, that time o' day, used to drive round in a pony-cart, a straw boatin' hat on his head wi' a cabbage leaf stuck in the back on it to keep the flies off his neck. That was about the most that shepherd knew o' the ways in which these parsonical gents gits theyselves up.

'Arter a while, currossity gits the better part o' Shepherd's good manners. He coughs a bit and then he says: "Scuse me, Sir, but ain't you some sort of a Rarverand?"

'The Bishop looks up, gives owd Shepherd a squint, crook an' all, and, says he: "As a matter of fact, my dear friend, I'm in the same sort of business that you are. I'm a shepherd."

'"Shepherd! Cor blast! You're a rum-lookin' shepherd," says owd Shepherd, took right a-back. 'I ain't never sin a shepherd done up like you afore. Hev you got a very big flock, master?"

'"Well, as a matter of fact," said the Bishop, "I've got a flock of 30,000 or more, I suppose."

'"Tharty-thousand," says owd Shepherd, garpin' like a fish. 'Tharty-thousand on 'em! Cor blast, you must be a rare busy owd boy come a-lambin' time. D'yew reckon to lose many on 'em, Sir, wi' a rare big flock like that o' yourn?"

'"Well," says the Bishop, solemn as an owl in a tree, but with his optics a-twinklin', "We always say in my particular line of shepherding that 99 are saved and one is lost."

'"Ah!" says Shepherd, jumpin' up and slappin' the Bishop on the back, till his teeth near sprung out of his head: "Thass where you don't know your job, boy. Thass the owd ram what git away. He allus is a rum owd b--- to ketch."'

Thomas, wiping the outer perimeter of a rock cake from his upper lip, considered the professional devastation of the prelate with slow relish.

'I count that owd shepherd were right,' he said slowly. 'Bulls is bad, sheep is fools, but rams is the wussest o' the lot.'

A DEAL IN BULLOCKS

THE CAR ground to a teeth-shuddering stop in the forecourt of the house. A face, aquiline, sun-reddened as a pippin, peered out. Eyebrows, grizzled, formidable as barbed-wire, shot out in a double-barrelled discharge, calculated to intimidate the innocent.

'Jes' going over to Runningfield to look at a bunch,' the voice beneath the eyebrows announced. 'Nice afternoon. Thought you might like to come.'

Since the wise man realises that education, like the brook, goes on for ever, I opened the door and got in. We rattled off to view 'the bunch'.

'I might buy 'em and I might not,' the voice went on. 'They're a tidy bunch. Old Frank's, you know.'

I nodded with the gravity of the half-educated.

Old Frank is 85, looks like the Madras Cavalry, hunts, shoots, dances until the stars reel and passes for an uninhibited 60. He owns a thousand acres or more, farms the lot and dwells in a gabled old house that was young when Elizabeth rode down to Tilbury. It sits between a garden full of summer scents and pigeon-dotted lawn and a sprawl of stables, coach houses, barns and stock-yards.

William, the power behind the eyebrows, is farmer-cum-cattle-dealer with half the county in the hollow of his hand. His father and grandfather were dealers before him, yeomen of sound repute, not mere catch-as-catch-can pawnbrokers of farming ill-luck. They thought nothing of walking 50 miles with their drovers to take a herd of beasts to Smithfield.

You will observe that 'buying a bunch' has nothing to do with choosing a spray of gardenias or sheaf of lilies for the charmer of one's choice. We were after bullocks.

''Course I'm not calling on old Frank on purpose,' William confided with a sidelong glance. 'We're just dropping in on the way home from somewhere else. Musn't let him think I want to see his bunch 'specially.'

Since William has been buying bulls, bullocks and

heifers from old Frank for 40 years, while his father bought them from Frank for a quarter century before that, the subterfuge seemed a little transparent. But that is the way of dealers. They foster eternally the pretence that the deal is purely an incidental aside, a pleasant interlude, in a day utterly preoccupied with other things.

'I've a friend who's just bought a house near Runningfield,' I suggested casually.

'Just the idea!' said William enthusiastically. 'We're going over to see him on a matter o' business. Old Frank can tell us where he lives.' The solution had been found.

Twenty minutes later the car ground to a stop in Frank's yard, scattering pigeons, ducks and barking dogs.

Old Frank in khaki shorts, spotless shirt and careful bow tie appeared, neatly as an antelope, from among the runner beans. One got the impression that he had just changed after winning the Parents' Hundred Yards.

'Whisky? Sherry? Or something long with ice in it? Come in.'

The room was long, cool, beamed and panelled, dappled with green shadows and shifting sunlight. Honey-coloured oak. Bristol glass, winking like rubies. John Leech over the fireplace. A marmalade cat on green and gold damask. Iced innocuous drinks in long glasses.

'Nice of you to look in, William. Didn't expect to see you today.'

'Didn't expect to see you either, Frank. James wants to see a friend who's bought an old house over at Deephedge - thought you'd know where it is.'

'Yes, yes. I know the place - top o' my medders on Brocksett Hill.'

'Ah! Jesso. Good medders those. Always good feed in those deep bottoms. Why, that old pasture of yours must be a hundred years old, Frank.'

'Dessay. Dessay. 'Member you bought a bunch o' heifers off me there last summer.'

'Ah! So I did.' William registered surprised but pleasant recollection. 'Tidy bunch too. Market's different this summer, though. This hot spell's knocked the bottom out of prices - no trade at all.'

'Isn't there now, William? Well, you see, I don't know values at all. Haven't been to market this last month. You never miss a market, old friend, so you have the advantage of me there.'

The bright, blue, boyish eyes of 85 fell innocently upon William. I began to feel sorry for Frank.

'Well, then, that makes two of us,' replied William genially. Babyish innocence flooded his rosy countenance. 'I don't know the values either. What with the heat and the thunder, there's no knowing how it'll be. Next we shall get the fly and any cattle with fat on 'em will run it all off with the fly a-chasing on 'em.'

'That's true. That's true. Cattle just eat your money out of the bank this weather. Hardly worth selling 'em, is it?'

''Tain't worth buying 'em, Frank, old friend. When you've got 'em you've got to unload 'em. Where and how? Now, I know a man up in Nottingham wants a nice bunch o' bullicks. He must have some of those Trentside medders where they never lack feed. But if I did buy a bunch there wouldn't be a penny profit in it. But there - I've done many a deal with him, so I suppose I'll have to look round for a nice bunch one o' these days. After we've had a spell of rain though. We need that to freshen the feed.'

'We had a nice drop last night, William.'

'Only a drop, Frank. Only a drop. Not enough to lay the dust, let alone fat a bullick.'

'Depends on where they're feeding, William,' Frank replied soberly. 'If you've got bullicks in a nice deep bottom, with plenty of shade, where the grass never goes dry and a hillside above 'em where they can get sun and fresh air on the move, without the flies to bother 'em, they'll stay fat through the hottest summer. That's a rule of nature.' He gazed solemnly at William. Diogenes never looked out of his tub with more detached philosophy.

'Jesso,' remarked William, rising to his feet. He had taken the hint. 'Well, we must get along to Deephedge to find out where that friend of James is hiding himself. Like to come for a ride with us, Frank?'

'Might as well,' assented Frank. 'We've finished hay-carting. If I stop round here, the Missus will find me a job. You can drive me round and I'll enjoy it. Getting too old to go to market nowadays and too old to drive, you know.'

'Didn't stop you hopping round with one young woman after another, till two o'clock t'other morning, at the Farmers' Ball, did it?' remarked William, climbing into the driver's seat.

We rattled out of the yard, through broad, bright fields of barley, swung down a dog-rose lane, where giant elms sailed like galleons against white clouds, and came to Deephedge. There the high upland falls to the luminous marshes in deep, steep, little valleys, like Devon combes. Each field, elm-bordered, is divided from the next by a great double hedgerow where magpies shake their watchmen's rattles and resurgent rabbits flourish white scuts. Hence Deephedge. In the green tree-shadows of a field which rises from a lush green bottom to a hillside half as steep as the side of a house, there moved a dappled tide of black-and-white Friesian bullocks. Twenty or 30 of them.

'Tidy-looking bunch. Yourn?' remarked William casually. He had inspected them closely at six that morning while Frank was at breakfast.

'Yes - mine,' said Frank with modest pride. He knew well that William knew just as well that the field had belonged to him for the past 45 years, and had never held any cattle other than his own. 'Like to look at 'em while you're here?'

'Might as well, Frank. Can't stop long though. Got to see this friend of James's. Special business. We come over here a-purpose for that.'

'Jusso, William. Musn't waste your time. However you 'on't miss a minute or so. P'haps you can tell me what they're worth, seeing as I haven't been near the market for a month.'

He placed one foot on the bottom bar of a five-barred gate and vaulted over into the field like a skip-springer. William, a mere infant of 55, followed with equal aerial grace. I managed to get over.

'Not a lot, Frank. All this heat. All that fly to come. All this long summer ahead. Cold ham and lettuces. Why, the beef trade's as bad as bad. What do you think Frank? '

'What do I think, William? I think £60 a-piece.' He fired the words like a gun. A magpie shot out of the oak tree scandalised. William regarded it with interest.

'Do you know Frank, I got scraped off me hoss by a low branch under that old oak out huntin' 40 year ago. Went straight into your brook. Full o' water then - not all mud and flies like it is today.'

'Ah! Jesso,' Frank replied. 'That would be when old

Squire Mashiter was Master. I recollect . . . .'

They dived into straight-necked runs of 40 years gone, as though such crudities as money had never been mentioned in terms so definite as to scare magpies out of oak-trees. I knew the form. The giants would now engage. Battle would be resumed by indirect flanking attacks, by feint and counterfeint, by suggestion and question - but never, until the bitter end, by a direct offer to buy or sell. Half an hour later I returned from a visit to the friend at the top of the lane.

'Fifty-two pun 10, Frank. There's my hand on it.' William's great fist, which takes a 17-hand hunter over the worst marsh ditches in England, shot out like a battering ram. Frank ignored it, with courtly politeness.

'Wild pheasants look like doing well this year and I do believe the poor old partridge is going to come back a bit,' he remarked cheerfully. 'Thank God we didn't have any heavy rains to drown 'em. But Lord! We had a downpour last night. And blow. I thought it'd blow the roof off.'

'Tell you what I'll do, being as dad always bought from you and so have I - I'll give you 53.'

William shot out his hand again and blew out his chest with sheer magnanimity.

Tea lasted half an hour. Deep ploughing; the folly of using deadly crop sprays; the return of the rabbit; the dumping of cheap Norwegian hay and Russian wheat in bygone days and the possibility that high prices for potatoes this autumn would lead to the dumping of cheap French potatoes, filled the conversation. Not a word about bullocks.

Tea over, William picked up his hat, shook hands with his hostess, patted his host on the back, strode purposefully out of the house, stepped into his car, slammed the door and put his foot on the clutch. Suddenly he wound down the side-window and shot out eye-brows and the words: 'Fifty-three.'

'Fifty-five,' shot back Frank, hopping from one leg to another like a pea on a hot plate.

William touched the self-starter. The car shuddered into demoniac life. It jangled. It jittered. It chattered. Frank, mouthing inaudibilities, sprang forward, clipped white moustache bristling. He thrust his head in at the car window and snapped: 'Fifty-five pounds. No less.'

'Right,' said William, shooting out a piston of a hand. 'I'll give you £55 apiece.' Frank grasped the outstretched hand. For an instant old age was betrayed by the guile of merciless youth. 'If you give me back a pound on every bullick for luck-money,' William continued.

Frank dropped the hand and snapped back as though the Scarlet Pimpernel had snatched him from the guillotine:

'That's not a price. That's a trick.'

''Tain't a trick,' William replied blandly. ''You said you'd take 55. I'm giving you 55. You merely give me back a pound apiece luck-money.'

William eyed him blandly. 'I'll give you 55. 'Tain't worth arguing about.' Their hands met like lightning.

'I'll come for 'em next week,' he added. 'Sort 'em out myself and pay you on the dot.'

'Leave 'em as long as you like,' Frank replied. 'Sort 'em to suit yourself, but you know my rule with everybody - I want the cheque three days before the cattle go. A cheque's only a bit o' paper till you get the money.'

William nodded. They gripped again. He drove off.

'You took an hour and a half over that, not counting tea-time,' I remarked accusingly.

'That took a minute or two more than I reckoned,' he admitted.

'What'll you get for 'em?' I asked.

'Sixty-two pun 10 apiece,' he remarked complacently. 'I've sold 'em already. I got 'em at the price I reckoned I would. But I jes' thought I might save a bob or two. It was worth tryin' - on anyone but Old Frank.'

We drove home, simple, contented countrymen, alone with the innocence of the dusk.

Four days later William's car slid up. The back springs seemed abnormally depressed.

'We're going over to pay Frank,' he remarked innocently. 'He likes hard cash - so he's getting it, hard. A couple of hundred-weight. Lift that.'

He pointed to a sack on the back seat. I could just shift it.

'All tanners, bobs and half-dollars - 440 quids' worth,' he remarked succinctly. 'That'll teach him to question my cheques.'

We took tea with Frank. Cream and strawberry jam,

plastered on bread without a hint of butter. A home-made plum cake which whispered of the bad old days of pre-1914 misrule. Money was not mentioned.

Finally -

'Will you take a post-dated cheque, Frank?'

'No damn fear. I like hard cash. Three days to clear a cheque - that's my rule.'

William rose without a word. A minute later he re-entered slightly rosier than usual about the gills. He dumped the sack with a thud that shook the farm-house to its foundations.

'There you are - all hard cash.'

Frank's face registered marble disbelief. He tugged at the sack. He opened it. Disbelief changed, chameleon-like, to amazement, glee, concern, defeat.

'How on earth am I to count this?' he gasped.

'You've got three days - what you wanted,' William replied. 'I'll come for them bullicks on Friday.'

We did. They were worth the price. There the matter now rests. Frank, it is whispered, plans a come-back.

BEWARE OF THE BULL

'THERE AIN'T sich a thing as a good bull - some is jist wusser'n others,' remarked the stockman, spitting expertly at a bumble bee buzzing ponderously about the lupins which stand sentinel by the yellow plaster walls of the farmhouse. The house, with half a score of steep-cocked gables and a rose-red cluster of Elizabethan chimneys built of that most delicate narrow brick whose like we no longer make, lies beneath slumbrous elms, in a green vale within smell of the North Sea.

Buttercup pastures, and hairy willows, witch-like by the slow brook, lead the eye through a lush landscape to the glittering mallard-haunted waters of a great lake which lies like beaten silver between the slow bosoms of the Essex uplands which lie to west and east of the waters that cover the one-time valley of the smugglers. Not even the concrete power house glimmering miles away in the haze of distance nor the hideous concrete fence which bound the 14-mile perimeter of that great reservoir, can quite destroy the new beauty of long waters and shining distances which this modern lake has brought to an old countryside.

So you would say, standing there in the sun, with the Tudor house behind us, and the great barns of the first Elizabeth set about the stockyard, with ducks white on the ponds, and butterflies gay in the garden, geese waddling and pigeons cooing, that here was a sentient cameo of English peace. An undertone of bees in the border. A baaing of lambs, in the home meadow starred with daisies.

And then it came again - a long, shuddering moan, a groan of menace. It had the cold smell of blood, a shiver of death. It paralysed, suddenly, the peace of that sunlit afternoon. It mocked the summer. It throbbed like a threat.

'He's a killer, that one,' the stockman remarked, taking a second shot at the bumble bee. 'You can't go nigh him without a pitchfork, and I hain't even bin able to get a ringle in his nose. He'd jump a five barred gate like a hunter - thass why we've got eight iron bars in the walls of his pen. Why, he got out on'y last week an' we had to round him up with a caterpillar tractor. He charged the tractor head on and hit it like a battering ram. There's a dent in it you wouldn't believe. He'll hev somebody's blood one day. The pity is he was took in hand too late.'

We walked across the yard to the bull pen, a tiny enclosure, walled on three sides by a seven-foot fence of stout iron bars set in concrete pillars. Behind it, from the dark door of the stall, lowered a solid ton of black and white ferocity, a Friesian bull, eyes red and bloodshot, a wild wreath of straw like demoniac vine leaves in his horns. One forefoot pawed the ground. Twin jets of steam hissed from his nostrils. And, from the deep chest, came again that shuddering moan with the threat of blood.

Bulls have, for me, an unholy fascination. They are my jinx, my hoodoo, my fear in waking moments, my nightmare in the small hours. If I am in the same parish with a bull, it is six to four that he will single me out from the rest of the inhabitants.

I have been hunted by horned beasts over cattle marsh and meadow, since that first paralysing moment of childhood when a cow, her calf lately weaned, and mad as only cows can be at such times, charged my nanny in the home close, sent her screaming in terror for the house and then, as I, a mere five-year-old, scuttled under her chair, the animal horned the chair high into the branches of the walnut tree and, lowering its head, missed my posterior by less than a foot as I bolted like a shot rabbit into the hedge. That laid the foundations of fear. The rot set in, and has not diminished. I confess, freely and without shame, that until the age of 15 I could not pass through a field of grazing cows without a twinge of fear, a sneaking backward glance.

And for that matter, there is no animal more ferocious in these isles than a cow, either when she has calved, or when when she has just lost her calf. Some are far worse than others. A really bad one goes through a period of definite madness. Such a cow should always be put on a long chain before she is due to calve and kept on it until after the babe is born. Then she will usually be quite quiet. But few cows with calves are really safe either with dogs or little children. The fear of the dog is the inherited fear of the wolf. It is latent and understandable. But the mad fear of little children, which sometimes causes cows to attack them on sight, is not so easily explained. Can it be that they are unable to distinguish between the form of the dog, the shadow of their hereditary enemy, and the forms and size of small children?

I am reminded of a foolish Sunday-school teacher who, in 1937, led her class of small children into a field near Amersham 'to look at the new little calf with her mummy'. The cow gored the teacher, scattered the children and for years after was highly dangerous with women and small children. It would attack a woman on sight. Men it ignored.

Whereas cows can react with insensate fury usually only in defence of their young, no bull is ever safe. Not even the mildest mannered old bull - and I know a man who rides without rein or rope, calmly smoking his pipe on the back of his eight-year-old bull and leads it to its stall on a length of binder twine - no bull, I repeat, is safe. Sooner or later, even with the best of them, there comes a red moment. And then the stockman, or the owner, is suddenly 'dunted' from behind, pinned against the wall, knelt on or gored to death.

I remember with undiminished horror the spectacle, a quarter of a century ago, of the limp, crumpled, blood-spattered body of a 70 year old marsh shepherd, lying sprawled on a half-cut haystack on the edge of an Essex marsh whilst, a hundred yards away, the bull, his horn black with congealed blood, was grazing peacefully among the cuckoo flowers and marsh grasses. When they rounded him up with a pitchfork, he trotted up the lane to the farm without a murmur, docile as a dog.

Twice in my life I have shot a bull - not dead - but in sheer self defence. The first was a strawberry roan brute who charged me on the lonely miles of the 'washes' of the Cam, in the heart of the Fens. There was no fence or man in sight, and the river at my back. So I let drive at him at 60 yards range. As the charge of No. 4 shot stung his hide and peppered his legs, he jinked to one side like a polo pony and, with a flourish of his tail, and a roar that shook the marsh, he galloped off. But for the accident of having a gun in my hand, I should have been gored to death or drowned in the river.

The second was on Langenhoe Hall Marshes on the Essex coast. We were coming back from shooting with a load of duck and rabbits when, suddenly, I saw a bull leave his herd of cows, walk towards us, stop and stare. That is always the first sign of trouble. Then down he went on his knees and horned up great clods of earth in a frenzy. That is the fatal sign. Then he broke into a trot, his tail straight as a poker with that kink in the middle which is the inevitable herald of bad business. We started to run for the marsh gate, stumbling along in thigh boots. I stubbed my toe on an ant hill and went headlong. As I staggered up, the bull was not 60 yards away, coming like a thunderbolt, head down.

'Shoot him, master! Shoot him or he'll hev us,' shouted Ted Allan the marshman. So swinging up a double 10 bore I let him have an ounce and a half of No. 3 full in the head. That bull swerved to one side as though he had struck a brick wall. Up went his head, a blood curdling roar shook the silent marsh. He lumbered off, shaking his head, his tail up like a poker. 'Tiddle him up agin,' shouted Allan and, clapping the heavy duck gun to my shoulder, I let him have the choke barrel at 80 yards or so. That bull did not stop until he reached the sea wall three quarters of a mile away, where he stood shaking and shivering, moaning softly to himself, sadder but wiser.

Now Ted Allan, who alas, is dead, was the most famous bull tamer and adder catcher in all Essex. He caught scores of adders with a forked stick and his bare hands. They were sent to hospitals and to the Zoo. He and his old retriever Nell had been bitten so often that both were of cast-iron immunity.

Ted's technique with bulls would have turned a matador green with envy. Armed only with a stout ash cudgel, he would creep up on hands and knees to a marsh bull and fling up handsful of earth and tufts of grass, in its chest, as it stood grumbling indecisively. This was guaranteed to puzzle even the most belligerent bull. Two legged humans they could understand. Four-legged humans that cast up clods were beyond their understanding. When within a few yards of the bull, Ted would spring to his feet rush forward before the animal could lower its head and fetch it the most fearful clout on the snout with his ash-plant. Inevitably the bull threw up its head, turned and lumbered off.

Then Ted, with a Red Indian yell, seized it by the tail and, belabouring its rump with his club, galloped after it. This proceeding, which I do not recommend to anybody, never failed to act. Ted explained it to me.

'I larnt that little owd trick when I was a titty-totty owd boy no more'n 10. I was on this here marsh with me catapult, stalkin' a lot of larks on me hands and knees when a herd o' cattle cum latherin' round me. I worn't no bigger'n tuppence, so I makes a run at 'em on me hands and knees, and off they goes. All 'cept one. He was an owd bull. He stood and moaned. So, thinks I, if I can make the cows run I can make the master run too. I hulls up a lot of grass and lets out a horrible row and makes a run at the guv'nor on my hands and knees. Blast! he went off like a train! You can allus scare a bull if you do something he can't make out.'

Of all the bull tales, the most remarkable was told me by the head stockman at the Manor Farm at Wells-next-the-Sea in Norfolk. He was leading a bull that had been quiet for years, down the back lane, with a length of binder twine on the ring in its nose. Suddenly the bull groaned, turned and pinned the man against a flint-built wall. Here are his own words.

'I was right atween his horns. His eyes was up agin' mine like bike-lamps, an' his snout in me belly. That first dosh ripped all me clothes off up the right side. There I stud in me shirt with me britches down an' the bull gloutin' in me face, snortin' like a steam ingin'.

'"Bill, yu owd b------r," I hollered. "Stop it, yu bloody owd fule."

'Damn! He tarned round and dashed through a hole in the hedge arter the cows. That was my voice what done it, I reckon. Warn't that a funny job?'

And believe it or not, that man, half naked, bruised and breathless, went straight into the field after the bull, drove him back to the farm with the cows and penned him. He went as quietly as a lamb.

'You see,' the stockman explained to me, 'I dussen't go home to the missus like that, wi' half me shirt off me back, an' I couldn't leave that owd bull roamin' the parish to do a mischief to summon else.'

The man was laid up with shock and bruises for six-weeks afterwards. When he returned to the farm he found the bull still in the pen. Not another man on the place had dared to move him.

The same man was leading a Jersey bull, the most dangerous of all, over the level crossing at Holkham Station. He had the bull by a pole fixed to a ring in its nose, usually the safest way to lead a bad bull. Suddenly the bull charged him. He stepped back, tripped on a railway sleeper and fell flat on his back between the railway lines. The bull lowered its head to gore him, head down. Luckily the pole twisted between its forelegs and jerked its head up. There lay the man on his back with the bull's face not more than a foot from his own, scalding drops of saliva dripping from its mouth into his face, its snorting breath blinding him and its blood-red eyes glaring in frenzy into his.

'So I drew back me fist, an' punched the owd b------r straight on the snout,' he told me. The bull threw up its head and galloped down the line. The man slipped through the wire fence and, pelting the bull with stones, followed it to an open gate, where he drove it on to the marsh. Such men, the unknown, unsung heroes of the farm, face such perils as a matter of everyday routine.

Jersey bulls are, as I said, the worst of all; but Shorthorns run them close, and Ayrshires are not far behind, whilst a Friesian, when he is bad, can be the devil incarnate. Perhaps the best of a bad lot is the Hereford.

The problem of how to handle a bad bull - and no bull is safe after his third birthday - is a difficult one. To begin with no bull should be let out in any field through which passes a public footpath. If he is, report the owner to the police. Most bulls are safe when with cows; but that is by no means a certainty. Nowadays bulls are often tethered by a long chain attached to a stout steel peg driven well into the ground. This allows them freedom to graze and to roam in a circle and at the same time keeps their heads down. So long as you can keep a bull's head down, he is moderately safe. But if he can lift his head, stare straight at you and 'get his direction' he is a danger.

Personally I consider that all bulls should have a short length of chain with a short pole on the end of it dangling from the ring in the nose. The weight of the chain keeps the head down. If the bull charges, the pole, rattling against his knees, is almost certain to pull him up.

Really bad bulls should be masked and kept masked. Metal bull masks can be bought in any market town. If a mask is not handy and the bull shows signs of becoming troublesome, a sack thrown over his horns and lashed on with a rope, is almost as good.

If a bull is penned and has to have his feet trimmed, there is one certain way to throw him with ease. Take a long, strong rope, loop one end round his horns, then take a loose half hitch round his neck, make another one just behind his foreleg, and another just in front of his hips. Lead the rope between his hind legs, and when you want him thrown, get two men to pull steadily on it. He will be down in a second. One man should then kneel on his neck to keep his head straight, whilst his feet are tied to a fence or a tractor or to iron stakes driven into the ground. After that you can trim his feet, or perform any other necessary operation.

De-horning should be done when the animal is young. One merely puts on caustic potash when the calf is a few days old, and burns round the bud of the horn with a hot iron. Not only does a de-horned bull fatten better than a horned one, but you have the dubious satisfaction of knowing that if, in later life, he gets you down, he can merely batter you to death with his head, instead of disembowelling you with his horns.

Personally I prefer my bulls half a parish away, and approach none without a double-barrelled gun. They are best on a dish, piecemeal, with plenty of onions.

PIG'S FRY

'A PIG'S a lovely creature,' said Efrum. He gazed into the sty. 'Look at owd Nance: she'll die kind. Ten score, if an ounce.'

Nance, her snout deep in straw, grunted appreciatively. Efrum spat. A philosophic pause ensued.

'Same as pigs,' said the Councillor, weightily. He deals in them. Old bedsteads, hens, second-hand bicycles, ships' anchors, bottles, boats, donkeys and a gallimaufrey of other necessities also contribute to his magpie economy. 'Same as pigs. I knowd a man name of Zeke Cantelow what allus killed a pig reg'lar, time the owd War was on. That was all legal-like. He had his papers all writ out, signed 'em an' they was passed by the owd War Ag. boys, straight as a gun. He killed his pig once a year, jest a'fore Christmas. He sold the hams and sides, kept the fry and chitlins and the owd head and chaps and trotters an' tail an' a bit o' sparrib, so as his owd belly never hollered at him.'

'"Never no waste in a pig" Zeke allus said. "That's good from snout to tail, from ears to trotters. You can eat every bit. That piy, a pig doos."

'Well, owd Zeke done so well, that, come the last Christmas o' the War, he up and killed two pigs. Niver said a word, o' course. His owd woman held the pigs while he slit their throats.

'He got his permit for the fust one, killed it, clent (cleaned) it and hung it up in the backus. The second owd pig he killed and hung up in the loft over the gig-house. He kept his owd mouth shut about *that* one. He jest went round in his owd hoss and trap and seed his pals like, time that was dark.

'"If you want a bit o' pig like, for Christmas, I kin oblige ye," he says. "Jest gimme your order now and piy up. I'll drop the bit o' pig in at yourn come next Wednesday night, arter dark. Money down now, though."

'That was owd Zeke all over. A cunnin', grabbin',

ungodly owd muck as ever walked. That was allus money fust wi' him.

'Well, his pals all paid up like men. Zeke got forever o' pound notes that dark night - most 20 pound - and they kep' their traps shut.

'Not Zeke though. Arter he'd got an order for a nice leg from the landlord of *The Oyster Pit,* down at Cod End, and sold another leg to the Missus at *The Gunners' Rest,* and a nice bit of sparrib in *The Eel Shear* and a pound or two o' chops in *The Hare's Foot* and a ham to owd Bill Blow what keep *The Decoy-Man and Dog* and had a pint along o' each and all on 'em, his owd tongue was loose. He reckoned he was the saviour of the parish. He reckoned he'd make their Christmas for them. So when he gits to the *Shepherd and Crook* he starts a-tellin' one o' two on 'em how the mucky owd Government would have kept 'em all short of meat for Christmas, if he hadn't up and killed this second pig of his'n. He'd got a rare skin-full aboard by that time.

'The next day, Zeke is a-settin' down in his kitch-place with a dish o' tea and a nice plate o' winkles, when a moty-car draws up at the front gate. Out gits two men in bowler hats, wi' little bags in their hand. "Rap! Rap!" they goes on the door. Away goo Zeke's missus for to see. Back she come right smart.

'"Two gents from the Ministry o' Food want you," she says. Zeke looked like that owd pig arter he's stuck it. Right blanched. Out he goes and sees the men.

'"We're from the Ministry of Food," they says. "We understand you've killed a pig in excess of the animal for which a licence was granted. We must see the animal at once."

'Zeke near dropped dead. He never said a word - jest took 'em to the loft where the pig hung.'

'"Most improper, Mr. Cantelow," says one of the gents, right severe.

'"You've broken the law, as you well know. You lay yourself open to a very heavy fine, not to speak of a possible term of imprisonment."

'When they talked o' prison, old Zeke shook like a jelly-fish. His owd teeth fair chattered.

'"Moreover we understand you collected a considerable sum of money last night from people willing to buy parts of this illegal pig from you. One of our Agents shadowed you from public house to public house, so it's no good denying the fact. You must hand over the money at once and we will give you a receipt for it. Proceedings will be taken in due course against the other persons involved. Meanwhile, we shall of course impound the two pigs. Load them into the van."

'Well, poor owd Zeke, tremblin' like a leaf, fishes out his wallet, hands over the 20 pound and then humps they two pigs, with a bit of 'sistance-like, into the van. He was so frit that he never asked for no receipt for the money and the two gents was too busy helping load the pigs that they forgot to give him one. Then they druv off sayin' :

'"You'll be hearing more from the Ministry about this."'

'Did he?,' asked Efrum all agog.

'Not likely,' said the Councillor scornfully. 'They was two "wide boys"from Easterend-on-Sea. They'd bin a-settin' in the saloon bar at *The Oyster Pit* when Zeke was a-blowin' his top off in the public bar and they heard it all through the partition and jist foller'd he around. That done him wi' pig killin' for a time - fair ruined Christmas for the lot on 'em.'

'Talkin' o' Christmas,' remarked Efrum thoughtfully, 'I went to Harvest Festival las' Sunday. Owd Rarverand was right owdacious. He rapped some on 'em.

'"That's nice to see you all here and the church full," he says from the pulpit, nice as pie. "I only wish I could see some of you here more often. Too many of you only turn up at Harvest Festival.

'"However, allow me to wish all those of you here now, a very happy Christmas."'

The Councillor disregarded this ecclesiastical interlude. Pigs were more important than parsons.

''Member owd Jimmy Dunch, the scrap dealer, what come from Rumford?' he say. 'Him and his owd woman come down here one day during the war. They druv down to mine in their moty-car. Jimmy could allus get petrol, being as he was a dealer. Like the rest of me pals from London-way, they was arter a bit o' grub.

'Well, I fixed 'em with a dozen eggs, two pound o' butter, a pair o' nice young rabbits, a bag full o' oysters and a nice young leg of pork. That was the bit of pig what done it.

'They left here arter dark and jest as they gets to the Layer-de-la-Zouche cross-roads, they sees light a-flashin' across the road and a police whistle blows.

'Jimmy knowd what that meant. Too many London folk had been gittin' bits o' meat, eggs and the like from us chaps on the quiet. The police had orders to stop all cars and search them.

'Smart as lightning, Jimmy grabs the leg o' pork and rams that up the skirts of his owd missus Gert, what sat beside him. Well, you know the size o' Gert. Once round Gert is twice round my pony stable. Time she had that leg of pork up her frontage, she was as big as a barn.

'Next minnit, the car stops. A torch shines in at the winder, an' a police-sergeant says:

'"Sorry, sir, we have instructions to search all cars proceeding in the direction of London for suspected black-market goods."

'"Oh Lor! Oh dear! Oh sargeant!" says owd Jimmy. 'I'm jist a-rushin' my poor dear wife orf to horspital. She's expectin' any minute now. Can't you let me pass - or do you want twins on your hands? They run in the family."

'The sargeant, he switches his torch on to owd Gert what sits there in the front seat, a-groanin', all swole up, like one o' them barrige balloons. He steps back right smart, salutes, and say most civil.

'"Sorry sir. I didn't know the lady was expecting. On your way - and good luck, Madam."

'Jimmy lets in the clutch and his owd Beelzebub Minor roars off down the road like a runaway hoss-rake. Gert sets there, a-larfin' like owd Mount Etna in eruption. She'd given up expectin' years past. All she was expectin' now was a port-and-lemon.'

'Ah! pigs kin lead to trouble - but mostly pigs lead to joyfulness,' said Efrum solemnly. He takes his pigs seriously. The sacred Hindoo cow shines with no greater effulgence before the eyes of its worshippers, than does the pig before the blue-eyed gaze of Efrum.

'I was frit out o' me life by bits of bacon rind, time I was a nipper,' he remarked slowly, his mind turning the pages of halcyon boyhood.

'Remember owd Stumpy Jennings and Bob D'Wit, years agoo?' he remarked. 'They was two owd fishing chaps, what went a-gunnin' every winter on the Main. They'd lay up their smack in Chapel Crick and with two punts, trawls and peter-nets, they'd stop there half the winter, shooting black geese and wigeon, trawling in the deeps and peter-netting up all the rills. They got forever o' fish and fowl.

'Me dad laid up that crick one October mornin' time I was a nipper. That was hazy over the shore-ends and still as glass on the water. I gets in Dad's punt, shoves up the crick and comes right under the stern of owd Stumpy Jennings's smack. All of a sudden, them two owd boys, the wickedest, most ungodly men afloat, pops their wicked owd heads out o' the hatchway and glouts (glares) at me.

'They'd bin havin' their breakfast and they'd stuffed long bacon rinds up their wicked owd snouts.

'"Ooh! We hev got nasty old colds this mornin', boy," they sings out. "Fetch a doctor quick, we're a-dyin'. If you don't we'll haunt yer."'

I am reminded of a certain day when a slight misunderstanding concerning a dog led to my appearance on a charge of dog-stealing before the unpaid, over-worked magistracy of our marshland levels. They were all there from the Chief Constable to a neighbouring squire, who was chairman. Never, in canine history, had a half-crown mongrel excited such portentous contention. When the case was dismissed, I repaired, with the chairman of the neighbouring Petty Sessions, the editor of the county newspaper and the squire of a nearby parish, who had all given testimony to my rectitude of character, to the local hostelry.

As we entered the raftered bar of that inn which was new when the Tudors came from Wales, a ribald voice shouted:

'Dog-robbers.'

There emerged a highly respected doctor, holding high office under local Government.

'I insist on standing you all a drink . . . You've done me the most excellent good turn. I am in all your debts for evermore.'

'What on earth have we done to warrant this?' I asked.

'Done? my dear fellow, done? It's not what *you've* done. It's what *I've* done. Whilst you had the chairman, the Chief Constable, most of the beaks and half the county police assembled to decide whether you had, or had not, stolen a nameless mongrel, I drove through the chairman's park, got a couple of his pheasants with an air-gun and then helped Squire ---'s keeper to cut up an illicit pig in the willow holt at the back of the old decoy pond. While there's a war on, there's a way.'

Which merely emphasises Efrum's profound truth that 'pigs kin lead to trouble, but mostly pigs lead to joyfulness'.

SMUGGLERS OF THE ESSEX ISLANDS

THE ROAD ends at an inn, barge-boarded, white-painted, whose roof of old red shingles, which hold all the summer suns of three centuries, sweeps almost to the ground. That long glowing roof lifts like the crest of a breaking wave to chimney pots where starlings sing. And there, where the road ends in a bower of tall elms, is that ancient inn, called, with the rural rightness of words , *The Plough and Sail* for this is a country where men live with one foot on land and one in the sea, by plough handle and ship's tiller.

It is a No-Man's Land of great islands that lie within grassy sea walls, their lands lower than the surrounding seas. Between the islands wind sea-channels where tides suck endlessly. Channels that bare to luminous mud-flats as the tides fall to the pull of the moon. And, fringing the mud flats, are wide ribbons of sea lavender. They blush and plum as summer suns warm their flowers to the glory of moorlands, until autumn frosts dull this sheeted magnificence and bleach it to winter's uniformity.

It is a country of wide skies and high clouds. Red sails of barges go sailing above the land and masts of anchored smacks dance on the waves above sea walls. A country of grazing bullocks, of an endless undertone of baa-ing sheep. Curlews whistle under the moon, duck pass on high notes of wings and herons fish solemnly. Sea-swallows fall like white plummets in the shining tides of summer and wild geese cronk and gabble far out on the misty flats when winter is cold.

A country of ancient mysteries, of rough, unwritten history. A lonely land where great farm houses and mighty barns stand humped, like little hills, on the endless, treeless flats. It is the loneliest land in all England within a short 50 miles of London.

For in these Essex islands that lie between the estuary of the Thames and the mouth of the Crouch there are few roads but many waterways. On half a dozen islands, perhaps 10,000 acres in all, there is only one hard road. There are islands without houses and islands where houses have fallen in ruin, barns are roofless and gardens run wild because neither men nor women will dwell in such hard solitude. There, if you like, is a forgotten and a secret land, a place to play on the imagination, to stir the roots of imagery, to repel the timid and enchant the few.

There is nothing else quite like this seaward end of the Rochford Hundred in Essex where the isles of Foulness and Wallasea, of Potten and tiny Rushley, of New England and Havengore bake in the summer suns or glimmer ghostly in the drifting sea-fogs of winter.

Go to it by the winding road that runs from Rochford, that ancient town on its sea river, where Anne Boleyn was born in her great sprawling Hall of endless gables and twisted chimneys, and you pass through a pastoral land. A countryside of tall cloud-topped elms, of yellow-walled farm houses that are manor houses in little, moated and ancient. Arthur Young called it the English 'Land of Goshen', for hereabouts is some of the richest land in all England - and some of the poorest. The good land will grow anything.

It is yeoman farmers' country where men have farmed their broad acres, century after century, tenants of great landowners who, in the past, dwelt at a distance such as the Dukes of Manchester, the Earls of Mornington, the great Lord Rich, the Earls of Nottingham and Winchelsea, noblemen whose names are like a roll of drums in English history. Today, most of the land is owned by the yeomen. Their roots, as long and deep as those of duke or earl, endure long after the great estates have been broken up, long after the pageantry and heraldry have faded and no trumpets blow beneath the walls of Rayleigh's vanished castle or Rochford's part-ruined Hall.

Life has not changed a lot in a hundred years on the islands, for if the smugglers no longer fight the coastguards, the old beliefs in ghosts and witches still linger.

Even in this year of enlightened retrogression my own two maids, strong, buxom, strapping girls, whose father, a horseman and cow-doctor, came from 'The Islands' - he was born next to the old *Shepherd and Dog* at Ballards Gore - complained to me that a ghost, 'a tall white thing, like a woman,' constantly visits them each night, standing between their beds and bending first over the one and then over the other. Yet my house was built somewhere about 1650, and has, as far as I know, no legend of a ghost.

Yet the two girls, insist that their nightly ghostly visitant is as real and actual as the Seven White Horses who, mounted by knights in armour, gallop spiritedly each midnight up the lane by their parents' house at Herongate.

It is only six years ago since Alfred Martin, who worked as a farm labourer on 'The Islands' for 40 years, told me that his mate was 'collared by a davvle', who plucked him out of his bed one night in Devil's House on Wallasea Island and threw him downstairs. Alfred knew a witch on Foulness who commonly crossed the creeks by moonlight at midnight on a wooden hurdle without sails or oars.

Paglesham, where stands that inn, the *Plough and Sail* is one of the remotest villages in the whole Hundred. Twenty-five years ago I had the shooting on Potton Island, a great lonely prairie of grass marshes, more than a thousand acres. Then it had no roads, no trees, no fresh water, only two houses and four grown-up inhabitants. It lies opposite Paglesham Hard, girdled by creeks where wildfowl today take the place of the smugglers who once infested them.

Paglesham is full of smuggling stories. That white-bearded old veteran, Captain Kemp, of the *Plough and Sail*, knew more than he would ever tell. My late boatman, poor Fred Keeble, knew much more of battles by moonlight in these lonely creeks and on the misty marshes. It is a living part of village history. Benton, the local historian, gives us the flavour when he says:

'Smuggling was carried on in this parish to a great extent . . . and the entire population seem to have been implicated. The three old elm pollards against Pound Pond, near East-hall, are known to have had £200 worth of silk at a time secreted within their hollow cavities, and several houses (one of them Stannet's) are pointed out as having receptacles for concealing goods.

'The roof of an old cottage, lately demolished, at East-end, formerly inhabited by one Taylor, who destroyed himself, was denominated "The Smuggler's Hoard".

'From a diary left by John Loten, Collector of Customs at the Port of Leigh, it appears that in 1786 , there were 10 vessels from 13 to 30 tons burthen, employed in illicit traffic in this district. The Paglesham smugglers chiefly carried on the exportation of wool, which was prohibited, and made large fortunes. In this parish likewise 13,476 gallons of geneva and brandy, were imported in one year.

'A notorious place for the temporary deposit of spirits was an Island on the Kentish coast, called "Gantlet" or "Yantlet", formed of shells, where there was only one house, and rendered the discovery of the place of concealment almost impossible. Even the Magistrates were corrupt, and their servants and horses were employed in conveying smuggled liquor.'

Harriott, a magistrate who lived at Great Stambridge, throws considerable light upon the doings of these smugglers. Travelling from Lille to Dunkirk in France, in 1786, he put up at an inn generally frequented by Englishmen where 'he fell in with some half a dozen Kentish smugglers, who knew Blyth, Emberson, and Brown, from Paglesham, who were engaged in that pursuit, and were expected at every tide.

'Regaling himself with them in a sup of good punch, he was called upon to drink "D . . . n to all Revenue laws and officers", which he strongly objected to, and finally betted, amidst furious oaths, a bowl of punch with the chairman, who proposed the toast, and a bottle of the best Burgundy with each of the others, that he was right in refusing the toast and they wrong in proposing it.

'His bets being accepted, he inquired if in wishing destruction to the revenue laws and officers they did not mean that there should be neither one or the other. "Certainly" was the answer from all, and Harriott went on to show if they were abolished, so would smuggling, and they would be common traders.

'"Lost," said the chairman, so here goes. "Revenue laws and officers for ever."

'His Essex friends arriving, made merry with the men of Kent, at being taught how to toast by an Essex magistrate. He sailed at midnight, and landed within a mile and a half of his own door.'

Loten tried to put a stop to this bare-faced smuggling by procuring a small decked ship which he armed with three brass swivel guns and appointed her to cruise in the estuaries of the Thames and the Crouch, and up all the channels and creeks connecting the two rivers. This preventive cutter made a good many seizures and fought more than one 'small naval engagement'.

John Dowsett, one of the principal Paglesham smugglers, immediately answered this challenge by equipping a cutter called the *Big Jane*, which he armed with six brass six-pounders. The grassy flats of Wallasea and Foulness Islands echoed more than once to the thudding boom of the smugglers and the Government vessels fighting it out.

Blyth, the king of the Paglesham smugglers, commonly known as 'body and bones', was both a diplomat as well as a fighting man. He was boarded one day by the king's cutter in the River Roach when his ship was carrying a cargo of smuggled tubs of brandy. Blyth immediately tried to drive a bargain with the revenue officer and apparently offered so many tubs of brandy instead of a fight for the lot. Along confabulation followed between the king's man and the smuggler. Whilst this was going on, tubs of brandy were carried from the smuggler to the revenue cutter and toasts were drunk in rum on both sides. The revenue cutter already had a considerable cargo of seized brandy in her hold. Blyth soon had the king's officer under the table and most of his crew paralytic.

Then the tubs of brandy were transferred from the king's ship back to the smuggler until, when they finally parted company, Blyth had not only recovered the whole of his own cargo but had added to it most of the brandy previously captured by the king's cutter from another. smuggler. He landed the lot safely at Paglesham.

Blyth was once captured at sea and taken on board a revenue vessel. A storm blew up and the king's ship went ashore on the Goodwins. The crew immediately commenced throwing the guns over to leeward. Meanwhile Blyth was down below fast in irons expecting the ship to break up at any moment.

The revenue officer, knowing that he was a first-class seaman, appealed to Blyth to save the ship. Blyth replied that it did not matter a damn to him whether they sank or not, for if they escaped he would sure to be hanged as soon as they put him on shore.

'Show me how to get my ship off,' said the revenue officer, 'and I will promise that you go free when we land.'

And so it was.

If you go to Paglesham today you will find near the church a field called Church Field. On that field when village grandfathers were boys, the smugglers regularly played cricket. 'Taking the precaution to have their pistols loaded, which, with their cutlasses, were laid upon their jackets.' Blyth was a great cricketer.

One afternoon a bull charged the cricketers, head down and tail up.

'Body and Bones!' roared Blyth. 'Don't think to frighten me!' And seizing a great cudgel he grabbed the bull by the tail, wrapped the tail round his arm and thundered on its ribs with his cudgel to such effect that the bull bolted, cleared hedge and ditch with Blyth still hanging on and then, according to the village tale 'completely exhausted, it dropped down and died'.

Another great local smuggler was 'Fiddler, the Pirate', otherwise Hynes, who was arrested in the tap room of the White Hart at Burnham on Crouch and was executed and hung in chains with two other pirates at Fiddlers' Point on the foreshore of the Thames near Greenhithe.

Such are the mighty ghosts of the boisterous past who haunt the shimmering creeks and sheep dappled marshes of these forgotten islands on the Essex coast.

BERT BAILEY—'FEN TIGER'

HE STANDS out in youthful memory, long, lean, hawk-eyed, and cheerful, peering into the peat-brown waters of a fenland dyke, an eel-spear poised like a great lance in his right hand. There was something Grecian about the whole attitude of the man. A whisper of the primitive, a throw-back to the hunter and fisher who was the tribal ancestor of mankind.

To-day Bert Bailey of Wicken, that remote Cambridgeshire parish which still contains the last great reedy relic of the old primaeval fen, is 69, veering on the end of the natural span of man but still as lithe and lively as the eels who are his natural prey.

For Bert is one of the last of the almost extinct race of true fenmen. In my youth he and his like were a little tribe apart. They dug turf on the wild wastes of Burwell and Swaffham Fens. They cut the sword-sharp harvests of sedge amid the jungles of Wicken Fen. They scythed acres upon acres of the surrounding 'litter fens', where cream-yellow seas of meadow-sweet melted into an ocean of many coloured grasses that undulated in the autumn sun. They netted the fen dykes and shining lodes, splashing the fish into the nets with 'spreads', the fenland equivalent of the Norfolk 'quant', with which they pole the black, tarred turf-barges up the waters of Wicken Lode. It was illegal, but the law ran on wooden legs on those wet wildernesses. Their fathers and grandfathers had done the same thing, and long generations of forbears before them, away back to the dim days of Hereward.

And, in the same tradition of the Saxons, they speared eels with broad-bladed 'glaives' - which is a fine Saxon word - and transfixed the lurking pike with thin-bladed 'darts', like unto the trident of Neptune himself. Old Ernie Rose, the village blacksmith, beat out glaives and darts alike on the ringing anvil of the village smithy which reeked of wood smoke and the tang of horse-feet shavings and, as any proper village smithy should, stood within the shadow of a mighty chestnut tree. The best blades were made from old carriage springs, for they had all the whippiness and tensile strength, for if a glaive should strike a submerged prehistoric fen oak, as hard as iron, inferior steel would snap. I have one such in the gun room among the old muzzle-loading 'bank'-guns, punt-guns, hand-guns, shot-flasks, powder-flasks, otter-traps and other relics of the old fen. The head alone weighs five pounds. Mount that on a stout wooden shaft 12 feet long, and you have a weapon which no weakling could handle.

Yet I remember Bert, soon after the end of the First World War, spearing a 3½ lb. perch in nine feet of water at Pout Hall Corner, which is where Reach and Burwell Lodes meet, a rare place for big fish. That alone is a rare testimony to the skill of hand and eye.

'Bout that time I saw a pike in Reach Lode as long as this table and as black as a bit of old fen-oak,' said Bert to me not long ago in the stone-paved bar of the thatched *Maids Head* at Wicken. 'That must have weighed a hundredweight. They said that when it got up to Reach it had to swim backwards all the way to Pout Hall, near on three miles, before it could find room to turn round in.

'I darted a pike that weighed nine pounds in Wicken Lode soon after that, and then I got a seven pounder. He looked a bit fat like, and when I cut him open, so he should have been. He'd swallowed a four and a half pound pike - more than half his own weight.

'One morning I was out early, when the water was as clear as glass, down at Wicken Cock-Up Bridge, and I saw an eel lying on the bottom of the Lode as thick as my arm and as long as that table. I darted him quick! Lord! He did wriggle and fight. I hulled him in the barge and he scuffled all round the bottom board and got covered as black as a nigger in turf dust. He was opening and shutting his old mouth and snapping like a dog - damned nearly scairt me. He weighed 7½ lbs, and that is a rare big eel for the fens - very near a record I reckon.

'Then I darted a 5 lb. bream and a 3 lb. tench in my time; but the best we ever did was when old Ted Palmer, Jack Hall, his brother Fred and Billy Day and me netted the Runawater and Wicken Lode and took 11 stone of fish. All sorts. Jack, perch, bream, roach, dace, rudd and tench - everything you can think of barring eel pouts.'

Bert puffed a cloud of tobacco smoke into the raftered ceiling, and his eyes went back in memory a quarter of a century. I thought, as he was thinking, of that jolly, piratical crew, the old fenmen, who were the pith and soul of the fen, as utterly different from the average farm-labourer as chalk is from cheese. There was his father, old 'John Bunyan', so called because as a boy he went into service with old Dr. Willis at Soham, which was at least three miles away and, therefore, deep in foreign parts. When he returned from this perilous venture in the abyss of the outer world, he was greeted as John Bunyan, the man who had returned from the 'Pilgrim's Progress'.

And there was that long, lanky, bearded prophet Bob 'Fal-lal' Simpkin, the village Sunday postman, who was a fenman every other day of the week. And Jake Barton, who once speared a pole-cat on a flooded fen with a hay-fork. I reminded Bert.

'Ah! Pole-cats always were about this fen,' he remarked. 'Bob Simpkins' dog ran a pole-cat into a rabbit hole on Fodder Fen about 1910. He put in his hand and pulled it out and my heart! Didn't that bite him. He got blood poisoning from that. Then I recollect your father killing one in the willow holt at the edge of the Sheep Walk at High Fen about 50 years ago, and they got another one out of Treen's Holt at the bottom of your home paddocks. Jake Barton killed his one in Spinney Fen. But Lord bless you, they are still about in the Fens.' I reminded Bert that just recently Mr. Horace Bull, the well-known wildfowler and pike fisherman of Waterbeach, had reported one in his neighbourhood, whilst another has lived in a willow-holt near Oxlode on the Bedford River washes for at least five or six years.

Those who imagine that pole-cats are confined to Wales and the Lake District little realise that the true wild fenland strain is still extant.

Bert reminisced on to otters which, to the fenman, are as the fox is to the foxhunter.

'I was out early one morning when the copper was still snoring his roof off, and I went down in me boat down Wicken Lode to the mouth of Drainer's Ditch. A rare big dog otter jumped in off the bank. I thrust at him with my dart. It slid off his shoulder. Up he came for air, and I got him with the second thrust right in the mouth. Another day I was carrying the game bag and the jumping pole on Lapwing, when your cousin, Mr. Fred Johnson of the Hall, was out shooting. We saw two otters, and believe me or not, 11 young uns with them. But the funniest job of all happened to old Ben Pamment and 'Lal' Barton, one down at Pout Hall Corner. They were squatting under a litter stack with their trousers down in a storm of wind and rain, when suddenly two old otters slid off the stack and landed slap on 'Lal's' shoulders. He nearly had a fit.

'But Lor', them old fen "tigers", when I were a boy, were up to all manner of tricks. Scared o' nobody. Why, they killed the first policeman we had. Name o' Peacock.

'The copper that came after him very nearly went the same way. There were two titty-totty little old men in them days called Joe Eli and Bob Layton. Neither on 'em weighed more than nine stone apiece, but they were as tough as brass monkeys. They went up to the Hall, your cousin's place, one night just before Christmas to get their Christmas dinners out o' the fowl run.

'Joe creeps in. Presently there is a squawk and a flutter. Out he comes and mutters "I've got the old brown cock, Bob."

'"And I've got you me boy," says the policeman, and he jumps out and grabs Joe. Down goes Joe with the copper on top of him and they fit like cats. Joe wriggles clear, sharp as a needle, gets astride o' the copper, pulls out his knife and draws it across his throat, and says "Shall I do him, Bob?"

'Well, the copper he knowed well enough what had happened to the man before him. He knowed the Wicken chaps didn't love a policeman. So he begged and prayed for mercy, and promised not to split on 'em. Well, they let him go, but when they got up here later that night, the policeman was waiting for them with the parish constable and one or two others. Bob Layton was arrested, but Joe got away because his wrists were bigger than his hands, and he slipped through the handcuffs. I don't believe they ever did catch him.

Now Bert, as befits a man of ancient lineage and robust character, scorns modern ways of travel. Not for him the cushioned ease of the automobile, or the expensive risks of the aircraft. You may lie under your roof of thatch in the pearly dawn, when the mists are stealing off the fen and the willows stand above the woolly sea like wild-haired witches, and you will hear suddenly the soft quick padding of little fairy feet and the tinkling silver chime of little fairy bells - elfin sounds from another world. Let there be no vain imaginings that Titania is afoot, or that Puck is passing by. Bert and his 10 year old donkey Polly have taken their early morning road down to the misty vastnesses of the fen.

A true fenman, Bert is faithful to his 'moke'. Unshod, Polly trots or gallops from cottage to inn, from inn to fen, bearing her master abroad on secret envoys, seated upright as a centurion in a two-wheeled chariot mounted on rubber tyres, their passage heralded by the chime of harness-bells. The chariot, is the pride of our village. It began life as the punt carriage in which my big duck-punt voyaged over the roads from the Essex Blackwater to the reedy meres of Burwell Fen, that Paradise which was drained in 1941. Before that Bert had a two-wheeled 'Dickey' cart of his own but, being a stout Tory, he thumped the bottom boards out and wrecked most of the rest of it when the Conservatives won a smashing victory over the Radicals in battles far away and long ago.

As for donkeys, he owned that nationally famous asinine swell, the great Ocean Swell who won the Donkey Derby at Newmarket at the noble age of 33, ridden by Ken Gethin, the jockey. There is no doubt that Ocean Swell would have lived honoured by all men and saluted by small boys to the better part of a hundred years, had he not, when rolling in summer ecstasy on the banks of the Runawater, rolled himself into the river and there drowned.

Apart from bold donkeys, Bert has owned notable greyhounds. Your true fenman has always been a lover of the long dogs, a great poacher, an inveterate hunter of 'Aunt Sally'. Indeed it was always a point of honour that on Boxing Day every field on the place was free and open to those who chose to take their long-dogs abroad.

Bert's pride was a big red dog named 'Grip'. Grip was surely unique, for he would regularly catch wild-duck in the deep peat-cuttings on the fen called Lapwing, by springing at them and catching them as they jumped from the trenches. This grand dog broke his neck one day when poaching on land at Fordy Gate, when jumping a cross-ditch. Bert was so distressed that he jumped a 16 foot dyke to retrieve the body of his beloved hound. That dog weighed no less than four and a half stone.

John 'Bunyan' Bailey, Bert's father, owned not only long dogs, but two donkeys, both of whom lived to be more than 70 years of age. Then, one day, one of them died.

'Mum,' said old 'Bunyan' proudly to his spouse, 'I've got more than any man in England. I've got a live donkey and a dead 'un.'

'Mum' died not long ago, just over her century. A grand old lady, living alone with her sprightly son in the cottage which has sheltered her family since it was built. A woman, moreover, of stirring memories for, warming the teapot on the hob and glancing at me with an eye of roguish reminiscence, she vouchsafed: 'Ah, that does me good to see you again, Master Wentworth. That minds me o' the time when my daughter Lizzie was in service at the house and used to pin your nappies on and smack your bottom for you.'

On which note we drank tea in honour of battles long ago.

CAMP FOLLOWERS OF THE LORD

RELIGION is a business with us. Whole-time on Sundays and part-time on week-days. It dominates the village. It has zip. It has zoom. Likewise zingaree. This is is said in no spirit of irreverence. Consider the facts.

In a grove of wind-twisted, rook-noisy oaks, stands the church. Hard by is the Hall, with the little wicket-gate in the churchyard wall, through which my grandmother would sweep, in black silken majesty, attended by poodles. They went to church also.

The church is of a grey dignity. It lurches a little to one side. This is no tribute to the port-drinking proclivities of ancestors who held the presentation of the living and charged the parson a rent of a shilling a year for the use of the chancel. It is due to the draining of the great Mere, across which they once ferried, in barges, the Barnack stone from which the church is built.

A covey of Cromwells lie in the chancel. They are on the maternal side. A fact of which we are not proud, since Strafford would have disapproved. It may be, therefore, that this overburdening of Roundhead dust has caused the church tower to tip a little.

Whatever the cause of subsidence in stone, the subsidence in worshippers, now reduced to an antediluvian handful, is more easily explained.

Proceed to the other end of this ancient village. Lowering over a bevy of reed thatched cottages with pink-washed walls, is a sort of grey fort. Built of that hideous white Cambridge brick, which, with age, becomes a dirty blot upon the earth. This fort or factory houses the Ranters. They are an odd sect. Praise-God-Barebones is their patron saint. Uriah Heep would have rubbed his hands in slinking ecstasy. Religion to them is a cold thing. Except the Hell part. That is hot enough. It burns everlasting. Each Sunday, sinners are consigned to those insatiable flames. We will return to Hell and the Ranters in a moment.

At the far end of the village where the old track, which the turf-diggers' donkeys have trod for centuries, goes wandering off down to the Fen - the fen of wet reeds, and bitterns in the spring dusk, and the tench among the lily-pads - there stands another edifice of God. White brick again. But it has an ecclesiastical sort of façade. A trace of tracery in the windows. A cross on the crow-stepped gable. There the respectable followers of John Wesley worship in respectable fashion. Hell takes a seat. No stokers need apply.

Between the lot of them, the Wesleyans, the Ranters, and the 'Camp Followers' - not what you think, for a minute - Sunday is pretty lively. The church, poor old grey thing among the trees, sits in almost unattended majesty.

This is hardly surprising, for we are in Roundhead country. Old Noll, the self-styled, tawdry 'King of the Fens', raised most of his troops hereabouts. Sour faced fellows. Always ready to break a saint's head, behead a stone angel, shatter a lovely window to which medieval monks gave their souls and beauty or 'buss' a Cavalier maid, since she was fair game. A chanting, Bible-banging crew, long dead, but far from forgotten. Their spiritual descendants are the 'Ranters' and the 'Camp Followers'.

The difference between the two latter is that, whereas the 'Ranters' rant in their grey factory of Hell-fire and brimstone, the 'Camp Followers' take to the village green.

A Camp Meeting must be seen to be believed. The Holy Rollers of America are damp squibs by comparison. The Peculiar People of Essex are monuments of prim orthodoxy. The Elim Brotherhood become positively archiepiscopal.

'Camp Followers' go the whole hog. Here, according to Mrs. Glasse, had she been that way inclined, is the recipe. Take, first, a four-wheeled farm wagon. Built like a ship, cocked up fore and aft with a curved and girlish waist, painted red, blue and yellow, and at least a hundred years old. Place firmly in the midst of the village green and garnish with worshippers. Then insert in the middle of the pie, or wagon, one local preacher. He is the 'main dish', as the soulless jargon of canteen cookery has it. The intake and output. Mainly he outputs.

My favourite is a gaunt, sallow, black-haired, black

avised, long-chopped Fen-man, with blazing eyes, named Brother Zebedee. Others of this kin are Brothers Ezekiel, Nehemiah, Titus, Hosea and Daniel - the defier of lions. Privily, Brother Zebedee, he is known to his intimates as 'Skin o' Snake'.

Then there is Brother Solomon, that wise man from the willow holt on the riverbank, known from Monday to Saturday as 'Sawny Sol by the Dyke'.

Finally, Brother Tobias, the pork butcher. His is small, round and fat with little porcine eyes and a rare memory for minute debts. From Monday to Saturday he holds the village in pawn. Cottage wives tremble at his frown. Somehow he has always 'suffin marked up ag'in you, Mum, in me little owd black book'.

In the eclectic conclaves of *The Eel Pick* he is referred to as 'Toby the Tick'. That is merely because he holds all households on eternal 'tick'.

'Skin o' Snake' draws dykes, cuts sedge, harvests osiers, digs turf, glaives eels, nets tench and rudd, sets bow-nets for jack, shoots partridges sitting and catches pheasants on fish-hooks baited with raisins.

In the course of these near-to-Nature communes with earth and water, fish and fowl, he stokes up the fires of oratory for Sunday. Windscale can produce no comparable fall-out. He also shoes horses. Thereby hangs my first tale. True, whether you believe it or not.

Came Sunday. The wagon was drawn up. The shafts firmly bedded in the turf. Once upon a time they were raised suppliantly to Heaven. There came, however, a day when, whilst Toby the Tick was in full cry, certain God-forsaken youths crept under the wagon and with pre-concerted heave and a masterpiece of discipline and co-operation sent the whole contraption hurtling into the pond. Since then they dig the shafts well in.

This unholy gambit, one should explain in passing, was due to the fact that, having gathered his choir in the fort for practice on the previous Saturday night, Toby had exhorted them in the following unparsonical terms:

'Sing! You little b------rs, sing! Draw the hair into yar guts and let it goo. Lift up yar hearts to the Lord - an' sing. Do you don't, I'll flee the hides off ye.'

True, he had returned from Newmarket that day, where he has a stall in the High Street and is said - bate the whisper - to frequent the *Black Horse* or the *Bushel,* or the *Wagon and Horses,* purely in pursuit of custom and by the back door only.

Our preacher, exalted upon his wagon, gazes upon the worshippers. They stand in a close pack, like hounds round the huntsman, waiting for the fox to be thrown.

Young and old, man or woman, they have that dark, high-cheeked, Jutish-look, the mark of your true Fenman. There may be Dutch blood there, a far-off Jutlander's or an immemorial echo from those old Gyrvil, the little black aboriginals of the Fens, who were creeping about the reed-beds and skimming across the meres in their punts and coracles, when Hereward lay embattled in the Isle and William the Mamzer was raising his great wooden tower at Aldreth with a hired witch in the top of it to rain curses upon the Saxons and rally the iron-clad hearts of his Normans.

With such a run of mixed turgid blood, do you wonder that, as the preacher exhorts, condemns, exalts, arraigns, exults and ex-communicates, they nod their heads, first like the slow swell of a tide, then in a mounting frenzy, until they weep, beat their breasts, confess their sins and - it has happened - roll upon the grass pop-eyed and frothing.

Homely similes are still in. Witness Toby the Tick, when he arose the other Sunday, smug and pink, and, opening his mouth, disclosed a horrid abyss of gap-toothed gums.

'Brothers and sisters all,' he began. 'I can't give ye much of the Word o' the Lord today 'cos a mucky owd hoss kicked fower o' me teeth down me throat las' Wensday, when I were a-shoeing on him down at Dog-in-a-Doubtlet. So I'm a-goin' to let ye have it, short, sharp and sweet.'

He leered at them confidentially.

'All on ye work in the filds. All on ye work for a master. If ye don't muck them fields o' his'n, your master don't harvest no crops. And ye don't draw no harvest money. Thass a true piece, ain't it?'

'Ah!' a deep-drawn intake of breath from a glassy-eyed audience bespoke the home thrust of profound truth: 'Thass a true piece an' all, Brother Tobias.' They bowed their heads solemnly three times. Encouraged,

Toby expatiated.

'Well, then, brothers and sisters, the Good Lord above is your Master, ain't He? Your souls are his fields, ain't they? Do ye mind you muck them owd souls o' yourn with plenty o' good deeds. Do ye don't, brothers and sisters, ye 'on't git no harvest money from the Lord above - that mean no harps in Heaven. Yew 'on't git no harps. You'll git Hell-fire and brimstone everlastin' and perish in that there Pit of Abomination, what's a-garpin' for ye right now, flames an' all. So muck yar souls with good deeds - else yew perish. Thass all I've got for ye today. Now, lift up yar hearts - and *sing*.'

They sang. The rooks took off in a body. The ducks flew off the pond. Dogs bolted for their kennels. And to beat of drum, blare of bugle, blast of trumpet and clash of tambourines, the 'Camp Followers' of the Lord pledged themselves, heart and lung, to muck their immortal souls with benevolence, righteousness and kindliness.

'Skin o' Snake', otherwise Brother Zebedee, is a kindly soul, with a simple dignity expressed best, I think in that definition given one Sunday as Great Uncle Isaac, the Squire, in Inverness cape and Westbury hat, passed by to church.

'There, my friends, goo the Quality. They give 14 pence a pound for lamb. Yew come here and git the Lamb o' God for nawthin'.'

His exposition of the Bible is equally masterly. Hear him on Strife: 'They was all a quarrellen'. One says I'm for Paul. Another says, "I ain't, I'm for Cephas". And another for summon else. Paul, he hears on it, and down he comes and sune squares 'em all up. "You don't belong to me," says he, "you don't belong to Cephas; you don't belong to none on us, only to the Lord".'

Brother Solomon is even more down to earth. His thatched cottage by the dyke includes a tidy little orchard of old apple trees. Blenheims, Cox's Oranges, Golden Pippins and D'Arcy Spice. They are the mecca of boys who go darkly by starlit nights. Hence Solomon, fixing some of the gang one Sunday with a steely eye, and letting fly on Disobedience:

'Arter the Lord had made Adam and Eve out of the clay, he put 'em in a garden for to dress it and keep it; and he calls 'em up and says, "Look you here, Adam and Eve," he says, "you've got this here garden for yer very own, to do just what yer like with it. You may have pears and plums, and strawberries, and all sorts o' things, and make jam or what yer please, but yer ain't to touch this here tree - *them's* my winter apples.'"

Do you wonder that we attenuated church folk feel that we are missing a lot? When the presentation of the living comes my way, I think I shall give the job to Brother Solomon. We need pepping up.

THE LAST OF THE FEN FOWLERS

THE EARNEST bird-watcher, horn-rimmed with curiosity, stuffed with sandwiches, who mounts the steps to the thatched observatory on the edge of Wicken Fen, in Cambridgeshire, gazes out over a reed-edged mere of some 10 or a dozen acres of water, alive with mallard, teal, widgeon and coots. It looks the genuine article. It is nothing of the sort.

It was created a few years ago from the benevolence of a lady, who gave sufficient funds to the National Trust to enable this replica of a small, fenland mere to be bulldozed out of the peaty acres of Adventurer's Fen.

The fact that my own nearby fenland meres, covering nearly 200 acres of reeds and water, had been drained a few years earlier, at great expense to the tax-payer, is a sardonic sidelight on the bogus economics of this time and age.

The bird-watcher, gazing from his eyrie, will see away in the misty fens to the right of the glistening mere a tall wind-twisted grove of leaning poplars and hoary-headed willows. They call it Harrison's Spinney.

There, in the dim days of the '70's and'80's, lived old Tom Harrison, the last of the Burwell Fen punt-gunners.

He lived in a hut whose walls, two feet thick, were of turf blocks - black peat cut from the wild fen, revetted with withies and plastered outside with stiff clay to make it waterproof. Village legend said that it was no more than the height of a man inside, with a hole in the roof through which the smoke went, and a tiny window or two lit dimly by horn panes. In it Tom lived the life of an aborigine. He seldom took off his clothes, never washed unless he fell in the dyke.

His gunning punt, some 16 feet long, clinker-built and open from end to end, much like the 'shouts' still in use on Cowbit and Guyhirn Washes, lay in a reedy dyke. The great muzzle-loading gun, an inch and a quarter in bore, was slung from leathern loops in the hut. His double-barrelled muzzle-loader hung below it.

His plover nets draped the walls. His 'glaive' and his 'dart', poking up out of mounds of unmentionable old clothing leaned against the thatch. His long leathern water-boots stood drying in a corner while a rusty, long-legged, curly-coated mongrel, half-retriever and half-spaniel, snoozed by the creamy ashes of the turf fire in the middle of the hut. A thin, aromatic whorl of smoke spiralled upward to the hole in the roof and the rude chimney pot which kept out most, but not all, of the rain.

Thus he lived, a hermit of the Fens, a man of the primitive wild, the last of the Fen fowlers. Not perhaps quite the last, for there was old Joe Phypers, who dwelt in a tiny, squat brick cottage on the edge of Fodder Fen Pits, hard by the 'washes' of the Cam, less than a mile down river from that delectable inn, the *Five Miles From Anywhere, No Hurry,* then the gathering place of fowlers and fishermen, turf-diggers and river bargees.

But Harrison was, in a sense, the last of our true fen fowlers, for his hut was in the heart of a wild fen, his shooting grounds were the trackless and, in many places, bottomless fens that stretched from the foot of Burwell Village to the old black, tarred and sedge-thatched turf-sheds at the head of Wicken Lode. That was his territory. On it he shot and netted in winter, fished, cut sedge, and dug peat in the kinder months of the year. It mattered not a jot or a tittle to him who was the actual owner of the land or water.

As for the owners, among whom my great-uncle and cousin were the main proprietors, they simply regarded Tom as an essential part of the landscape. In his veins ran the wild blood of Hereward's Saxons. In his face, with its aquiline nose, high cheek-bones, and lank black hair, was some foreign strain of Dutch or Jutish forbears. Like enough they came over with the raiding Jutes when the Vikings sailed their beaked galleys up the slow Fenland rivers, through glittering meres that spread like scattered shields beneath the winking stars of the wide Fen skies.

Or, perhaps, it was that later strain of blood, scattered strong and potent through the Fens when Vermuyden brought his Dutch and Flemish bands to dig the great lodes, to rise the river walls, to build the draining mills, whose black sails revolved like witches' arms against the flat, red sunsets. They built the sluices which the Fen gunners blew up. By night the fenmen came slinking through the reeds in their flat punts and shot and stabbed the foreigners patrolling the lock gates, laid their gunpowder charges and blew their devilish works sky-high, to let in 'Old Captain Flood', their patron saint of spreading waters.

Tom Harrison was yellow of face and racked with ague. In summer he gathered 'paigles' in the fen meadows and made 'paigle tea' or cowslip wine. When he sold his ducks and geese, his eels and tench, part of the payment was in laudanum - the foundation of that 'ager mixter' which doped his shivering limbs and kept the ague at bay for a few delirious hours.

As Tom stood at the low doorway of his thatched hut, which looked like a huge, grass-grown hump under the sighing poplars, turning their shivering silver leaves to the fen sun, he gazed upon a scene wild and desolate. Not a house was in sight. To the north-east the black hooded shape of Norman's Mill revolved its bat-like sails, churning out the brown peat-stained waters in a creamy flood. That old mill fought an ever-losing battle.

Away to the north, the low rise of the Wicken uplands was screened by a marching frieze of shock-headed willows, soaring elms, and wind-twisted oaks above which the great white Tudor chimneys of my old home had gazed for more than 400 years over the glittering wastes of Soham Mere, once one of the largest lakes in England, and the brown wastes of Wick and Adventurer's Fens.

That was the nearest outpost of civilisation, a place so remote that the one road to it petered out at High Fen in a sodden, grassy drove, an old forgotten road, where once the Roman legions marched and the brazen eagles glittered in the sun.

In winter the high road through the village was a running river of mud and water, which, in a silver thaw, froze from end to end so that village boys might skate from door to door.

The haunting bittern was Tom's ghostly companion by night. The flickering, ghastly gleam of the Jack-o'-Lantern, dipping over the fen pools like 'a little owd man with a hoppity leg', were his terrifying nightlights. The grey geese clanged overhead beneath the winking stars, and the windy threnody of wild swans filled the immense skies.

Throughout the year, lapwings, in white-waistcoated multitudes, wept and wailed above his soggy home and drilled themselves in regimental companies upon the peat-diggings. That is why they call that wild corner Lapwing to this day.

He knew the black oozy spots where the snipe probed their long bills, where the ruffs and reeves fought on the hillocks, and the red-shanks - he called them 'clews' - flirted their thin red legs, graceful as dancers. There, on frosty days, he laid his horse-hair nooses and took snipe by the dozen.

I can see him in mind's eye, poling his grey punt over the flooded Fen, standing immobile in the bows. In his right hand he poised an eight-foot dart. The sliding shadow of a jack or the bronze-gold swirl of a shoal of rudd or tench was the signal. The dart flew, straight as a lance, and pike or tench was brought squirming inboard.

He knew the workings of the eels in the mud. The tell-tale blow-holes in the lode bottom where the 'glaive', shooting through the water, transfixed his serpent-like quarry. He set bow-nets in the gault-pits and under the bridges and, with a man or boy to help him, netted the Lode or the slow stream of the Runawater with a net which stretched from bank to bank. Then they would go 200 yards upstream and, with punt poles or darts, splash and drive the fish into the net.

Today, the lonely hut under the wind-riven trees is a shadow in the ground. The fens about it are a bird sanctuary. The wild geese are a passing memory. The bittern still booms on nights of spring from the reedy fastness of Wicken Fen - but the wild waste of Lapwing is tamed. Joe's great gun is a rusty, vanished relic. No longer the flash and boom comes over the waste on a wet Fen wind. The lapwings drill in untroubled multitudes with no brown spectre of a net to fall upon them. But, to this day, few among the Fen villagers would walk by night on the peaty track that leads to Harrison's Spinney. For they say the ghost of the old Fen gunner is still lord by night. One day, they say, the waters will return.

Tom Harrison was a true 'Fen Tiger', that ancient nickname for a fiece and ancient race.

For centuries men in 'the Sheers' have labelled the

fenmen 'Fen Tigers', because the average fenman is an independent, combative, and often secretive man. The nickname, I think, derives from Carolean and Georgian days when the fenmen fought the imported Dutch drainers with shot-gun and bludgeon.

The average fenman today is still sturdily independent, utterly parochial, often narrow-minded, suspicious of strangers, frequently a fanatical Nonconformist and a virulent Radical. If he is a churchman and a Conservative, he is still as independent, combative, and suspicious of his religious and political opposite number. He counts it a disgrace to owe money and almost a disgrace to marry a girl from an upland shire. He is a grave soldier in war, and a hard worker in peace. In fine, that typical paradox, a good Englishman, blent of Jutish, Dutch, Huguenot and Norse strains.

A century or more ago the uplanders dubbed us 'Cambridgeshire Camels'. That was because, in the old days, when the goose fens and horse fens, which, in summer were more or less dry, tussocky commonlands, became flooded by the autumn rush of waters from the highlands of Bedfordshire, Northamptonshire and Huntingdon, the fenmen stalked through the shallow floods mounted on high stilts.

When I was a boy the old race of fenmen still survived in highly individual form.

I treasure the word-picture given me 40 years ago by old Charlie Crisp, of Upware, the champion snipe-shot, skater, and beer drinker of that fen hamlet, that clusters about the lock and the pumping station and, now vanished, the *Five Miles From Anywhere, No Hurry.*

Sticking his water-boots straight out in front of the winter fire in the sanded bar and puffing at his clay pipe, Charlie said:

Joe Phypers would net forever o' lapwings and send 'em to Cambridge Market wi' stones o' eels. He was a little sharp owd chap, quick as a tarrier dawg, an' he'd fight any man what ast for it. When he'd had a skinful, he'd dance a jig in this here bar till the sparks flew - and there was old Paddy Carey, the fiddler, fiddlin' away like mad. Tew proper owd Fen-Tigers.'

Tom Harrison was followed in Burwell Fen by the Badcocks, who thought nothing of having a 'mess o' water-rats' for supper. Old Daddy Badcock, whom I remember as a little, sharp, fox-like man, burnt brown by fen suns, and tough as wire nails, would sleep any summer night curled up on a litter stack or bedded down like a dog in the heart of a dry reed-bed. He drank 'poppyhead tea' to ward off the ague, believed that the wills-o'-the-wisps which danced over the fen on hot summer nights were 'Jack-o'-Lanterns', small and evil spirits, whose mission was to lure innocent humans to a watery death.

In summer he made 'paigle tea' and distilled potato wine, raw and potent enough to drive a train. A good and genuine little man, who worked 'all the hours that God sent', attended chapel though it meant a six-mile trudge each Sunday, and died sure in the faith of Heaven.

At home, in Wicken, the true fenman flourished. Perhaps the most notable was Albert Houghton, the village shoemaker. Houghton was a great self-taught naturalist, an entomologist of national repute. He knew every bird, moth, butterfly, plant and beetle in Wicken Fen. Their Latin names were as plain to him as English. Entomologists and botanists came to him from all over the world. He was the friend and confidant of the fifth Lord Walsingham, the greatest game-shot that ever lived - to whom the Natural History Museum at South Kensington owes so much - of Adam Sedgwick and Ducane Godman and of every Cambridge don who came to dredge beetles from the fen pools or lure moths to a lamp-lit sheet at night. Houghton's collection of swallow-tail butterflies and other rarities was probably one of the largest in the country.

His introduction to Lord Walsingham was amusing and typical. Walsingham first came to the Fens about the beginning of the century, and stayed with my uncle, the late Isaac Aspland of Wicken. A brilliant man with a mind that ranged like an eagle over half a dozen different fields of science, Walsingham dressed with individuality. Norfolk breeches were topped by a moleskin jacket. Beneath it he wore a snakeskin waistcoat. The whole was crowned by a fearful looking cap made of hedgehog skin with the bristles erect. The snout was pulled well over his nose as a peak, and a pair of black, evil little glass eyes glittered wickedly above.

Houghton encountered this apparition one summer night, laden with a butterfly net, tin collecting boxes and a fen lamp.

'Who the hell are you?' demanded Houghton.

'I'm a friend of Mr. Aspland, and I'm staying with him,' Walsingham explained mildly.

'Not you! The Master wouldn't have a rum-lookin' owd pup like you - not in his house, I'll warrant,' retorted Houghton. 'If I catch you down on the fen again, I'll hull you in the dyke.' On that note they bade adieu.

Walsingham, with many chuckles, told my uncle the story.

Next morning Houghton called at the house as breakfast was ending. He was asked into the breakfast room. My uncle said: 'Albert, I want to introduce you to a very good friend of mine who is one of the best entomologists in the world. This is Lord Walsingham.'

Houghton took one swift look, scratched his head and burst out bluntly:

'Well, I'm damned, if you ain't the rum old b— that I run up agin in the lane last night. Cor, blast! Well, that is, me Sir, me Lord, your Lordship - how the davvle was I to know who yew were, if yew will dress up like that?'

After that Walsingham and Houghton were fast friends. When Albert Houghton died, Lord Walsingham was the first to send his family a practical token of his appreciation of the old man's knowledge and forthright character.

A FENLAND BIRD CHARMER

HE WAS short, swarthy and thickset, with bright gipsy eyes and a soul packed with guile. He wore gold ear-rings, a peaked cap, a seaman's pea jacket, a moleskin waistcoat and trousers of some strange old fustian material. He was the Lothario of the village belles, a great fighter when the beer was in him, an invincible snapper up of hares and rabbits and the greatest bird catcher for miles around. I adored him. He was my boyhood hero.

His name was Uriah Marshall and he lived a hermit's, but far from monastic life, in a thatched cottage at the head of Wicken Lode where now eager 'bug hunters' and bird watchers debouch in pop-eyed anticipation from their motor coaches as soon as the weather is warm enough for them to be abroad.

Where now the National Trust has neatly parcelled out the Fen and labelled its ancient acres with academic names which have no relation to the old village place names, Ury set out his nets, planted his bird-lime twigs, laid his springes and took his toll of linnets and goldfinches, peewits and hares. He was a natural hunter, though not before the Lord, and something of a true bird lover, for all his dealings in them. The upper floor of his thatched cottage was an aviary. Both bedrooms were full of a chattering crowd of goldfinches, chaffinches, linnets, bullfinches, twites and other small birds.

'Ury' slept, ate, cooked and seldom washed in one big room on the ground floor. His bed hid behind a filthy curtain. A stuffed cormorant, a barn owl, a case of wooden-looking French partridges, and a stuffed hawk or two lulled his slumbers. You could cut the smell with a knife. Nets of all sorts, clap-nets, fall-over nets, plover nets, purse nets and gate nets hung in bundles from nails in the walls. His only weapon was a walking-stick gun. He never used a 12 bore.

'Guns is for gennelmen and dam fules,' he impressed on me with a wicked wink. 'I gits me buds quick and nat'ral. Why, bless yer, young Master Wentworth, the little own bewties don't know I've ketched 'em till they're in me nets.'

'Ury' was the greatest poacher for miles around. He

'ate rough, slept rough and fought rough'. In flood-time he took his plover nets down Fodder Fen Drove and caught scores of white-waistcoated peewits on the 'washes' at Dimocks Cote and High Fen. Other fowlers did likewise on the Welney, Mepal, Guyhirn and Crowland 'washes'.

Ury's nets, mounted on hinged poles on the fall-over principle, were spread out on one of the grassy islands in the middle of the washes. The old reprobate operated them with a long cord, about 200 yards in length. He built a hide of bushes, old sacks, and general flotsam, squatted in it, set out his live decoys, tethered to pegs, round the perimeter of the area to be covered when the net swept over and among them he placed a dozen or so 'stales' or stuffed decoys, which he mounted himself with fair skill.

Then, squatting in his hide, he waited until he saw a great mob of peewits swooping and wailing over the glittering waters, or spied a 'congregation' of them standing in the shallows, all facing one way, their white waistcoats gleaming in the sun, like so many pipe-clayed soldiers on parade. Then his wild whistle went wailing over the waters. It was the most lifelike, mellifluous and fetching call.

The peewits came to it, tumbling like black and white blown leaves through the windy skies, whilst the tethered decoys leapt and flapped on their short strings, crying wildly to their bretheren. Down came the whole flock in a great rush of wings, with a sound like falling waters. They pitched on the net, round it, and ran back and forth on the fatal plat of grass.

The old man's eyes glittered. His brown, tattooed hand pulled on the long cord, up rose the net, a curtain of doom, and swept over, falling in a billowing cloud upon the frightened whistling multitude beneath. A hundred or more birds sprang aloft, keening their fright on the cold wind, sweeping away like bullets over the water. But anything from 50 to a hundred or more were prisoned beneath the net, some half drowned in the shallow water. And upon them advanced the water-booted, crouching figure of the old Fenman, to set about his deadly work of neck-breaking.

Hundreds of birds were taken in this fashion each season. Often they included not only peewits, but golden plover, dunlin, redshank, knots, occasionally ruffs and reeves, now and then a bar-tailed godwit and sometimes a curlew, or, more rarely a spotted redshank. As many as 50 peewits were often taken at a time, and sometimes 10 or 20 dozen in a day. They sold in the market for about 6d. each, and were every bit as good to eat as a partridge. Today such netting is illegal.

Another old Fenman, Old Levi Bulman of Wicken, told me that in about the 1850's he well remembered setting out in a duck punt from 'The Dolvers' - a dolver is a seven acre allotment - and punting the whole day in early spring, over the flooded bed of Soham Mere, whence he returned with 'a clothes-basket full of peewits' eggs'.

Little enough can be found in old records to tell us much of Soham Mere. Alas, unlike Whittlesey Mere, it seems to have had no chronicler, although, before it was drained just prior to 1800, it covered no less than 1,400 acres of water — a vast expanse indeed.

I have found some particulars, however, in an old copy of *The Antiquary* for November 1888, concerning John Helder, a yeoman farmer who lived on the Soham Mere-side from about 1710 - 45 onward. He was a man of education, and erudite tastes, well read, and with good handwriting.

In May, 1724, he married 'a young woman, who, before unknown, had appeared to him in a vision during a dangerous illness in the previous year'. During his illness he renounced 'carding and dicing, dancing and reading ungodly ballads, unchaste songs, and lascivious discourses in play books'. In 1758 he was made a 'Commissioner for Ely and Soham Levell in Middle Fen, etc., being encouraged to undertake and go through this business by the hopes and prospects of being serviceable to the poor inhabitants of these drowned parishes.'

He was nearly drowned in Soham 'Meer' when a storm hit him as he was crossing it in a small, open sailing boat, and was nearly overset. In December 1747, during a great flood, he sent his son with other men to rescue some horses out of Beach Fen. Crossing the 'charn' in a boat with three horses, the current drove great ice floes against the boat. His son and two horses fell overboard, and the son was half drowned.

In February, 1745/6, 'the wind lying north east, and blowing very hard brought the water against the "Meer" bank, and raised it higher than I have ever seen it before and kept it rising so much as made me believe ye "Meer" was in danger of being drowned; ye bank then was very dry and consequently light, and upon a break of a frost not so solid as usual. The wind increased in the night and was very stormy. I got up soon after two of ye clock in ye morning and took my Bible to read in as usual before going out . . . I knew if ye Meer was drounded it wd be a great loss to Ld Townsend to my neighbours and to myself. But the "Meer" was all right.'

Another great Fen character in my youth was Mark Parr, who roared like a bull and kept the old Anchor Inn at Upware Sluice, a tiny old cottage, with dormer windows and crooked roof huddled under ancient apple trees. It has gone. A commonplace bungalow takes its place. In a bad winter the flood waters came in at the back door, where Mark used to moor his gunning punt. Mark, was a true 'Fen Tiger', a born fighter - always ready for a 'turn-up' with a friend or enemy. His language, thundered out in a voice like half a gale, was momentous. It 'blistered the tar off the barn'.

The Fenman's love of fisticuffs was beautifully put one day by old Bob King, my uncle's one-time bailiff, when he returned home from Ely Fair. Bob with his rubicund face, white side-whiskers, bright twinkling blue eyes, full-skirted green shooting coat, and beautifully sprigged and flowered double-breasted waistcoat, a relic of my grandfather's Victorian finery - was a great character. A handsome, robust man, of simple philosophy, with a great faith in God. He was one of nature's noblemen. But there was nothing of the sly, hypocritical 'bible-banger' about Robert. He was proud of the fact that three, if not four generations of his family had worked for ours, but he was equally proud of the fact that he could drink 16 pints of beer, and walk home straight afterwards. He thought nothing of walking the six or seven miles across the Fens to Newmarket in his 76th year, having an uproarious day with trainers and jockeys, and then striding home again across the Fens, puffing at what he proudly described as 'a gennelman's half-crown cigar'. On this particular occasion Robert sat down to his tea in the kitchen, having walked the eight or nine miles to Ely and back again in the day. My mother, who always insisted on serving him herself instead of leaving it to one of the maids, said solicitously:

'Well Bob, what sort of a day did you have at Ely Fair?'

'Not much of a day, Miss'. (She was always Miss to him from her childhood upwards.) 'There worn't no gaiety at all. No gaiety. Not till I got in a pub on the Fore Hill. Then tew chaps got argufying. One called t'other a liar. Then that chap he gied t'other one a draw o' the snout what knocked him head over heels under the table. He sprung up and the chap gie him a clink o' the skull what onsensed him. He was a-bleedin' like a pig on a pig-killin' day. But - Lor bless yer, Miss, apart from that there worn't no gaiety at all. In the owd days at Ely Fair I've sin min stand up and fit each other fer 15 or 16 rounds with bare fists. They was gay boys.

'And when they had the Bandy Matches (an ancient form of ice-hockey) on Spinney Fen, you'd see harf a score o' min lam each other on the shins with their sticks, and kick each other till they fell down and had to be tuk home on turf barrows. They was the gay days.'

It was in the 'gay days' somewhere about 1860, that Peacock the first policeman ever sent to Wicken Village, was killed after he had tried to stop a Saturday night brawl in the Maid's Head Inn. Two Fen Tigers, Jim Bacon and another, are believed to have followed him outside, hit him on the head with a bludgeon, put the body on a turf barrow, and then wheeled it across the Bredes to the now-vanished brick kiln, standing among the reed-beds of Solomon Bailey's Pits at the top end of Sedge Fen Drove. There the body is said to have been cremated in the glowing kiln. It was whispered that the wretched policeman's truncheon, with its brass crown of office, was many years later dredged out of one of the pits - and thrown away.

Bob, on the morning after the brawl, was driving my uncle's gig to Upware, when Jim Bacon and the other man suddenly appeared out of the hedge, and asked for a lift to the Ferry. As they climbed up beside him, Bob noticed that their huge hairy hands were smothered with dried blood. He remarked on it.

'We bin a pig-killin',' Jim Bacon said laconically. Bob asked no more. At Upware, the men took the Ferry across the River and disappeared down the Black Fen Drove towards Waterbeach. They were never seen again.

Many years later, an old woman who lay dying in the Almshouses, sent for my mother, who was universal nurse, comforter, companion and confidante to all in trouble, at the point of death or in the pains of childbirth. Feebly, the old lady fished out a scrawled, ill-written missive, bearing an American post-mark, 30 years old or more.

'That's from me boy, Miss,' she gasped. 'Him what's in Ameriky. I've had that thutty year or more, and bein' as I can't read, I want you to tell me what that say, as I ain't got long now afore I go to the dear Lord up above.' Briefly, the letter told the old lady that the two murderers, one of whom was her son, the writer of the letter, had got safely to Liverpool, taken ship to America, and were in work and prospering. That, I believe, is the true answer to the hitherto unsolved mystery of the murdered Wicken policeman. My mother kept the old lady's secret for more than a quarter of a century after her death.

In those days, when a Fen village held its annual fair or 'feast', it was a point of honour for a gang of men and youths from the next village to come over and break it up. Thus Soham men usually broke up Wicken Feast, and Wicken 'Fen Tigers' descended, impartially and with gusto, upon the merry-makers of Soham and Burwell.

Burwell has always had a particularly tough race of Fen Tigers. They are of the true Fen breed. Ted Jarvis was one, and the Badcock family, who lived and slept in the Fen like otters, and 'Fenner' Bob, who made his living by selling cart-loads of Fen litter to the owners of the wretched cab-horses of London.

The Crawleys mixed up with a lawless gang of sheep-stealers and farm robbers, who were the terror of the district for many years, until they were finally rounded-up by Police Sergeant Plant. Some were transported, and others left the village for good.

This gang had their headquarters at Pout Hall, an old house, with a thatched roof and dormer windows, which stood in a grove of willows and poplars, at the junction of Reach and Burwell Lodes, on a little patch of some 30 acres of undrained fenland, now owned by the National Trust, and marching with my own Fen.

No wilder, out-of-the-way place could be imagined than this old, secret house, with its black, tarred wooden walls, and little winking windows, peering over the high river bank. It was built to serve as an inn, but the licence was refused, so the sheep-stealers made it their headquarters. There they brewed illicit beer and went on forays at night to lonely farms. Sheep were rounded up, taken to Pout Hall, 'fleed' (skinned), cut up, and taken in the small hours by boat, to a wharf belonging to the last house in North Street, Burwell, an old building with a great underground room, built in the 17th century by one of the Dutch drainers.

At harvest time, the gang stole boatloads of corn,

thrashed it with wooden flails on a sail cloth, bagged it up, and took it by boat to the underground granary in the old house at North Street. These raids went on to such an extent that they virtually held many of the outlying farmers and cottagers in terror of their lives.

Finally, Police Sergeant Plant, with only one or two constables, surprised the gang with a boatload of plunder one night. They resisted arrest. He went for them like a fury, broke one man's arm with his truncheon, laid out several others stunned and bleeding, and captured the ring-leaders. Those who escaped disappeared for good.

Another old 'Fen Tiger' in Burwell, Jonathan Casburn, alias 'Old Desperate', inherited a small legacy. He immediately hired a chaise and pair, picked up two women of loose morals, and with his fiddle and a purse-full of money, toured the fenland inns, fighting, fiddling and carousing, until the last penny had gone.

Burwell in those days, had a famous parson called Baines. At the back of his garden ran a lane, called the Back Way or Back Side. Old Dinah, the letter carrier, was coming down the road one day, carrying a basketfull of rich, ripe elderberries, for the making of elderberry wine, when she was stopped by a lady, who remarked on the size and lusciousness of the berries.

'Yes Miss,' said Old Dinah, 'I ha' just picked 'em off Parson Baines's Back Side.'

Despite the Fenmens' reputation for hard fighting, hard living and hard drinking, they were, in some villages, sticklers for the proprieties. If a Chatteris girl was so unfortunate as to present the world with an illegitimate child, her neighbours paraded under her bedroom window, beating saucepans, rattling kettles and frying pans, whooping and holloaing like devils. In our Fen, such a small matter as a love child 'did't si'nnify'.

At Whittlesey, a much more interesting and less inhuman custom prevailed until recently. It is referred to by Sir James Frazer in *The Golden Bough* in the following words:—

The Strawbear at Whittlesey.

'a custom . . . still prevails at Whittlesey in Cambridgeshire on the Tuesday after Plough Monday, as I learn from an obliging communication of Professor G. C. Moore Smith, of Sheffield University, dated 13th January 1909. He writes: "When I was at Whittlesey yesterday I had the pleasure of meeting a 'Straw-bear', if not two, in the street. I had not been at Whittlesey on the day for nearly 40 years, and feared the custom had died out. In my boyhood the Straw-bear was a man completely swathed in straw, led by a string by another and made to dance in front of people's houses, in return for which money was expected. This always took place on the Tuesday following Plough-Monday. Yesterday the Straw-bear was a boy and I saw no dancing. Otherwise there was no change."'

When my cousins by marriage, the Johnson family, were Squires of Burwell, before they moved to Wicken Hall - they lived at Burwell Hall, a largish, picturesque old 16th century house, with two gables, a curtain wall, and an ancient porch. It was partly moated, and when some of the house was pulled down a few years ago, a long perpendicular cusped window was revealed, about 18 feet high, probably the west window of the banqueting hall. A thousand acres went with the property, and a witch named Judy Finch enlightened the daily gossip of their lives.

Old Judy lived in the Squatters' Cottages on the Fen side of the Weirs, half a dozen primitive, one-storyed hovels, built of wattle and daub, with white clunch chimneys, and thatched with sedge and litter. They lived, a little colony of typical fenmen, tall, big men, with very black hair, sallow or swarthy skinned, rough manners, gruff speech, tenacious and cunning, highly independent and lawless to a degree. They existed chiefly by fowling and fishing, a little harvesting, turf-digging and sedge-cutting. Old Judy lived in the most northerly cottage, and was credited with every sort of witchcraft. Indeed, the great pit of about an acre and a half of water nearby, is called Judy's Hole to this day, and a doggerel verse about her says she was:

A wicked old croen,
Who lived all alone
In a hut beside of the reeds,
With a high-crowned hat
And a black tom-cat,
Whose looks were as bad as her deeds.

THE OLD FEN ROAD OF GHOSTS

THE OLD green droveway runs along the corn-bright ridge from the hamlet of Upware where the Romans had a quay on the banks of the Cam to High Fen Farm, white-washed and lonely in fields above the misty fens. Thence it wanders along the upland to Barway. There, before the fens were drained, you could take boat to the holy isle of Ely.

They call this old green trackway Fodder Fen Drove. Houseless, manless, lonely, a road of ghosts. The Legions tramped it, their bronze eagles glinting in the sun. Dutch drainers of Vermuyden's day clumped along it in wooden sabots, or long leather water boots. Sheep stealers went that way by night in Georgian days. Always, the Fenmen made it their secret road.

In that hedgeless, windy land the ridge of broad, bright stubble sweeps on the one side to the green, dyke-seamed cattle 'washes' of the slow and stealing Cam. There redshank nest in spring. It falls, on the other side, to the cattle-dappled pastures of Spinney Fen. Beyond lies the brooding wilderness of Wicken Fen, sanctuary of bittern and Montagu's harrier. A land of wild duck and peewits wailing in the green dawn. On the night-wind comes that old, ineluctable fen smell. The scent of wet reeds and peat waters, of fish and water weeds and turf smoke from cottage fires.

Far away and long ago, when Grandfather rode this old green drove on a 16 hand hunter and the internal combustion engine was no more than a horrid dream, there dwelt in a tiny cottage on the edge of Fodder Fen Pits almost the last of the old fowlers in the Wicken and Burwell Fens. Joe Phypers was his name.

Small, wizened, brown as a berry, quick as a weasel, he wore a round, otter-skin hat, corduroy trousers gartered below the knee with dried eel-skins - they kept the 'rheumaticks' away - a red waistcoat and a great double-breasted blue Melton jacket of seafaring cut. His long water-boots were made of leather and built to last a century. He dressed them with mutton fat and rubbed goose grease into his own skin to keep the fen mists and ague at bay. There were gold earrings in his ears for, as any good gypsy will tell you, they give a man long sight.

Fodder Fen Pits are deep and reedy pools lost in a cloud of windy willows. A lily-starred dyke leads thence to the river. Bream move in silver solemn shoals. And a great red bull is gamekeeper. They probably dug the pits of the coralline rag of that ridge of corn-bright land when men were draining the Fens and building the river walls a century or more before other diggers began prospecting at great profit for coprolites. That lasted from 1856 to 1875 or thereabouts.

Now coprolites were the petrified dung and other remains of huge prehistoric reptiles: Plesiosaurus, Dinosaur, Scelidosaurus and even a type of Armadillo which, with the Ichthyosaurus, flourished in the prehistoric fens. About a hundred years ago a long bed of coprolites, rich in phosphates of lime, was discovered at the foot of the chalk hills running by Soham, along Burwell, Swaffham, Horningsea, Cambridge, Grantchester, and as far as Barrington. For a quarter of a century small fortunes were made by local farmers and landowners who had coprolites on their land. The echoes of prehistory were carted along this old green road that the Romans made and dumped into long strings of barges under the giant willows which still shade the grassy quay at Upwell.

When the coprolite diggers went, the old green lane was left once more to silence and memories. Each winter the gypsies, mainly Lees, camped in their hooped tents hard by High Fen Pits which they dug about the same time as Fodder Fen Pits, and for the same purpose, when they needed the rag and the chalk to build the river walls of the Cam.

Joe Phypers lived in his little house by the willow-shaded pools where the pike plunge. From his windows he looked across the river 'washes' to the very site of Stretham Mere where, as Daniel tells you, in his *Rural Sports*, Old Merry of Stretham Ferry was the champion snipe shot of his day with a gun that was eight feet long in the barrel.

Not many years ago I came up the old green lane one autumn night with young John Diver of Upware. His father had just dredged from the river and brought me, in a barrow, bones of beaver and Bos Longifrons, of pelican and wolf, of Irish elk and red deer, of swan and fallow deer, and, last and rarest,the heel-bone of an anthropoid woman.

As we passed the ruined cottage of Fodder Fen Pits,

young John told me of Joe Phypers as his grandfather had known him 60 years ago.

'Owd Joe, Marster, had a gret owd muzzle-gun noine foot long what he lashed inter his gun-boat, and when he shot her off the gun-boat flew back yards in the water. I'er sin him come up ter Upwer wi' his owd boat loaden down ter the gunnel wi' mallard and teal and pockers an' chance toimes an owd guse or tew. He'd git his skinful o' beer at the "Foive Mile" and thin goo hum in his little owd gun-boat as tight as a looard. He were an owd masterpiece, an' no mistake.'

'Let's try the pits for a duck,' I suggested. But young John would not.

'That's ha'anted, that owd green lane.'

'Who by?' I demanded.

'Thim owd Roomans. They'll hae ye, sure as harvest.'

Which took me back to a certain day in the early 1920's. Two Cambridge undergraduates, Lord Cawdor and Tom Lethbridge, were digging on the side of Fodder Fen Drove. They came across the skeleton of a Roman soldier. He had fallen and been buried by the sand martins' holes within a few feet of the old trackway. And, so the tale went, they put him in a sack and bicycled back to Cambridge with him, across the black and misty fens.

That night, behind the beckoning, red-curtained windows of the old *Five Miles From Anywhere*, in the sanded bar, with its fen-caught goldfinch in the cage, Charlie Crisp sat in his corner and said solemnly:

'If they've dug up that owd Rooman, he'll ha'ant them, sure as harvest. There's Suffin what walk that owd road at night. That ain't human. I've bin there many a time and I know.'

Now Charlie was fat and round and merry, as strong as a horse. With his old spaniel at his feet, he was the epitome of rural, jolly philosophy.

Poor old Charlie. He is dead now and I mourn him.

Charlie could skate a mile against any man, bar the Smarts and Sees - a tub-like, red-faced little man who flew along the ice with the long fen stroke, his arms going like windmill sails, his short legs twinkling.

And he could drink beer. 'Sixteen pints, Master, an' I'm sober as a jedge - twinty-fower an' I can just git home straight.'

His long muzzle-loading eight bore, still with his last

charge of powder in it, hangs above the gun-room chimney piece as I write.

I remember Charlie, with the face of a bishop, the eye of a judge, telling a visitor one night that the winter before: 'the fowl was that thick on the owd fen, I set in this here bar, an' loaden me gun and stuck her snout up the chimbley and shot her orf. An' d'you believe me, sir, whin I runned ter the door tew open it, I couldn't. That wuz all blocked up wi' the bahds I'd killed.'

The visitor, stricken, departed, and Charlie remarked: 'Them Lunnoners fare tew be made for larfin' at.'

I thought of Charlie, his long brown gun, his rusty spaniel and his Roman ghost, as we came through the frost-rimmed reeds of Westmere Bank by the side of Wicken Fen in a cold dusk this winter. Pheasants were cock-cocking up to roost in the buckthorn and sallow bushes. The fen was alive with their crowing. A great skein of mallard went out over the Cock-Up Bridge by Burwell Lode. There followed, high against the green and saffron sky, a flight of pintail. Snipe were scaaping over the rushy fields. We had shot just under 100 pheasants that day off less than 200 acres of roots. And that is by no means a record for a wild pheasant in my native fens.

'Let's try Fodder Fen Pits for a duck or two,' I remarked to my host, Mr. Tom Fuller of Spinney Abbey.

'Might see a duck - might see a ghost,' he cackled. 'At any rate my old dog saw something mighty queer in that old green drove a few years ago. We were coming back from shooting, just as we are now. There were two or three of us and we had a retriever and, curiously enough, an Alsatian.

'Suddenly both dogs growled, stuck their hackles up, bristled all over - and then dashed forward and attacked an Invisible Man.'

'What on earth do you mean?'

'Just what I said. Both dogs were leaping up, barking and snapping, exactly as though they were attacking a man - one on either side of him. It was so realistic that I almost thought there must be a man there. There was nothing. It was perfectly light. We could see for hundreds of yards. Yet there were the dogs, growling and snapping, rushing forward, jumping up - biting - and then drawing back, all hunched up ready to attack again. Most extraordinary thing I have ever seen. It went on for quite two or three minutes. Then we called the dogs off - and walked on. And never saw a thing. How do you account for that?'

I could account for it no more easily than I can for that other equally strange story told me by his father, the late Robert Fuller, when I stayed with him during the course of my thousand mile ride on horseback in 1941. We set out, Jim Rodd, an Essex farmer, and myself to ride a thousand miles through rural England and write about the mechanical revolution in farming. In all we rode just over 130 miles on horse-back in two months and visited more than 100 farms and estates, totalling 164.000 acres. This is the story told me on that riding tour as I sat, booted and spurred at lunch, with Robert Fuller in Spinney Abbey. That gracious old house of grey stone with mullioned windows, beamed rooms and a haunted cellar, stands high above the fens with a few wind-musical firs to sentinel the Abbey fishpond.

Once it was the home of Henry Cromwell, one-time Lord Protector of Ireland. There after the Glorious Revolution of 1688 Charles II visited him on a hare hunting day and drank his claret.

And there at breakfast on Low Sunday in 1934 Robert Fuller, his two sons and a maidservant, heard suddenly, under a blue sky, the sweet, unearthly singing of monks in Latin. They all, at first, thought it was the wireless. But there was no wireless.

'It was high up in the air, 10 or 15 feet above the ground, the sweetest singing I have ever heard,' said Mr. Fuller. 'I know no Latin, but I do know English, and this was not English. It was over there,' and he waved his hand.

'And what was once over there?' I asked.

'That's were the old chapel once stood. We've traced out the walls and the foundations.'

Enough ghost tales cling about Spinney Abbey to fill a book. It was founded by Sir Hugh de Malabisse during the reign of King John. He and his wife Beatrix, Lady of the Manor of Wicken, built and endowed the Priory of the beginning of the reign of Henry III. Since then it has been through the hands of Mary Lady Bassingbourn who gave it further lands in 1321; later Sir Edward North, Sir George Somerset, Henry Cromwell, Phillip Welbore, Edward Russell Earl or Orford, the Duke of Somerset, the Earl of Aylesford and then my own maternal connection, Miss Mary Hatch. It is now in the hands of a family who have held lands in

Wicken for three centuries or more.

'We don't sit up at night looking for ghosts,' Tom Fuller remarked drily, 'although my young son Peter did spend the night in the cellar waiting for the old monks to come out of the tunnel, and we don't let ghosts bother us. There are enough tales about this old place and enough bones have been dug up in the garden to give one a nightmare - but I still say the oddest thing I've ever seen was the sight of those two dogs attacking an Invisible Man.'

BOB FAL-LAL—THE POSTAL GENIUS

BOB'S LONG, straggly, ginger-rusty beard glowed in the sun. His eyes were blue, his forehead high, his nose like an eagle's beak, cheekbones high and the bone structure of a Viking. His name was Simpkin, which is as old English as you can be. Clearly one of the Saxon 'kin' of Sim; and Sim like enough came up our East Anglian rivers in a beak-prowed long-ship, the banked oars thrashing, the deep sides of the well of the ship glittering with shields, the Raven of Odin at the mast-head and the wild, wild war cry of 'Yuch! Hey! Saa-Saa!' going before them on the wind. The blood-curdling cry of the Viking invaders.

He was always known as Bob Fal-lal since he declared, with pride, that he was 'no townboy but a pore simple owd Fen-tiger - with no fal-lals about me'.

There may have been no fal-lals, as we called fancy ribbons, dangling from Bob's neck, but his soul was deep in guile. He looked as innocent as a bearded babe could look but his long full-skirted game-keeper's coat in cutaway tweed with two brass buttons at the back - 'one of uncle's cast-offs' - had two of the deepest hare pockets I have ever known. Each could carry not one hare but a couple - or four or five rabbits. Slung across his shoulder was a game-bag big enough to hold a young pig.

He wore an old wideawake slouch hat, drab breeches, hob-nailed boots and brown leather buskins. He carried a stout cudgel, heavy enough to brain a bullock. Had you looked in his outer-pockets you would have found, neatly coiled, a dozen or more copper wire snares with wooden pegs attached. At Bob's heels trotted a little rangy, wiry, prick-eared mongrel terrier with one black eye, four brown boots, a villainous wavy tail and the brains of Beelzebub. He was named, aptly, Satan. Such was the get-up, the uniform and accoutrements of our village Sunday postman, letter carrier, newspaper seller, perambulating poacher, doctor's messenger, and medicine man all in one.

Bob took his orders from our family and the rest of the

village, in strict rotation every Saturday night, winding up with a duty call on the Parson. There were orders for newspapers, bottles of medicine, boxes of pills, 'hoss iles' and those invaluable rural dab-ons known as liniments. They cured everything from nettle-rash to dog bites.

On Sunday, no matter how many fights there had been in the *Maids Head* on Saturday night, or poaching of rabbits in uncle's closes, we all went to Church or Chapel. Uncle Isaac, tall, broad-shouldered, with a strong handsome face, the hand-grip of a boxer and eyes of kindliness, was hereditary Squire of the Parish and Lord of the Manor. As such he seemed to stand next door to God in the eyes of small boys.

We all trundled up to church in dog-carts, Governess carts, tub carts, high-wheeled gigs, low-wheeled flat carts, donkey carts, or on our flat feet. There was a double row of waiting parishioners, headed by the rubicund smiling face of Woollard Barton, the miller, and Robert Mortlock Treen, a bearded gentleman farmer, who always wore a top hat and a tweed suit for church.

They were waiting for uncle to arrive. He strode up in his flat-topped hat - a flattened bowler - his great Inverness cape flapping in the shrewd Fen winds, his hand and heart open to greet all his friends, neighbours and workers.

There was a word of inquiry for everyone in every family, young, old, sick, dying, or just hatched. After all, we in the village had known each others' secrets since birth and fathers, grandfathers and great-grandfathers likewise before them.

We tolerated no 'furriners'. A man from Soham, four miles away across the fields, was pretty sure to have a heart full of black deeds; while any man from Burwell, five miles in the opposite direction across the Black Fens, was a Fen-tiger and as such a sworn enemy.

There was no nonsense about the fellowship of mankind. We might say our prayers in church, but had a Sohamite erupted from behind a gravestone he would, like as not, have been thrown in the horsepond.

As for the chapel-goers - known as dissenters or 'ranters' - although of the village, and often blood relations of church-goers, they were definitely a heathen race apart. Church regarded chapel with distrust, disdain and icy aloofness.

Chapel-goers passed church-goers on the opposite side of the road, with their bibles clasped unctuously in their hands, black-suited as any Puritan. And as Bob tersely put it: 'Snouts cocked in the air, and a blast o' spit about their ears.'

Meanwhile, Bob Fal-lal had set off by the field path across the meadows whilst the rest of mankind was sitting down to breakfast.

He was a man of importance on Sunday, our unique link with the outer world. He was a blend between Mercury and St. Hubert, with a touch of Diana the Huntress.

Bob's Sunday mission had been artfully worked out by him many years before. He calculated that if he left while the squire and cousin Alec at the hall were still at breakfast, and Jingler, the gamekeeper-cum-groom, was getting out the trap to take the ladies to church, he was - in his divine mission of newsgathering and balm-bearing - not only above suspicion but unhampered by prying eyes.

So cutting across the Hall meadows, which fell from the slope on which stood Hall and church, to the vanished bed of the great mere, he could put down his 'yokes' or snares at the foot of cousin Alec's rabbit warren where a tall thorn hedge made an admirable screen.

On the mere itself, dyke-seamed black fields, which stretched into infinity, were inhabited by bouncing great hares. Bob knew every runway. Down went a few more yokes.

'One fist high for a rabbit. Two fists high for a hare,' was his Sunday matins song.

And in one broad dyke were the Jacks - any pike under 7 lb. was known as a Jack.

Bob knew exactly how to snare them, working his copper noose stealthily up the long barred body from the tail to just beyond the dorsal fin. The art of the trick was to touch neither the tail, fins or skin of the fish until the noose encompassed the fish at just about the point of balance.

Then the noose, hanging from the end of Bob's cudgel, was jerked smartly upwards and a 5 or 6 lb. Jack was swept into the air and flung kicking into the wheelruts of the old green droveway behind.

All this went on while God-fearing folk were purring over psalms, or roaring out hymns in rollicking discordance.

When he arrived at Soham, Bob collected the letters from the post office, the newspapers from the newspaper shop, the medicines from Doctor Willis's surgery, the 'hoss iles' from the vet's house and put the lot, with a few other oddments, into the game bag.

The newspapers went into the outer netted compartment. Somehow they gave a touch of official importance. With them there, no one would think of looking in the bag itself to see if it contained a Jack or for that matter a hare, picked up an hour before from a yoke which had been put down overnight.

All this took about three hours. Then Bob set off for home at midday. He reckoned to take the best part of an hour to trudge across Soham Horse Fen, along Mereside, into the Dolvers and emerge from the Black Fens into the gently sloping grass fields and wheat stubble of Wicken, where tall, rambling old hedges full of spindle-berries, lovely in the sun, dog-roses, wild honeysuckle, old-man's beard, blackthorn and blackberry bushes glowed, blossomed, swelled and ripened in their seasons.

There were watercresses to be gathered in a running dyke on the way; unwary rabbits to be picked up in their yokes; perhaps an 'owd Sally' kicking and squirming in a snare on the Fens. These were Soham hares, so any right-thinking Wicken man did a public and a Christian service if he snapped them up for a Wicken cottage dinner. Even uncle's keeper would have turned a blind eye to that.

Just as one was sitting down to luncheon there came a tap at the door and a maid entered to say: 'Bob Fal-lal's brought the letters, Mam.'

Bob was ushered into the kitchen, given a pint of home-brew, rewarded with twopence for each letter and joyfully relieved of letters and magazines and 'doctor's pills'.

The rabbits, the hare and the Jack found grateful, discreet customers in thatched cottages. We were glad to buy the watercress, without asking further questions. It was delicious with brown bread and honey for tea in the garden, with the sun shining and rooks cawing.

And then Bob Fal-lal, his mission accomplished, trudged off with Satan trotting importantly at his heels. His mind fixed on a great stew-pot waiting in the cottage kitchen, his soul at peace with the world and with his God.

Somehow Bob Fal-lal seems to have done his job rather better than the post office does its job today. Neither sleet nor snow, rain, nor burning sun diminished his vigour or defeated the time-table of Bob Fal-lal.

If Mr. Bill Rylands, Chairman of the Post Office, can get

a knighthood for an inefficient telephone service and bemuse one's eyes with the incomprehensible letters and numbers attached to the simplest address, then Bob Fal-lal deserves a posthumous peerage.

Drawing by Sidney Parker, reproduced by courtesy of the Basildon Evening Echo.

GUNNERS' WINTER

THE NIGHT before, 'Lucka' had come up on the tide with a boat-load of fowl. They laid them out on the Inn floor by the water-side, in that low bar, with its skittle-table and glowing fire, its faded paintings of sailing barges and prints of great yachts, magnificent in stiff breezes.

There were geese and strings of wigeon; mallard, teal and pin-tail, etched and graceful in death. There were 'marl plover' and a sackful of knots, dunlin and shank, all slain at one shot of the great muzzle-loading punt gun. The butcher and the game-dealer, the cottage house-wives and the fishermen were all there. Bunches and strings of fowl changed hands in rough-and-ready auction.

'Lucka' had earned, not only his week's rent, but his keep for a month. That fisherman-fowler, with the Viking shoulders and the Cromagnon face, slow in speech, mighty in muscle, deadly in a punt, had, as usual, scooped the pool.

For a week he had lain in his smack in Death Creek, fast in the ice, three miles down the broad estuary, stealing forth at dawn and dusk in the long, grey punt that slides like the shadow of death itself over the grey waters. This was his reward. For hard weather had come at last. The inland fields were iron-frozen. Dykes were six inches thick in ice. Saltings and mudflats were sheets of tumbled, glistening slush-ice. Nights were bitter and stars winked frostily. And the fowl were there, fleeing down from the frozen North in thousands.

By day they moved in black clouds, in long straggling skeins, over the ice and the glittering tide. By night they passed over in a river of wings. It was the winter of which wildfowlers dream. Such clouds of fowl, such wastes of ice and snow, such bitter nights of stars as you see only in steel engravings of our grandfathers' days.

'Never seen anything like it,' said Alf. 'That's very near the worst I've knowed in me time. And I've been gunnin' on this river 40 odd year.'

'Ha! You're only a younker,' said an ear-ringed old

reprobate from the window settle. 'Time I was a little owd boy it really *were* a winter. Snow was right up to me bedroom winders. Yew couldn't git out of the door. That was shut fast by the snow, right above the lintel. Me Dad and me Mum and us nippers was held fast in the house for a week. Couldn't git out nor in. We lived on salt hog an' a sack of spuds. An' when me Mum wanted to bile the kittle, me Dad shoved me out o' the top winder with a bucket to git some snow to fill the kittle. That *wuss* a winter.'

'Liars I've knowed in me time,' remarked Alf casually, looking fixedly out of the window. 'Big 'uns too, in foreign parts. 'An yew can *enjoy* their yarns - but bloody liars I allus run from. Come on, mates, let's git gunning.'

Out we went, to an icy street where dogs moved stiffly. Fishermen shuffled by with mufflers round their ears. House-doors and windows were shut fast. And thence, in a motor-car that rolled like a ship over frozen ruts, we voyaged afield to pick up those three fowlers whom neither snow nor ice can daunt - Lord Lisle, Colonel 'Chutney' Gordon-Dickson and Major Philip Martin. Now these are three mighty men, proven in the ways of marsh and mudflat.

Five or six miles out of the town we turned left by a farm road, so deep in snow that you could only tell it was a road by the tops of the fences on either side. Cattle marshes stretched in a white prairie. Carrion-crows beat the bitter waste like hounds. Woe betide the partridge crouching under the lee of a snow-drifted hedge, if those cold eyes came near.

We topped the sea-wall. Beyond lay the estuary. Three miles wide, void of ships, the near shore a white and broken land of grinding floes, of icebergs and snowdrifts. The far shore was a glimmer of ghostly white - a faint fantastic land of little white hills crowned by ghostly farmhouses.

In middle distance rose an island, elm-crowned and lonely. Great floes of ice, an acre or more in extent, moved solemnly down on the tide. Black masses of duck were sitting on them, riding down-river like marooned sailors.

Decoy Point ran out into the estuary. On the lee shore, sitting in the sun, were fleets of fowl. I picked them up through the glasses in the cold sunlight. Forty or 50 geese strutted in their calm, deliberate way. A big parcel of wigeon were asleep on the mud. Half a dozen pintail sailed, graceful as yachts, on the water. Three herons waded in the shallows. A host of small waders flickered back and forth.

Beyond, five or six huge birds rode at anchor. They looked like Canada geese. Alf had shot one with his punt gun a week earlier, before the punt was locked in the ice. It weighed 15 pounds. And that was something of an event, for the Canada goose has only begun to visit our flats in the last ten years or so. Driven south by gales and snow and ice, they may, who knows, before long become a resident goose. And that will be a notable gain to the fauna of our long and lonely coast.

Half an hour passed. The wind came out of the East like a knife. Geese and duck passed up and down river in constant trips and flights. Gradually the flats bared. Weed-grown piles stood up, black and glistening. A stranded buoy tipped sideways on the mud, like a gigantic fishing float. We straggled out across the flats, following Alf, ankle-deep in frozen mud and spaced out across a mile of mud where rills of salt water ran like mill races. All the vast flats scintillated in the sun.

Up-river, a great lagoon of salt water, a mile and a half wide and three miles long, was dotted with fowl. Down river, the estuary glittered mile after mile to a far snow-misty horizon where a great four-masted Finnish barque, a timber ship, swung at anchor, spars and rigging glistening. It might have been mid-winter in the England of three centuries before.

I settled down on a bit of old board, a stranded ice floe at my back, a pile of frozen ice in front. It made a perfect butt. That ring-tailed mongrel, Mr. Soapy Sponge, whose heart is of gold, whose mother was a flat-coated retriever, whose father, they say, was a Norfolk harrier whose cost was 30 shillings and whose price was above rubies, squatted, flailing snow and mud with a ceaseless tail, searching sky and sea with amber, questing eyes. Not a feather that moves escapes him. No tide nor mud could daunt him. Not a whimper of wings missed his ear. That day he was to set the high peak on all dog endeavour. It is a true tale, worth telling.

Presently the birds began to come. First seven bar-geese swept by, shining in chestnut and white. I let them go. We do not shoot the gaudy, lovely shelduck, too lovely to be killed, too fishy to be eaten.

Then, through the glasses, I saw seven geese coming low over the water, beating along in that deceptive, slow-seeming way of theirs. Raggedly they flew, with pointed wings, seeming to travel at all too easy a pace. They were coming straight for me. I crouched low behind the piled ice. Behind, in a deep gut, a pool of salt water gurgled. A great block of ice popped suddenly to the surface like a grey-backed seal. Soapy turned his head. And that, I think, turned the geese.

I swung up the double eight-bore, which weighs near 17 pounds, and fires five ounces of shot, and let drive. A thunderous boom, a billow of white smoke, another boom, a billow of white smoke, another boom, and I sat back as though a horse had kicked me. Not a goose fell. Clean missed, with both barrels at under 40 yards. And that, my masters, points the moral that although a heavy gun may give you much greater range, infinitely more penetration and a bigger pattern, it is no gun for quick, close shooting or for low shots.

I let pass a trip of a dozen gray plover, scything low over the water. An easy shot for a game-gun but far too fast and close to risk the waste of a four and a quarter cartridge from the big gun.

Other trips and bunches of waders passed quickly. Redshank flew within 15 yards. Stints, or ox-birds as we call them, flashed past, a foot above the mud in shimmering clouds. They turned and wheeled in the winter sunshine like falling silver. Once I heard an oyster catcher, a rarish bird on those flats. Yet they bred there 40 years ago. What looked like a trip of ruffs and reeves fled past at a distance.

Great saddle-backed gulls swung high overhead on slow wings, barking like dogs. They were hunting the slain, on the track of wounded.

Once a peregrine falcon swished past, not 15 yards away, beating a bare yard above the ebbing tide. I could see its dark moustache, its tiger eyes and hooked beak perfectly. An easy shot. But why shoot a peregrine for the mere sake of killing a rare bird? There are too few of them in a world bent on destroying beauty when it finds it.

Then, far ahead, a bunch of geese lifted from a mud-bank where a red and black can-buoy tipped sideways on the flood. They swung past the end of the island, winging against the background of spidery elms. They were wide of me. They would pass over Jack Lisle. They did. A double flash, far twin reports. One goose crumpled up its neck and thudded in the mud with a 'sock'. A second glided forward on bent wings, suddenly doubled up and came down in a shallow, emptying lagoon. Soapy was out of the butt like a flash. He reached the pool, grabbed the goose and came trotting back to my butt and delivered it to hand.

Other geese passed wide. A cock wigeon came over, high as an archangel. James Gordon-Dickson pulled it out of the clouds.

Then from behind, came a whicker of wings, a hoarse, startled 'Cr-onk! Cr-onk!' and, dead overhead, nine geese, huddled in a startled bunch. The first barrel missed, for one sea-boot on the trailing corner of the oilskin threw me off balance. The second barrel cut down a goose as they planed away 40 yards off. Nothing to be proud of.

As the great gun boomed across the flats, duck and geese sprang from the water and swept back and forth. Straight towards me were coming seven geese. Soapy was plodding across the flats with the dead goose. Would the oncoming birds see him and veer? They came straight on.

A hundred yards, necks outstretched, wings beating evenly, all seven in that perfect V which you see so often in pictures and so seldom in actuality. Eighty yards, fifty.

I threw up the gun, swung that mass of metal a yard and a half in front of the leader, pulled: 'Br - oomp!' Down he came like a sack of wheat. They bunched suddenly, fled away to windward. I fired again. Down came a second, winged. Soapy was on him like a flash, leaving the dead bird to lie. There was the quick mongrel intelligence.

More shots across the mud from Jack Lisle. A goose toppling headlong. A double shot from Alf and another goose socked into the mud on the far island foreshore. Five pintail and 30 wigeon went over 'Colonel Chutney'. James' long-chambered 12 cut one down and sent another away in a long, planing dive to light, far out in the river, near half a mile away. A great cloud of green plover went over in a fantasia of wings.

Far down the river off Decoy Point, Philip's gun cracked, thin and whip-like - five times running. Through the glasses a great ragged cloud of fowl, geese, ducks and waders, veered back and forth over the point. Seven great birds lumbered up river on heavy, beating wings. Wild swans or Canada geese. It was too far to see, even with the glasses.

A bunch of wigeon were coming straight for us. Soapy's eyes watched intently. His tail hammered the mud, splashing me from head to foot. Sixty yards up, and I let drive. One to the first barrel and a pricked bird to the second, a bird that went wide towards the island and was cut down handsomely by Alf. As neat an eye-wipe as one could wish. And Alf, be it said with praise, was shooting with an old, rusty 12-bore whose barrels were so loose that you can see daylight at the breech-face.

A moment later a solitary goose came past him like the wind, travelling low. He cut it over headlong.

Time passed. The salt pool behind my butt gurgled and swirled. Great floors of ice, stained grey by mud, suddenly caved in. Swirling water, alive with snow bubbles, hissed and rustled on its under-ice journey to the sea. A party of ox-birds lit on the mud not 20 feet in front and ran about like mice. Odd shots came from left and right. But the main flight was over. It was near low water and, by the sun, two in the afternoon.

Lines of geese honked on distant mudbanks. A cormorant went over like a black crossbow. A heron was fishing in the shallows of Death Creek. Far away in the main channel, a great white shape, long, low and turretted, moved slowly with the tide. It looked like a frost-encrusted gunboat. I slewed the glasses on it. An ice-berg, the biggest berg I have ever seen on that coast, an odd, fantastic ship which sailed, manless, out to sea.

Presently Alf came plodding across the mud, gun under one arm, a bunch of mud-draggled ducks and geese in the other hand. He picked up Jack Lisle, who sat, crouched like a fox, in a gut in the mud, and the twain joined me.

'Dead low water now,' said Alf. 'They on't fly much more now till that turn. Better get back to the car and have our grub.'

Back at the car, in the lee of the sea-wall, hot rum and

coffee, pork pie and bread and cheese and onions went their proper way. The wind blew keener. It came out of the East like a knife. It bit nose and ears and seared necks like a whiplash. Snow on the gun barrels crystallized, sugar-like. The iron latch on a field gate stuck to one's hand when it was touched. It was below zero, freezing harder.

Presently the tide turned. We went back to our places. For an hour, for two hours, birds passed to and fro, shots rang out. Some fell, some were missed. I gathered three more geese and lost a fourth; picked a pair of wigeon and missed more than I should have done.

Then the tide flooded us out. We waded back, loaded with birds, plunging once into a hidden, hurrying rill that nearly topped our thigh boots. Soapy had to swim for it.

Back at the sea-wall we retired to the car to get out of the wind and get into the rum.

The tide flooded over the flats. Ice-floes were grinding along the shore. Between us and the island stretched near three quarters of a mile of running sea. Ten minutes more out on those flats would have meant certain death.

Suddenly a goose came from nowhere over Jack Lisle. He fired. It swung out over the salt water, flying low, suddenly crumpled and pitched dead into the flowing tide. The next moment Soapy was swimming strongly. Whatever the misdeeds and malfeasances of his master, the dog at least was determined to redeem them. The goose was a good 200 yards out. The tide was flowing at four knots and swinging the bird off-shore. The water was thick with floating ice. It was actually two degrees below freezing point.

I watched that dog with my heart in my mouth. Yapping incessantly, he cut the tide like a motor boat, that frightful ringtail brandishing above the freezing water. The black, yapping head and that ridiculous tail faded behind a floating floe. Would he be seized by sudden cramp, throw up his paws and sink? I got out the glasses. He emerged from the other side of the floe, still swimming strongly. The goose was drifting steadily out 200 yards from the shore. And the tide was taking dog and bird still further out. High, determined yaps floated shoreward. The glasses followed that gallant little head.

He reached the goose, grabbed it, swung round and

started to battle back against the tide-set. I wondered whether the bird would drag his head down, whether icy water would fill and choke his throat - wondered too, if a cramp-stricken dog suddenly sank or floated.

No need for such fears. Steadily he forged through the tide, the goose held high above the water, that monstrous, unforgivable tail wagging gaily.

He brought the bird, blinded though his eyes were by its heavy body, straight to the water's edge in front of me, wallowed through mud and ice, dropped it at my feet, smiled broadly - and proceeded to roll frantically on a floe. Then he swallowed a mouthful of snow. A hand tapped me on the shoulder. There stood a stranger, thigh-booted, head and neck muffled in a great balaclava wool helmet, a heavy 10 bore across his oilskin coated shoulder.

'I don't know you, sir, but I'd like to raise my hat to your dog', he said, quietly. 'It's the longest swim I've ever seen in salt water - 500 yards if it was an inch. I've never seen a dog before that would even face the water on a day like this. I watched it from the sea wall. It crowned the day for me.'